"I think I've made myself clear. I'm not planning on marrying. I have a calling, a vocation, and certainly one Seattle sorely needs. I intended to stay another day, but if you all can't understand my position, then perhaps I should leave now."

Drew met her gaze, and this time she had no doubt the emotion flickering in that expanse of blue-green was regret. She felt it, too, just as she felt herself leaning toward him, as if her body vied with her mind as to where she belonged.

Beth spoke before he did. "No, you can't go, Miss Stanway. Not until Ma's well."

"Your mother is on the mend, Beth," Catherine said. "There's nothing more for me to do here."

Catherine waited for Drew to argue. She wasn't sure why she expected it. Some part of her believed him when he said he didn't wish to wed, either. If he truly did intend to court her or marry her to one of his brothers, he ought to protest her leaving. And if he actually cared about her…

She shut that thought away. She didn't want Drew to care about her.

Because that meant she'd have to care about him more than she already did.

Regina Scott has always wanted to be a writer. Since her first book was published in 1998, her stories have traveled the globe, with translations in many languages. Fascinated by history, she learned to fence and sail a tall ship. She and her husband reside in Washington state with their overactive Irish terrier. You can find her online blogging at nineteenteen.com. Learn more about her at reginascott.com or connect with her on Facebook at facebook.com/authorreginascott.

Books by Regina Scott

Love Inspired Historical

Frontier Bachelors Series

The Bride Ship
Would-Be Wilderness Wife

The Master Matchmakers Series

The Courting Campaign
The Wife Campaign
The Husband Campaign

The Everard Legacy Series

The Rogue's Reform
The Captain's Courtship
The Rake's Redemption
The Heiress's Homecoming

Visit the Author Profile page at Harlequin.com for more titles.

Would-Be Wilderness Wife

REGINA SCOTT

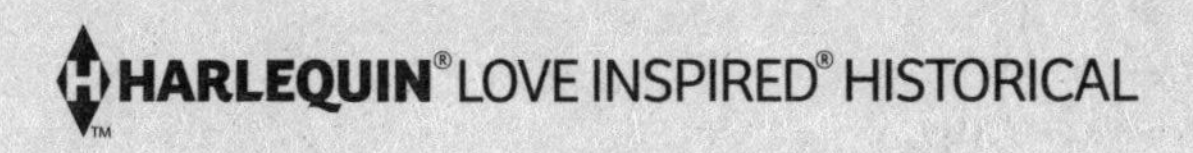

If you purchased this book without a cover you should be aware that this book is stolen property. It was reported as "unsold and destroyed" to the publisher, and neither the author nor the publisher has received any payment for this "stripped book."

PLEASE RECYCLE · THIS PRODUCT IS RECYCLABLE

Recycling programs for this product may not exist in your area.

ISBN-13: 978-0-373-28302-6

Would-Be Wilderness Wife

This edition published by arrangement with Love Inspired Books.

www.Harlequin.com

Printed in U.S.A.

For this reason a man will leave his father
and mother and be united with his wife,
and they will become one flesh.

—*Genesis* 2:24

To Joe Mullins and Angela Rush,
real estate agents extraordinaire,
who helped us find a house on the new frontier,
and to the Lord, who makes a house a home

Chapter One

Seattle, Washington Territory
May 1866

"I need a doctor."

The commanding male voice echoed through the dispensary of Doc Maynard's hospital like a trumpet call. Catherine Stanway straightened from where she'd been bending over a patient, fully prepared to offer assistance. But one look at the man in the doorway, lit from behind by the rare Seattle sun, and words failed her.

He carried himself as proudly as a knight from the tales of King Arthur her father had read to her as a child. His rough-cut light brown hair brushed the top of the doorjamb; his shoulders in the wrinkled blue cotton shirt reached either side. He took a step into the room, and she was certain she felt the floor tremble.

Finding her voice, she raised her chin. "I can help you."

He walked down the narrow room toward her, the thud of his worn leather boots like the sound of a hammer on the planks of the floor. The blue apothecary bottles lined up on the shelves behind the counter chimed against one another as he passed. He was like a warrior approaching his leader, a soldier his commanding officer. Mrs. Witherspoon, waiting on a chair for the doctor to reset her shoulder, clutched her arm close, wide-eyed. Others stared at him or quickly looked away.

He stopped beside Catherine and laid his fingers on the curved back of the chair where the elderly Mr. Jenkins snoozed while he waited for his monthly dose of medicine. Scars crossed the skin of the massive hand, white against the bronze.

Up close, Catherine could see that his face was more heart-shaped than oval, his unkempt hair drawing down in a peak over his forehead. His liberally lashed eyes were a mixture of clear green and blue, like the waves that lapped the Puget Sound shores. The gold of his skin said he worked outdoors; the wear on this clothes said he made little income from it.

He was easily the most healthy male she'd ever seen, so why did he need medical assistance?

"Are you a doctor?" he asked. Everything from the way he cocked his head to the slow cadence of the question spoke of his doubt.

Her spine stiffened, lifting her blue skirts off the floor and bringing her head level with his breastbone. She was used to the surprise, the doubts about her vocation here in Seattle. Even where she'd been raised, a few had questioned that the prominent physician George Stanway had trained his daughter to be a nurse. More had wondered why their beloved doctor and his promising son had felt it necessary to get themselves killed serving in the Union Army. At times, Catherine wondered the same thing.

"I'm a nurse," she told their visitor, keeping her voice calm, professional. "I was trained by my father, a practicing physician, and served for a year at the New England Hospital for Women and Children. I came West with the Mercer expedition. Doctor Maynard was sufficiently pleased with my credentials to hire me to assist him and his wife."

"So you're a Mercer belle." He straightened, towering over her. "I didn't come looking for a bride. I need a doctor."

A Mercer belle. That, she knew from the newspapers back East, was synonymous with *husband hunter*. Obviously her credentials as a medical practitioner meant nothing to him.

Well, he might not have come to the hospital seeking a bride, but she hadn't come to Seattle after a husband, either. She'd already refused three offers of marriage since arriving two weeks ago. Her friend Madeleine O'Rourke had turned away six. Even her friend Allegra had had to argue with two would-be suitors before she'd wed her childhood sweetheart, Clay Howard, a successful local businessman, only two days after landing.

None of them had left the East Coast expecting such attentions. When Seattle's self-proclaimed emigration agent, Asa Mercer, had recruited her and nearly seventy other women to settle in Washington Territory, he'd talked of the jobs that needed filling, the culture they could bring to the fledging community. Already some of her traveling companions were teaching schools in far-flung settlements. Others had taken jobs they had never dreamed of back home, including tending a lighthouse. They were innovative and industrious, just as Catherine had hoped she'd be when she'd journeyed West.

"I'm not interested in marriage either, sir," she told him. "And I assure you, I am perfectly suited to deal with medical emergencies. Now, what's the trouble?"

He glanced around as if determined to locate her employer. Doctor Maynard had converted the bottom floor of his house for his patients. This room was his dispensary, the medicines and curatives lined up in tall bottles on the triple row of shelves along one wall, with a dozen chairs, frequently all filled, opposite them. The other room held beds along either wall, with an area at the end curtained off and outfitted for surgeries. That room was used primarily as a laying-in ward for women about to give birth.

After conversations aboard ship about the dismal state of Seattle's medical establishment, Catherine hadn't been sure what to expect of Doctor Maynard and his hospital. She'd been greatly relieved to find the wood floors sanded clean, beds nicely made and light streaming through tall windows. The doctor shared her father's view that fresh water, healthy food and natural light went a long way to curing any ill.

"I appreciate your offer," the man said, returning his gaze to hers. "But I would prefer a doctor."

She could see herself reflected in his eyes, her pale blond hair neat and tidy, her face set. She refused to be the first one to look away. In the silence, she heard Mr. Jenkins mumble as he dozed.

"Well, greetings, Drew!" The call from her employer caused their visitor to raise his head, breaking his gaze from Catherine's. She suddenly found it easier to breathe.

Doctor Maynard didn't appear the least concerned to find a mountain of a man in his dispensary. He strolled toward them with his usual grin. A tall man, he had a broad face and dark hair that persisted in curling in the middle of his forehead as if it laughed at the world like he did. After helping her organized father, Catherine had found Seattle's famous founding father undisciplined, impractical and irrepressible. He was also endlessly cheerful and generous. In the two weeks she'd been working at his side, he'd never turned anyone down, regardless of gender, race or ability to pay.

"And what can we do for you today?" he asked their visitor as he approached. "Are all the Wallins healthy? No more bumps, bruises or broken bones among your logging crew, I trust?"

The man hesitated a moment, then nodded. "My brothers are well enough. I'm here about another matter."

"I told Mr. Wallin I could assist him," Catherine assured her employer.

"O-ho!" Maynard elbowed the man's side and didn't so much as cause their visitor to raise an eyebrow. "Are you after my nurse, Drew? Can't say I blame you. Allow me to introduce Miss Catherine Stanway. She's as pretty as a picture and twice as talented."

Catherine didn't blush at the praise. She'd heard it and far more in her hometown of Sudbury, while she'd worked as a nurse in Boston and while aboard the ship to Seattle. Much of the time it came from no sincere motive, she'd learned. She was more interested to see how this Drew fellow would answer. Would he continue to argue with her in the face of her employer's endorsement?

He did not look at her as he transferred his grip to the doctor's arm. "May I speak to you a moment in private?"

Maynard nodded, and the two withdrew to the end of the dispensary nearest the door. Fine. Lord knew she had plenty of work to do. She had only determined the needs of about half those currently filling the chairs, and two women were expected any day in the laying-in ward. If Mr. Wallin couldn't be bothered to make use of her services, the fault lay with him, not her. She was fully prepared to do her duty.

Yet Catherine could hear the low rumble of his voice as she spoke to the woman next to Mr. Jenkins to determine her complaint, then went to reposition the pillow that had slipped out from where it had been cushioning Mrs. Witherspoon's shoulder. But though she tried to focus on the needs around her, she couldn't help glancing up at Drew Wallin again.

Whatever he and Doctor Maynard had discussed seemed to have touched his heart at last. His mouth dipped; his broad shoulders sagged. She could almost see the weight he carried, bowing him lower. What worries forced a knight to bend his knee? Her hand lifted of its own accord, as if some part of her longed to help him shoulder his burden.

She dropped her hand. How silly. She had work to do, a purpose in coming to Seattle that didn't involve any emotional entanglements. She was a trained nurse in an area that badly needed medical assistance. And that was a great blessing.

Every time she eased the pain of another, she forgot the pain inside her. Every time she helped fight off death, she felt as if she'd somehow made up for the deaths of her brother and father on those bloody battlefields. Surely God did not intend her to leave her profession to serve as any man's bride.

Besides, she liked nursing. Medicine was clinical, precise, measured. It kept her from remembering all she had lost. And each time someone passed beyond her help, she watched their grieving loved ones and knew she could not allow herself to hurt like that again.

No, whatever way she looked at it, she had no business mooning over a wild mountain logger like Drew Wallin. He was a knight with no shining armor, no crusade worthier than her own. The sooner she forgot him, the better.

Andrew Wallin stepped out onto the stone steps of Doc Maynard's hospital and pulled in a deep breath of the late-afternoon air. It never ceased to amaze him how Seattle changed between his visits to town. Another new building was going up across the street, and wagons slogged by in the mud, carrying supplies to camps farther out. The sun beamed down on the planed-wood buildings, the boardwalks stretching between them, anointing the treetops in the distance.

Yet he could not enjoy the sight, thinking about what lay waiting for him back at the Landing. If only he'd been able to counter Maynard's logic. But how could he argue one life against many?

He glanced back at the hospital. Something blue flashed past the tall windows, and he couldn't help thinking about Catherine Stanway. For a moment there, when he'd first spied her in the dispensary, he'd wondered whether his mother had been right to encourage him to find a bride among the ladies Asa Mercer had brought to the territory.

He hadn't been interested. The last thing he needed was a wife to look after when he already had the lives of six people to consider. Besides, he doubted that a lady brought from the big cities back East would know how to handle herself on a backwoods farm without more tutoring than he had time to give.

Catherine Stanway seemed a perfect example of a lady more suited to civilization. She was obviously well educated, her skills suited to a city. Her manners had been polished, her voice cultured and calm. Of course, he much preferred that attitude to the coy smiles and giggles that had marked his interaction with the few unmarried ladies of the Territory.

Then there was the fact that she was so pretty. Her hair was like sunlight shafting through the forest, her eyes resembled a pale winter's sky and the outline of her curves looked lovely behind the apron covering her crisp cotton gown. He knew exactly what would happen if his brothers ever laid eyes on her. Either he'd be standing up as best man in a wedding, or his brothers would hog-tie him and wrestle him to the altar. They seemed determined to see him settled with a wife. They couldn't understand that he already had enough on his hands taking care of them, Ma and Beth. There was nothing left of him to give to a wife.

With a sigh, he started down the steps toward where his team stood waiting farther along the block. The two youths arguing at the side of the wagon gave him as much concern as what was happening at home. As he approached, his youngest brother shoved his friend back. Scout Rankin, scrawnier than Levi despite being the same age, took one look at Drew and loped away. Drew grabbed his brother's shoulders and spun him around.

"What?" Levi snapped, fists raised protectively in front of his lean frame. "I was watching the wagon, just like you asked."

"You'd do better to watch the horses than fight," Drew told him with a shake of his head. He went to check that the sturdy brown farm horses were munching from their feed sacks. "What was Scout doing here?"

"Seeing some people for his father," Levi said, lowering his fists as Drew patted their horses down. "And I thought you were more worried about Ma than the horses. Isn't that why we came to town?"

It was, but he didn't like admitting his fears to Levi any more than he liked having to remind his brother why they didn't associate much with their nearest neighbor. The Wallin family had chosen homesteads at the northern end of Lake Union for the timber. Benjamin Rankin had other reasons entirely to avoid town. He'd turned his cabin into a high-stakes gambling den, and the smells issuing from the place told Drew he was likely making his own liquor, as well. Ma had tried befriending Scout, teaching him to read and write beside Levi, but the son's sullen behavior said he was turning out no better than the father. Drew didn't want any of Scout's bad habits rubbing off on Levi.

He removed the feed sacks and tossed them up to his brother. "Stow these."

"Why? Are we leaving?" his brother asked, clutching the dusty burlap close. "Where's Doc?"

"He's not coming," Drew reported. "Too many patients in town right now."

Levi frowned, dropping the sacks into the wagon. He glanced in the windows of the hospital as he tugged at the hem of his plaid cotton shirt. "I saw you jawin' at that gal. She's pretty enough. Maybe she could convince him to come."

Drew leaned against the rough wood of the wagon. "In the first place, it would take more than a pretty face to get Doc to abandon his patients. In the second place, the less we have to do with Nurse Stanway, the better."

Levi threw up his hands. "She's a nurse? That tears it, Drew. You know how bad Ma needs help. You get back in there and tell that gal she has to come with us!"

Frustration pushed him back from the wagon. "I asked Doc, Levi. He says he needs her here right now. Some women are expected in to give birth."

Levi shook his head, curly blond hair creating a halo he didn't deserve. "Women give birth all the time without someone standing over them. Leastways, that's how Ma did it."

"Ma didn't have a choice," Drew pointed out. "And if you recall, that's how we lost Mary, her giving birth without a doctor there to help. Now simmer down. I still need to check for mail and load the supplies we ordered before heading back."

Levi narrowed his dark blue eyes, a sure sign rebellion was brewing. Drew couldn't blame him. His brother had just turned eighteen and was feeling his oats. Drew had been the same way at that age. Then his father had died and left the responsibility for their mother and five siblings on Drew's shoulders. He'd settled down fast. He was glad Levi didn't have to face the same fate.

Drew slipped a two-bit coin from the pocket of his work trousers and flipped it to his brother, who caught it with one hand. "Tell you what. Take the wagon down to the mercantile and get yourself a sarsaparilla. Ask Mr. Quentin to load up the supplies we bought. I'll meet you there."

Levi was still boy enough that he grinned over the treat as he climbed over the backboard for the bench.

Drew continued on to the post office, but he found nothing waiting for him. He wasn't surprised. Most of his mother's and father's relatives didn't write often. They couldn't understand why his father had left Wisconsin for the far West. They thought themselves pioneers already. But his father had wanted more than the lakes and hills.

He'd wanted a town of his own.

So instead of settling in the hamlet that had been early Seattle, he'd claimed a parcel along Lake Union's shores for himself and his wife. As each Wallin son had come of age, he, too, had laid claim to an adjoining parcel. Drew and his next brother, Simon, had put in the five years of hard work necessary to prove up their own claims, building cabins, tapping springs and clearing land for crops they had yet to plant. John and James were a few years from doing the same. Someday, they all might even have the town his father had dreamed of building.

If Drew could see them all safely raised first.

He headed back toward the mercantile his mother favored. Several wagons were crowded in front, but none of them were his. Where had Levi gotten to now? With a rattle of tack and the rumble of hooves, the wagon pulled up beside him in the street, his brother at the reins, eyes wild. "Come on! Jump in!"

Drew slung himself up on the bench, but he hadn't

even settled in the seat before Levi whipped the reins and whistled to the team. Drew grabbed the sideboard to steady himself as the wagon careened out of town.

"At least tell me you loaded the supplies," he called over the thunder as the two horses galloped up the track that lead north.

"All squared away," Levi shouted back. "Yee-haw! Go!"

Drew was afraid to ask, but he had to know. "You tick off the sheriff again?"

"Naw," Levi yelled. "Just in a hurry to get back to Ma."

Drew felt a twinge of guilt that he wasn't as eager. In truth, he dreaded what he'd find at Wallin Landing, about a two-hour ride from Seattle.

He'd watched, helpless, the past two weeks as his mother had sunk beneath a virulent fever. At first he'd kept his brothers and sister away to prevent the disease from spreading and neglected his work to tend her. The past few days, Levi and Beth had served beside him. Only the combined insistence of his family that they needed help had driven him from Ma's side today.

He hated having to relay the news that Doc Maynard wasn't coming. But he hated more the thought that his mother might not be alive to find out.

So Drew let Levi drive the team more than four miles, until the road petered out to a narrow track near the south of the lake, before he insisted on stopping and giving them a rest. Only when the horses had quieted did he hear the muffled cries from the back of the wagon.

"Now, don't get angry, Drew," Levi said, edging away from him on the bench as Drew frowned toward the sound. "You know we have to have help."

Drew felt as if one of the firs he felled had toppled into his stomach. He stared at his brother. "What have you done?"

"Ma needs a nurse, and you need a bride," Levi insisted. "So I got you one."

Drew jerked around and yanked the canvas tarp off what he'd thought were only supplies in the bed of the wagon.

Rag stuffed in her mouth, hands trussed before her, Catherine Stanway lay on her back, her bun askew and hair framing her face. She had every right to be terrified, to cry, to swoon.

But the blue eyes glaring back at him were hot as lightning, and her look was nothing short of furious.

He'd have to do a lot of talking if he hoped to calm her down and keep Levi from ending up in jail for his behavior. But he feared no amount of talking was going to keep his brothers from interfering in his life, especially when Levi had just gone and kidnapped Drew a bride.

Chapter Two

"What do you think you're doing?" Catherine demanded the moment Drew Wallin set her on her feet and pulled the rag away. Her mouth felt as dry as dust, every inch of her body bruised by bouncing around on the wagon bed. "I am a citizen of the United States. I have rights! Untie me and return me to Seattle immediately, or I shall report you to the sheriff!"

"Bit on the spiteful side, ain't she?" the young man who had grabbed her said, sitting on the wagon's tongue, safely out of reach of both her and Mr. Wallin.

"Release her, Levi," Mr. Wallin said to him, jaw tight. "And apologize. Now."

The youth jumped down and hurried to Catherine's side. He didn't look the least bit contrite about snatching her out of the hospital, treating her as if she were no more than a bag of threshed wheat. She held out her hands toward him, and his fingers worked the knot he'd made in the rope that bound her wrists.

He'd looked so innocent when he'd appeared in the dispensary—a mop of curly blond hair, eyes turned down like a sad puppy's, cotton shirt and trousers worn but clean. He'd bounded up to her and seized her hands.

"Please," he'd said, lips trembling. "My ma's real sick. You have to come and help her."

She'd thought he'd had an ill woman in a wagon outside. He wouldn't have been the first to pull up to the hospital begging for help. It seemed Doctor Maynard tended to at least one logger a day with a broken arm or leg or a crushed skull. As soon as Mr. Wallin had left, her employer had gone into surgery with his wife, Susanna, assisting him. Catherine had known she couldn't call him away from that until she knew the severity of this young man's mother's illness.

"Show me," she'd said to the youth, taking only a moment to dry her hands before following him out the back of the hospital.

But instead of an older woman huddled on a bench, she'd found a long-bed wagon partially filled with supplies and tools and no other person in sight.

"Where's your mother?" she'd asked.

"About eight miles north," he'd said, wrapping one arm around her and pinioning her arms against her. "But don't you worry none. I'll get you there safe and sound."

She'd opened her mouth to call for help, and he'd shoved in that hideous rag. Though she'd twisted and lashed out with her arms and feet, his whip-cord-thin body was surprisingly strong. He'd tied her up, tossed her in the wagon and covered her with a tarp.

She supposed she should have been afraid, being abducted from her place of work with neither her employer nor any of her new friends to know what had become of her. In truth, she'd been furious that anyone would treat her like this. What, did he think her friendless, an easy victim? When Doctor Maynard realized she was gone, he would likely ask after her at the boardinghouse where she and some of the women who had come West with her were living.

That would concern her friend Madeleine. The feisty redhead would have no trouble enlisting the aid of the sheriff and his young deputy to find Catherine. A posse could be on its way even now.

If the men had any idea which way to go.

That thought gave her pause. As her young kidnapper worked on the rope and Mr. Wallin stood sentinel, arms crossed over his broad chest, she glanced around. The wagon was pulled over among the brush at the edge of the road, two horses waiting. A muddy track stretched in either direction, firs crowding close on both sides. In places she could still see the low stumps of trees that had been cut to carve out the road. She could make out blue sky above, but the forest blocked the view of any landmark that might tell her where she was.

Levi stepped back with a frustrated puff. "She went and pulled the rope too tight. We've going to have to cut it." His voice was nearly a whine at the loss of the cord.

"If you value your material so highly," Catherine said, "next time think before using it to kidnap someone."

"No one is kidnapping anyone," Mr. Wallin said, his firm voice brooking no argument.

She argued anyway. "I believe that is the correct term when one has been abducted and held against her will, sir."

He grimaced. "It may be the right term, but I refuse to allow it to be the right circumstance. We'll return you home as soon as possible."

He pulled out a long knife from the sheath at his waist, the blade honed to a point that gleamed in the sunlight. Though he towered over her as he reached for her, she felt no fear as he sawed through the rope and freed her.

"I haven't heard that apology, Levi," he reminded the boy with a look that would have blistered paint.

Levi shrugged. "Sorry to inconvenience you, but my mother is sick. Now, will you just get back in the wagon so we can go home?"

Catherine took a step away from them both. "I am going no farther. Return me to Seattle."

"Can't," Levi said, hopping back up onto the wagon's tongue. "Too far."

"He's right," Drew Wallin said before Catherine could argue with his brother, as well. He nodded to what must be the west, for she could see the light slanting low through the trees from that direction. "The horses are spent. We'll never make it back to Seattle before dark, and it isn't safe for the horses or us to be out here at night."

She could believe that. Since coming to the town, she'd rarely ventured beyond it. Those forests were dark, the underbrush dense in places. Allegra's husband, Clay Howard, who had accompanied them on their journey from New York, had explained all about the dangers of getting lost—bears, wolves and cougars; unfriendly natives; crumbling cliffs and rushing rivers. She certainly didn't want to blunder about in the dark.

She crossed her arms over her chest. "So where do you propose to take shelter tonight?"

"We'll make for the Landing," he assured her, "but I promise you I'll return you to Seattle tomorrow."

"But tomorrow we're supposed to fell that fir for Captain Collings," Levi protested before Catherine could answer. "We can't do that without you!"

Mr. Wallin turned away from them both. "As Miss Stanway said, there are consequences for your decision," he tossed back over his shoulder as he walked along the wagon to the team. "You should have thought before acting. Now get in the back. Miss Stanway will be riding with me."

Grumbling, the youth clambered deeper into the bed of the wagon and set his back to the sideboard, long legs stretching out over the supplies.

Catherine couldn't make herself follow the elder Mr. Wallin. She still wasn't sure where they were taking her.

"This landing," she said, "how far is it?"

"Another few miles," he replied, running his hands over the nearest horse as if checking for signs of strain. "On Lake Union."

Lake Union was north of Seattle's platted streets, she knew. The *Seattle Gazette*, the weekly newspaper, had been full of stories recently about how the lake could serve as Seattle's chief water source as the town grew. There'd been talk of building a navigable canal between Lake Washington to the east and Lake Union, perhaps even to Puget Sound for transporting logs.

But right now, all those were nothing but dreams. The only people she knew about who lived on Lake Union were Indians.

And, apparently, Drew Wallin.

"Are there any women at this landing?" she asked.

He had been frowning at her. Now his brow cleared as if he understood her concerns at last.

"My mother and my sister," he said. "Beth is only fourteen, but I think most of the gossips in Seattle would count her as a chaperone. Your reputation is safe, ma'am."

Still she couldn't make herself move. Was he telling the truth? Was Seattle really so far behind them? She glanced back the way they had come and saw only the mud of the track stretching into the distance—no sign of smoke from a campfire or cabin, no other travelers. A gull swooped low with a mournful call. They were close to water, then, but she could say that of any location near Seattle.

She was tempted to simply walk away, but if a wagon and team couldn't reach Seattle by dark, what chance did she have on foot?

She nodded. "Very well, Mr. Wallin."

She followed him back to the box of the wagon, passing Levi's narrowed look. He acted as if she should feel guilty for inconveniencing *him*! A shame she was entirely too mature to stick out her tongue at him, however highly satisfactory that would have been. A shame Maddie wasn't here with her. Her friend would have given him an earful.

They reached the front of the wagon, and she put out her hand to climb in. Before she knew what he was about, Drew Wallin put both hands on her waist and lifted her onto the bench as if she weighed nothing. For the first time since this adventure had started, her heart stuttered. She took a deep breath to steady herself and busied herself arranging her skirts as he jumped up beside her and took the reins.

"Give her your hat," he ordered Levi without so much as looking back.

The youth, who had been lounging against the side of the wagon, jerked upright. "Give her your own. You're the oldest."

"I don't require a hat," Catherine assured them both, but Mr. Wallin reached one arm over the back of the box and rapped his brother on the head. In answer, Levi tossed up a brown wool hat with a battered brim, which Mr. Wallin caught with one hand. He offered it to Catherine as if it were a jeweled ring on a velvet pillow.

"We still have a ways to go," he explained when she hesitated. "And I need to walk the horses, so it may take us a bit. I know my sister is always talking about how a lady needs to protect her complexion from the sun."

He was trying to be considerate, and though the hat had clearly seen better days, she knew it for a peace offering.

"Thank you," she said, accepting it and setting it on her hair. But one touch to her head, and she realized how disheveled she must appear. The bun she normally wore had come partially undone while she'd struggled. Strands clung to one ear; others hung down her back. As Drew clucked to the horses, setting them plodding up the track, she pulled out the last of her pins and let the tresses fall.

She had piled up the pins in the lap of her apron when something brushed the back of her hair. She jerked around to find Levi on his knees behind her, staring at her as he pulled back his hand.

"It's like moonlight on the lake," he said, voice hushed and eyes wide.

"Sit down," his brother grit out. He whipped the reins, and the horses darted forward. Levi fell with a thud onto the wagon bed.

Catherine faced front, mouth compressed to keep from laughing.

"I apologize for my brother," Drew said, slowing the horses once more. Catherine could see that his ruddy cheeks were darkening. "He's spent too much time in the woods."

"So have you," Levi grumbled, but Catherine could hear him settling himself against the wood.

Better not to encourage him. She twisted up her hair and pinned it carefully in place at the back of her head as the horses continued north. The track dwindled until the trees crowded on either side and the ruts evened out to ground covered by low bushes and broad-leafed vines. She sighted something long and dark hanging from a blackberry bramble, as if it had reached out to snag the last horse or human who had ventured this way.

Both Wallin men fell silent. The clatter of the wagon wasn't so loud that she could miss the scree of the hawk that crossed the opening between the trees. The breeze was coming in off the Sound, bringing the scent of brine like fingers combing through the bushes.

He leadeth me beside still waters. He restoreth my soul.

That chance for peace was what had brought her here so very far from what she'd planned for her life. She should not let the misguided actions of an impetuous boy change that.

Nor the fluttering of a heart she had sworn to keep safely cocooned from further pain.

How could his brother have been so boneheaded? Drew glanced over his shoulder at the youth. Levi had curled himself around the supplies on the wagon bed like a hound before the fire, and it wouldn't surprise Drew if his brother started snoring. The boy had absolutely no remorse for what he'd done. Where had Drew gone wrong?

"I'm really very sorry," he apologized again to Catherine as he faced front. "I don't know what got into him. He was raised better."

"Out in the woods, you said," she replied, gaze toward the front, as well. Her hair was once more confined behind her head, and he knew a moment of regret at its disappearance. Levi might have been the one to cry out at the sight of it, but the satiny tresses had held him nearly as captive.

"On the lake," he told her. "My father brought us to Seattle about fifteen years ago from Wisconsin and chose a spot far out. He said a man needed something to gaze out on in the morning besides his livestock or his neighbors."

She smiled as if the idea pleased her. "And your mother?" she asked, shifting on the wooden bench, her wide blue skirts filling the space at her feet. "Is she truly ill?"

It was difficult to even acknowledge the fact. He nodded, turning his gaze out over the horses. "She came down with a fever nearly a fortnight ago."

He could feel her watching him. "A fever that lasts that long is never good," she informed him in a pleasant voice he was sure must calm many a patient. "Do you open the windows daily to air her room?"

He'd fetched gallons of water from the spring, even trudged down to the lakeshore to draw it cold from the depths. He'd stoked up the fire, wrapped Ma tight in covers. But he hadn't considered opening the windows.

"No," he answered. "Doesn't cold air just make you sicker?"

She shook her head, Levi's hat sliding on the silk of her hair. "No, indeed. The fear of it is a common belief I have had to fight repeatedly. Fresh air, clean water, healthy food—those are what cure a body, sir. That is what my father taught. That is what I practice."

She was so sure of the facts that he couldn't argue. He knew from conversations with Doc Maynard that Seattle was woefully behind on recent medical advancements. As one of the few physicians, Doc was overwhelmed with the number of people ill or injured. He must have been overjoyed to have Catherine join his staff.

"I hope you'll be able to help her, then, ma'am," he told her. "Before we return you to Seattle tomorrow."

He glanced her way in time to see her gaze drift out over the horses. "You did not seem so sure of my skills earlier, sir."

With Levi right behind him, he wasn't about to admit that his initial concern had been for his brother's matchmaking, not the lack of her skills. "We've known Doc for years," he hedged.

He thought her shoulders relaxed a little. She sat so prim and proper it was hard to tell. "My father's patients felt the same way. There is nothing like the trusted relationship of your family doctor. But I will do whatever I can to help your mother."

Levi's smug voice floated up from behind. "I knew she'd come around."

Though Drew was relieved at the thought of Catherine's help, he wanted nothing more than to turn and thump Levi again.

"As you can see," he said instead to Catherine, "my brother has a bad habit of acting or talking without thinking." He glanced back into the wagon in time to see Levi making a face at him.

"My brother was the same way," she assured him as

he turned to the front again with a shake of his head. "He borrowed my father's carriage more than once, drove it all over the county. He joined the Union Army on his eighteenth birthday before he'd even received a draft notice."

"Sounds like my kind of fellow," Levi said, kneeling so that his head came between them. "Did he journey West with you?"

Though her smile didn't waver, her voice came out flat. "No. He was killed at the Battle of Five Forks in Virginia."

Levi looked stricken as he glanced between her and Drew. "I'm sorry, ma'am. I didn't know."

"Of course you didn't," she replied, but Drew saw that her hands were clasped tightly in her lap as if she were fighting with herself not to say more.

"I'm sorry for your loss," Drew said. "That must have been hard on you and your parents."

"My mother died when I was nine," she said, as if commenting on the weather. "My father served as a doctor in the army. He died within days of Nathan. It was a very bloody war."

How could she sit so calmly? If he'd lost so much he would have been railing at the sky.

Levi was obviously of a similar mind. "That's awful!" He threw himself back into the bed. "Pa died when I was eight, but I think I would have gone plumb crazy if I'd lost Drew and Simon and James and John, too."

Her brows went up as she glanced at Drew. "You have four brothers?"

He chuckled. "Yes, and most days I'm glad of it."

"We had another sister, too, besides Beth," Levi said, popping up again. "She died when she was a baby. Simon says it about broke Ma's heart."

It had almost broken Drew's heart, as well. His parents had been grieving so hard that he'd had to be the one to fashion the tiny coffin and dig the little grave at the edge of the family land. He'd never dreamed his father would be dead just five years later.

Please, Lord, don't make me bury another member of my family!

The prayer came quickly, and just as quickly he regretted it. It was selfish. If a man prayed, he should ask the Almighty for wisdom to lead, strength to safeguard those he loved. The Lord had blessed him with strength. Some days he wasn't too sure about the wisdom.

Beside him, Miss Stanway's face softened, as if his pain had touched her.

"I'm sorry for your loss, as well," she said. They were the expected words; he'd just used them on her. He'd heard them countless times at his father's passing and his sister's. Yet the look she cast him, the tears pooling in her blue eyes, told him she understood more than most.

He wanted to reach out, clasp her hand, promise her the future would be brighter. But that was nonsense! He couldn't control the future, and she was his to protect only until he returned her to Seattle. He had enough on his hands without taking on a woman new to the frontier.

Besides, every settlement within a hundred miles needed her help. Catherine Stanway might not have realized it yet, but a nurse was a valuable commodity, even if she wasn't so pretty or one of a few unmarried women in the Territory.

Which made him wonder how far his brothers might go to keep her at Wallin Landing.

Chapter Three

Twilight wrapped around the forest by the time Catherine's host guided the team into a grassy clearing crossed by moss-crusted split-rail fences. A large cabin and a barn made from logs and planed timber hugged the edges, with trees standing guard behind them as if honoring their fallen brothers and sisters. Another light through the trees told her at least one more cabin was nearby. The glow through the windows of the closest cabin beckoned to her.

"Where's the lake?" she asked as Drew hopped down and came around the wagon.

He nodded toward the cabin, a two-story affair with a pitched roof and a porch at one end. It was encircled by a walk of planed boards.

"Through the trees there," he said. "We're on a bench fifty feet or so above the waterline. Keeps us out of any flooding in the spring."

His father had obviously planned ahead. She wouldn't have thought about spring flooding when choosing a plot for a house. Of course, she'd never had to choose a homesite in the wilderness!

She turned to climb down, and once again Drew reached out and lifted her from the wagon to set her on her feet. For a moment it was as if she stood in his embrace. His eyes were a smoky blue in the dim light. She couldn't seem to remember why she was here, what she was supposed to do next.

The sound of Levi scrambling out of the wagon bed woke her, and she pulled away. As the youth started past, his brother put out an arm to stop him.

"See to the horses and bring in the supplies. I'll take our guest inside."

Levi's face tightened, but then he glanced at Catherine. As if he finally realized it was his fault she was here, he shrugged and went to do as he had been bid.

"This way," Drew said with another nod toward the cabin.

The Wallin home might have been made from peeled logs, but it appeared the family had taken pains to make the place attractive as well as functional. Stained glass panels decorated the top of each window on the two floors. Boxes filled with plants underpinned the two larger downstairs windows; she recognized several kinds of flowering herbs. Someone had plaited a wreath from fir branches and hung it from the thick front door. The resinous smell greeted Catherine as she approached.

Drew reached for the latch, but the panel swung open without his aid. Catherine only had time to register blond hair darker and a good foot lower than hers before a young lady launched herself into her arms.

"Thank you, oh, thank you!" The girl drew back to grin at Catherine. "I know this was a terrible long way to come, but we need a nurse badly. Simon and James and John will be so glad to see you! They'll be by later, my brothers, all of them. They thought you or Doc or whoever was coming should have some time to yourself before they came stampeding in, but I couldn't wait to get to know you better."

"Beth," Drew rumbled beside Catherine.

The girl didn't even pause for breath as she seized Catherine's hand and pulled her across the colorful braided rag rug into the wide, warm room, which was lit by a glowing fire. "I'll make an apron for you to wear. *Godey's Lady's Book* says they're all the rage for the fashionable lady of industry."

"Beth," Drew said a little more firmly as he followed them.

"I have stew ready for dinner," his sister continued, and Catherine could smell the tangy scent drifting through the cabin as Beth tugged her past a long table with ladder-back chairs at each end and benches along the sides. Similar chairs rested against the walls, cane seats partially covered by small quilts, and a bentwood rocker stood near the rounded stone fireplace. Through the openings on either side of the hearth she caught sight of a step stove with kettles simmering. A massive iron tub leaned against the outside wall.

"I know it's not much," Beth said, "but I wasn't sure when you'd get here and I was afraid I'd dry out the venison if I kept it on the stove too long. Do you like stew?"

"Yes," Catherine assured her, pulling herself to a stop in the middle of the room, "but..."

Beth didn't wait for more. "Oh, good! This time of year we only have early carrots, of course, but I still had potatoes and turnips left from the fall. We have our own garden behind the house. Drew cleared the land. In a few weeks, we'll have peas and beans and cabbage and…"

"Beth!"

Drew's thundering voice made Catherine cringe, but it finally stopped his sister, in word and in action. She turned to frown at him, firelight rippling across her straight golden hair. "What?"

"Doc Maynard couldn't come," he said without a hint of apology in his voice. "This is Miss Stanway. She's a nurse, but she'll only be staying the night with us. I'll return her to Seattle tomorrow."

"Oh." The single word seemed to echo in the room. She dropped her gaze and tucked a strand of hair behind her ear. Now that she was still, Catherine could see that she had a heart-shaped face like her brother, wide-spaced eyes and the beginnings of a figure. Her cheeks were turning as pink as the narrow-skirted gingham gown she wore.

"It was a natural mistake," Catherine assured her with a smile. "And I'll be happy to help your mother while I'm here."

Beth glanced up and brightened. Her eyes were darker than her older brother's, closer to the midnight blue of Levi's. Catherine had a feeling that one day a large number of suitors would be calling.

"Thank you," Beth said, good humor apparently restored. "And I truly am happy to make your acquaintance. Would you like to see Ma now?"

Before Catherine could answer, Drew stepped forward, gaze all for his sister, his brows drawn down heavily over his deep-set eyes. "How is she?"

Beth's light dimmed, and she seemed to shrink in on herself. "Still the same. I'm not sure she knows me."

Catherine felt as if her spine had lengthened, her shoulders strengthened. Her father had always said it was a powerful thing to have a purpose. She felt it now, wiping away her weariness and soothing her frustrations. *Thank You, Lord. Help me do what You fitted me to do.*

"Take me to her," she ordered them.

Beth clasped her hands in obvious relief. Drew merely motioned Catherine to where a set of open stairs, half logs driven into the wall, rose to the second story.

Upstairs were two more rooms, divided by the fireplace and the walls that supported it. One room held several straw ticks on the floor, but only one seemed to be in use; the others were piled with rumpled clothing, tools and chunks of wood. The other room contained two wooden beds—a smaller one in the corner with a carved chest beside it and a larger bedstead in the center with a side table holding a brass lamp. Both beds were covered with multicolored quilts that brightened the room.

A woman lay on the wider bed. She had hair that was more red than gold, plastered to her oval face. She'd been handsome once, but now pain had drawn lines about her eyes, nose and mouth. By the way the collar of her flannel nightgown bagged, Catherine guessed she'd lost some weight, as well. Her skin looked like parchment in the candlelight.

Catherine sat in the high-backed chair that had been placed next to the bed and reached for Mrs. Wallin's hand. Setting her fingers to the woman's wrist, she counted the heartbeats as her father had taught her. She could feel Drew and his sister watching her. She'd been watched by family members before, some doubting her, some worried. This time felt different somehow. Her shoulders tensed, and she forced them to relax.

"Her pulse is good," she reported, keeping her voice calm and her face composed. She had to remain objective. It was so much easier to do her job when she viewed the person before her as a patient in need of healing rather than someone's mother or wife. She leaned closer, listening to the shallow, panting breaths.

"Mrs. Wallin," she said, "can you hear me?"

The woman's eyelids fluttered. Drew and Beth leaned closer as well, crowding around Catherine. Their mother's eyes opened, as clear as her eldest son's but greener. She blinked as if surprised to find herself in bed, then focused on Catherine.

"Mary?" she asked.

Beth sucked in a breath, drawing back and hugging herself. Drew didn't move, but Catherine felt as if he also had distanced himself. Who was this Mary his mother had been expecting? Did Drew Wallin have a wife he'd neglected to mention?

Drew watched as Catherine tended to his mother. Ma had changed so much in the past two weeks that he hardly knew her. As Beth had said, he wasn't sure she knew them, either. It was as if the fire that had warmed them all their lives was growing dim.

He had feared Catherine might confirm the fact, tell them in her cool manner to prepare for the worst. Instead, she was all confidence. She opened the window beside the bed and ordered the one opposite it opened as well, drawing in the cool evening air and the scent of the Sound. She directed Drew to smother the fire and helped Beth pull off some of the covers they had piled on their mother in an attempt to sweat the fever from her. She even removed Ma's favorite feather pillow and requested a straw one. It was testimony to how ill their mother was that she protested none of this.

"Do you have a milk cow?" Catherine asked Drew as Beth dug through the chest their father had carved for Ma to find the clean nightgown Catherine had suggested.

Drew shook his head. "Four goats. But they produce enough milk for our purposes."

Catherine accepted the flannel gown from Beth with a nod of thanks. "What about lemons?"

"Simon brought some back from town last week," Beth said, tucking her hair behind her ear and hugging herself with her free hand. "I used some for lemonade."

"Fetch the lemonade," Catherine advised. "We'll start with that and see if she can tolerate it. Later, I'll show you how to make lemon whey. Mrs. Child recommends it for high fevers."

"Mrs. Child?" Drew asked, but his sister nodded eagerly.

"I know Mrs. Child! Ma has her book on being a good housewife. She's very clever."

Beth might have gone on as she often did, but Catherine directed her toward the stairs, then turned to Drew. "I'll need warm water, as well."

Drew frowned. "To drink?"

Pink crept across her cheekbones, as delicate as the porcelain cups his mother had safeguarded over the Rockies on their way West. "No," she said, gaze darting away from his. "To bathe your mother. Can you see that it's warmed properly? Not too hot."

"Coming right up," Drew promised, and left to find some help.

He managed to locate the rest of his family at Simon's cabin, which was a little ways into the woods. His brothers were cleaning up before dinner, but they all stopped what they were doing to listen to his explanation of what had happened in town. He thought at least one of them might agree with him that Levi's actions were rash. But to a man they were too concerned about Ma to consider how Catherine Stanway must feel.

"So this nurse," Simon said, draping the cloth he'd been using to dry his freshly shaven face over the porcelain basin in a corner of his cabin. "What do we know about her? What are her credentials?"

Figure on Simon, his next closest brother in age at about two years behind Drew's twenty-nine, to ask. He was the only one tall enough to look him in the eye, for all they rarely saw eye to eye. With his pale blond hair and angled features, Simon was too cool. Even looked different from Drew. Every movement of his lean body, word from his lips and look from his light green eyes seemed calculated.

The middle brother, James, leaned back where he sat near the fire, effortlessly balancing the stool on one of its three legs. "Does it really matter, Simon? She's here, and she's helping. Be grateful." He turned to Drew. His long face was a close match for Simon's in its seriousness, his short blond hair a shade darker, but there was a twinkle in his dark blue eyes. "Now, I have a more pressing question. Is she pretty?"

"That's not important," Drew started, but his second-youngest brother, John, slapped his hands down on his knees where he sat at a bench by the table.

"She must be! He's blushing!" He shook his head, red-gold hair straighter than his mother's like a flame in the light.

Drew took a deep breath to hold back a retort. Of all his brothers, John was the most sensible, the most studious. If he'd seen a change in Drew, it must be there.

But he wasn't about to admit it.

He started for the door. "Pretty or not, she has work for us to do. She wants lots of water warmed. You bring it in. I'll heat it up." He glanced back over his shoulder. "And John, find Levi. He should have finished in the barn by now. I don't want him wandering off."

"Where would he go?" James teased, letting the stool clatter back to the floor as he climbed to his feet. "It's not as if he has tickets to the theatre."

"Or one to attend within a hundred miles," John agreed, but he headed for the barn as Drew had requested.

For the next couple of hours everyone was too busy to joke. His brothers took turns bringing in the water to Drew, who heated it in his mother's largest pot on the step stove. Then they formed a line up the stairs and passed the warm water in buckets up to Beth and Miss Stanway.

"She washed Ma with a soft cloth, then rubbed her down with another," Beth marveled to Drew at the head of the stairs when he ventured up to check on them after he and his brothers had eaten. "And she changed the sheets on the bed without even making Ma get up. She's amazing!"

Drew had to agree, for when Catherine beckoned him closer, he found his mother much improved. No longer did she look like a wax figure on the bed, and she smiled at each of her sons as they clustered around to speak with her.

"I think it's time to rest," Catherine said to them all after a while. "I'll come talk to you after I've settled her."

Drew herded everyone down the stairs. They all found seats in the front room, Simon and James on opposite ends of the table, John on a bench alongside, Beth in Ma's rocking chair and Levi sprawled on the braided rug with Drew standing behind him leaning against the stairs. He caught himself counting heads, even though he knew everyone was present. Habit. He'd been watching over them for the past ten years, ever since the day his father had died.

It had been a widow-maker that had claimed their father. Drew had been eighteen then, and only Simon at sixteen and James at fourteen had been old enough and strong enough to help clear the timber for their family's original claim. None of them had seen the broken limb high on the massive fir before it came crashing down.

"Take care of them," his father had said when his brothers had pulled the limb off him and Drew had cradled him in his arms. Already his father's voice had started wheezing from punctured lungs, and blood had tinged his lips. "Take care of them all, Andrew. This family is your responsibility."

He had never forgotten. He hadn't lost another member of the family, though his brothers had made the job challenging. They'd broken arms and legs, cut themselves on saws and knives, fought off diseases he was afraid to name. Even sweet Beth had given him a scare a few months ago when she'd nearly succumbed to a fever much like their mother's.

He'd kept them safe, nursed them through any illness or injury. His had been the shoulders they'd cried on, the arms that had held them through the night. He'd been the one to ride for medicine, to cut cloths into bandages. He'd been the one to sit up with them night after night. Having someone help felt odd, as if he'd put on the wrong pair of boots.

That odd feeling didn't ease as Catherine came down the stairs to join them. As if she were a schoolmarm prepared to instruct, she took up her place by the fire. The crackling flames set her figure in silhouette.

"I thought you would all want to hear what I believe about your mother's condition," she said, and Drew knew he wasn't the only Wallin leaning forward to catch every word.

"Two culprits cause this type of fever," she continued, gaze moving from one brother to another until it met Drew's. "Typhus and typhoid fever."

Neither sounded good, and his stomach knotted.

"Aren't they the same thing?" John asked.

She shook her head. "Many people think so, and some doctors treat them the same, but they are very different beasts. With typhus, the fever never leaves, and the patient simply burns up."

Beth shivered and rubbed a hand up her arm.

"Typhoid fever, on the other hand," Catherine said as if she hadn't noticed, "is generally worse for the first two or three weeks and then starts to subside. Given how long you said she's suffered, I'm leaning toward typhoid fever, but we should know for sure within the week."

Simon seized on the word. "A week. Then, you'll stay with us for that long." It was a statement, not a question.

"I promised to return Miss Stanway to Seattle tomorrow," Drew said.

Simon scowled at him.

"We need her more than Seattle does," Levi complained.

His other brothers murmured their agreement.

"That isn't our decision to make," Drew argued.

"No," Catherine put in. "It's mine."

That silenced them. She clasped her hands in front of her blue gown. "Doctors take an oath to care for their patients. My father believed that nurses should take one, as well. It is my duty to care for your mother and for you, should you sicken."

A duty she took seriously, he could see. Her color was high, her face set with determination as she glanced around at them all. "I will stay until your mother is out of danger."

Simon stood. "It's settled, then. Drew, clear out your cabin and let her have it. You can bunk with me. I snore less than Levi or James."

John rolled his eyes. "That's what you think."

"Oh, I couldn't take anyone's cabin," Catherine started.

Drew held up his hand. "No, Simon's right. Not about his snoring. He's louder than Yesler's sawmill." As his other brothers laughed and Simon shook his head, Drew continued, "You need a place of your own. I'll clear out my cabin tonight so you can sleep when you finish with Ma."

"I intend to stay up with her tonight," Catherine warned him.

"Then the cabin will be waiting for you in the morning," Drew assured her.

She smiled at them. "Well, then, gentlemen, I will leave you for the night. I understand the youngest Mr.

Wallin sleeps upstairs. I'll send him if we need anything."

Again Levi looked as if he were going to protest, but one glance at Drew and he shrugged and settled back on the rug. Drew watched her climb the stairs, Beth right behind her.

"That's quite a woman," Simon mused, stretching his feet over Levi's prone form toward the fire.

"Never met one so determined," James mused.

"You never met one with that kind of education, either," John reminded him. "I like the fact that she isn't afraid to speak her mind."

"Bit on the bossy side," Levi said with a yawn. "But she'll do."

"That she will," Simon agreed. "The only question is, which one of us is going to marry her?"

Just what he'd feared. Drew stiffened. "No one said anything about marriage."

Simon glanced around at his brothers. "I believe I just did."

John nodded, brightening. "Inspired. She's smart, and she has a skill we sorely need."

"And she's not bad to look at," James added.

"You could do a lot worse, Drew," Levi agreed.

Drew shook his head. "You're mad, the lot of you. I'm not getting married."

"Suit yourself." Simon rose and went to the fireplace to scoop up a handful of kindling. "We'll draw straws. Short straw proposes."

Drew stared as his other brothers, except Levi, rose to their feet. "Don't be ridiculous. She wouldn't have any of you."

James shrugged. "Doesn't hurt to try."

Simon squared up the sticks and hid all but the tops in his hand, then held them out to his brothers. "Who wants to go first?"

Drew strode into their group. "Enough, I said. No one is proposing to Miss Stanway, and that's final."

His brothers exchanged glances. Simon lowered the sticks. "Very well, Drew. For now. But you have to marry someday if you want kin to inherit your land. You'll never build that town for Pa unless you do. I think you better ask yourself why you're so dead set against her."

"And why you're even more set against us courting her," John added.

Chapter Four

So one of the Wallin brothers was going to marry her. Catherine shook her head as she crossed the floor to the big bed. Either they didn't know voices carried in the log cabin or they didn't care that she realized their intentions. It truly didn't matter which was the truth. She wasn't getting married.

"Do you think bonnets or hats are more fetching on a lady?" Beth asked, following her. "I'm of a mind for bonnets. They cover more of your face from the sun, and they have extra room for decorations. Feathers are ever so flattering."

She was chattering again, voice quick and forceful, but it seemed a bit more strained than usual, and Catherine couldn't help noticing that Beth's color was high as she joined Catherine. Was she trying to pretend she wasn't aware of her brothers' intentions?

Her patient was awake, green eyes watchful. "You mustn't mind Simon," Mrs. Wallin murmured, proving that she, too, had heard at least part of the conversation downstairs. The ribbon ties on her nightcap brushed the skin of her cheek. "Being the second son after Drew has never been easy. He tends to assert himself even when there's no need."

As Beth tidied up the room, Catherine raised her patient's wrist to check her pulse. It seemed just a little stronger, but perhaps that was because Mrs. Wallin was embarrassed by her sons' behavior.

"And there is no need to assert himself in this situation," Catherine told her as she lowered Mrs. Wallin's hand. "I'm here to help you. Nothing more."

Mrs. Wallin shivered, and Catherine touched the woman's forehead. Still too hot, but did she perhaps feel a little cooler than earlier? Was Catherine so desperate to see hope that she had lost her ability to be objective?

"Am I going to die?" Mrs. Wallin whispered.

Beth gasped. Catherine pulled back her hand. "Not if I can help it."

As Beth hurried closer, Mrs. Wallin reached out and took Catherine's hand, for all the world as if Catherine was the one needing comfort. "I'm not afraid." Her eyes were bright, and Catherine told herself it was the fever. "I know in Whom I've put my trust. But my boys and Beth, oh, I hate the idea of leaving them!"

Beth threw herself onto the bed, wrapping her mother in a fierce hug. "You're not leaving us, Ma. I won't let you!"

The room seemed to be growing smaller, the air thinner. Catherine pulled out of the woman's grip.

"Now, then," she made herself say with brisk efficiency. "I see nothing to indicate your mother must leave you anytime soon. The best thing now would be for her to rest. I'll be right here if she needs me."

Beth straightened and wiped a tear from her face.

"Yes, of course. I'll just go help Drew." She hurried from the loft.

"She's a dear child," her mother murmured, settling in the bed. "She'll need someone besides me, another lady, to help guide her."

Someone besides Catherine. "Rest now," she urged, and Mrs. Wallin nodded and dutifully closed her eyes, head sinking deeper into the pillow, face at peace.

A shame Catherine couldn't find such peace. She perched on the chair beside the bed and tried to steady her breathing. Still, the woman's fears and Beth's reaction clung to her like cobwebs. Who was Catherine to promise Mrs. Wallin's return to health? Only the Lord knew what the future held. Her earthly father had drummed that into her.

We may be His hands for healing, he'd say as he washed his hands after surgery. *But He will determine the outcome of our work.*

And the outcome of a life.

Did he have to go, Lord? Did You need another physician in heaven? But why take Nathan, too? Did You have to leave me alone?

The tears were starting again, and she blinked them fiercely away. She'd had her fill of them months ago. She couldn't look at the sunny yellow rooms of their home in Sudbury without seeing the book her father had left before going to war, the galoshes her brother had forgotten to pack. The polished wood pew in their community church had felt empty even though another family had joined her in it. Every time she'd walked down the street, she'd seem nothing but stares of pity from her neighbors.

Still, her father had taught her well.

You cannot let sorrow touch you, Catherine, he'd admonished. *You are here to tend to their bodies. Let the Lord heal other hurts. Remember your calling.*

That was what she'd done in those dark days after her father and brother had died. None of the other physicians in the area had wanted to attach themselves professionally to an unmarried nurse. Even the big cities like Boston and New York had been loath to let an unmarried woman practice. Widowed men who had known her father well offered marriage, the opportunity to mother their motherless children. Even her minister had counseled her to find a good man to wed.

When she'd seen the notice advertising Asa Mercer's expedition to help settle Washington Territory, she'd known what to do. She'd put the house up for sale and donated their things to those in need. Then she'd packed her bags and sailed to the opposite side of the country.

All her experiences had taught her how to wall off her emotions. It did no good to question her past. She must look to her future, to the health of the community she could improve, the lives she could save. She had no intention of entering into marriage, with anyone.

For once she opened the door to feeling, she was very much afraid she'd never be able to close it again.

At the far edge of the clearing in his own cabin, Drew yanked a pair of suspenders off the ladder to the loft. As he tidied the place so Catherine could sleep there that night, all he could think about was Simon's ridiculous demand that one of them must marry the pretty nurse.

He ought to be immune to such antics by now. But after years of proximity, his brothers knew just how to get under his skin like a tick digging for blood.

Oh, he'd heard ministers preach on the subject. A man had a duty to marry, to raise children that would help him subdue the wilderness, make a home in this far land. Children were one way a man left a legacy. To him, the fact that his brothers had reached their manhood alive and ready to take on the world was enough of a legacy.

He knew the general course of things was for a man to find his own land, build a house, start a profession and marry. He had this house and was top in his profession, but he couldn't simply leave his mother, Beth or his brothers to fend for themselves. They were his responsibility, his to protect. That was what any man did who was worthy of the name. That was what his father had done.

How could he call himself a man and leave his family to tend to a wife? In his mind, a wife took time, attention. She'd have requirements, needs and expectations. He already felt stretched to the breaking point. How could he add more?

Oh, he had no doubt Simon and James were looking to marry one day, and John and Levi would eventually follow. But to stake a claim on a lady after a few hours of acquaintance? That was the stuff of madness.

Or legend.

He snorted as he gathered up the dishes he hadn't bothered to return to the main house. Their father had claimed he'd fallen in love with their mother at first sight when he'd met her at a barn raising. *Her hair was like a fire on a winter's night, calling me home*, he'd told his sons more than once.

Before his father had died, Drew had dreamed it would happen that way for him. Though there were few unmarried ladies in Seattle, he'd thought someday he might turn a corner, walk into church and there she'd be. But at twenty-nine, he knew better. Love was a choice built from prolonged presence. And with six lives already depending on him, he had chosen not to participate in adding more.

"Hello, brother Drew!" Beth sang out as she opened the door of his cabin, basket under one arm. She stepped inside, glanced around and wrinkled her nose. "Oh, you haven't gotten far, have you?"

Drew looked around as well, trying to see the place through Beth's eyes. He'd built the cabin himself, his brothers lending a hand with planing and notching the logs and chinking them with dried moss and rock. He'd crafted the fireplace in the center of one wall from rounded stones gathered along the lake. As his father had taught him from what he'd learned in his homeland of Sweden, Drew had built a cabinet for his bed tick, setting it next to the hearth for warmth. A table and chairs of lumber cut from trees he'd felled rested on the rag rug his mother had woven for him. A plain wood chest sat against the far wall, waiting for him to start carving. All in all, his cabin was a solid, practical place to sleep between long hours of working. Very likely, Beth considered it far too plain.

But it didn't matter what his sister thought. It mattered what Catherine Stanway thought, and he had no doubt she'd find it lacking.

He pointed his sister to the corn-tassel broom leaning against one wall. "If you think the cabin needs more work, feel free to lend a hand."

He busied himself with shaking out the quilt his mother had made for him.

Beth hummed to herself as she set down the basket and began sweeping dried mud off the floor. "I like her," she announced, and Drew knew she had to be talking about Catherine. "She knows a lot. And did you see that dress? There was one just like it in *Godey's*."

His sister devoured the ladies' magazine, which generally arrived in Seattle months after its publication back East. The editor of *Godey's*, Drew was convinced, had never laid eyes on a frontier settlement, or she'd never have suggested some of the outlandish fashions. What woman needed skirts so wide they couldn't fit through the door of a cabin or allow her to climb to the loft of her bed?

"I'm sure Miss Stanway was all the rage back home," Drew said, hauling the table back into place in the center of the room from where James and John had shoved it during a friendly wrestling match a few days ago.

"Here, too." Beth giggled as she paused. "I think Simon is smitten."

"Simon can go soak his head in the lake." The vehemence of his words surprised him, and so did the emotions riding on them. The first thought that had popped into his head at his sister's teasing was the word *mine*.

Beth must have noticed the change in his tone as well, for she turned to regard him wide-eyed. "You like her!"

Drew shoved the chairs into place with enough force to set the table to rocking on its wooden legs. "I like the fact that she can help Ma. That's what's important—not the rest of this tomfoolery."

"I suppose you're right." She resumed her sweeping, angling the pile of dust toward the doorway. "Still, I hope she'll let me talk to her about how they're wearing their hair back East. Every time I try the curling iron, I get it so hot I can hardly touch it. I bet she'll know how to do it right."

Hand on the wooden bucket to fill it with fresh water from the pump outside, Drew paused. "You think she curls her hair?"

"And irons her dresses." Beth nodded with great confidence. "She might even use rouge to get that glow in her cheeks."

What was he doing? This wasn't the sort of thing a man discussed, even with his little sister. He hefted the bucket and headed for the door. "You're too young to rouge your cheeks or curl your hair, Beth. And Miss Stanway is here to help Ma, not teach you things you don't need to know."

Beth made a face at him as he opened the door. "You don't get to decide what I need to know. You couldn't possibly understand. You're a man." When he turned to argue, she swept the dirt up into the air in a cloud of dust that nearly choked him.

Drew waved his hand, backing away. "I'm your brother, and the last time I checked, I'm responsible for your upbringing. If you can't leave Miss Stanway be on such matters, I'll make sure you have other things to do elsewhere."

"You would, too," Beth declared, lowering the broom. "But you're right. We should be thinking about Ma." Her face crumpled. "Oh, I sure hope Miss Stanway knows what's she's doing. I just can't lose Ma!"

Cold pierced him. Drew went to enfold his sister in his arms, getting a broom handle on the chin for his trouble. "We won't lose her, Beth. We won't let her go."

Beth nodded against his chest, and he heard her sniff.

When she pushed back, she wiped her face with her fingers, leaving two tracks of mud across her cheeks. This from the girl who admired rouge, of all things.

As Drew smiled, she turned to glance back into the cabin. "The place is looking better already. You go check on Ma, and I'll add a few finishing touches."

Drew cocked his head. "Like what? I'll have none of those doilies you're so fond of."

Beth turned to him, eyes wide. "Who could hate an innocent doily? They're so dainty and cultured."

Everything he was not, he realized, and trying to pretend otherwise served no one. "Just remember, this is a man's house," he told his sister as he stepped out onto the porch. "Miss Stanway may be staying awhile, but I'm the one who lives here."

With a feeling he was talking to the air, he left Beth humming to herself.

Rouge. He shook his head again. His mother had complained about the stuff from time to time.

A lady makes the most of what the good Lord gave her, she'd said after they'd visited Seattle a few weeks ago. *She doesn't need to paint herself or squeeze herself into a shape she wasn't born with.*

He had never considered the matter, but the thought of his sister prettying herself up made his stomach churn.

A few strides across the clearing brought him to their parents' house. Once, they had all lived there, his brothers curled up on beds on one side of the upstairs room, and Beth with their parents on the other. When he'd laid claim to the land next to his father's, he'd built his own house. Simon had done the same on the opposite side, clearing the land there. Now James was in the process of outfitting his cabin on the next set of acreage he had claimed. Tracts were already platted for John and Levi, as well. When they managed a town site, their father's name would go on even if he hadn't.

Simon, James and John had retired for the night, and Levi was still spread in front of the fire, rereading one of the adventure novels their father had brought with him across the plains. Drew could barely make out the words *The Last of the Mohicans* on the worn leather spine. Why his father and brothers wanted to read about the frontier when they lived on it Drew had never understood. He climbed the stairs to his mother's room.

At the top, he paused, almost afraid of what he might find. His mother lay asleep on the bed, her chest rising and falling under the quilt. He had not seen her so peaceful in days, and something inside him thawed at the sight. Beside her on the chair, Catherine Stanway put a finger to her lips before rising to join him at the stairwell.

His first thought on seeing her up close was that she was tired. A few tendrils of her pale hair had come undone and hung in soft curls about her face. Her blue eyes seemed to sag at the corners. But the smile she gave him was encouraging.

"Her fever appears to be coming down," she whispered. "But it's still higher than I'd like. The next two days will be very important in determining her recovery. Someone must be with her every moment."

Drew nodded. "We can take turns."

She gazed up at him, and he wondered what she was thinking. "I was under the impression you and your brothers had an important task to undertake tomorrow."

"Captain Collings's spar," Drew confirmed. "His

ship, the *Merry Maid*, was damaged in a storm crossing the mouth of the Columbia River. She managed to limp into Puget Sound, but she can't continue her journey to China without a new mast."

She stuck out her lower lip as if impressed, but the movement made his gaze stop at the soft pink of her mouth. Drew swallowed and looked away.

"I thought all trees felled around Seattle were destined for Mr. Yesler's mill," he heard her say.

"Most," Drew agreed, mentally counting the number of logs that made up the top story of the house. "My brothers and I specialize in filling orders for masts and yard arms for sailing ships. Simon's located the perfect tree not too far from the water, so it will be easy to transport, but it will take all of us to bring it down safely and haul it to the bay."

"If you should be working, sir, your sister and I can take care of things here."

He could hear the frown in her voice. She was probably used to being self-sufficient. Yet Drew had a hard time imagining her standing by to protect a frontier farm. She'd come on the bride ship, which meant she'd lived in Seattle for less than a month. By her own admission, she'd lived in larger towns back East. What could she know about surviving in the wilderness?

"Can you shoot?" he asked, gaze coming back to her.

She was indeed frowning, golden brows drawn over her nose. He had a strange urge to feather his fingers across her brow. "No," she said. "Do you expect me to need to shoot?"

"Very likely," Drew assured her, trying to master his feelings. "Pa made sure all of us knew how to protect each other and the farm. Ma can pick a heart from an ace at thirty paces, and Beth can hold her own. But if Beth is helping Ma, there will be no one left to protect you."

Her lips quirked as if she found it annoying that she needed such protection. And of course, his gaze latched on to the movement. He forced his eyes up.

"Is it truly so dangerous?" she asked. "You aren't living among the natives. You have homes, a garden, stock."

She needed to understand that the veneer of civilization was only as thick as the walls of the house. "James spotted a cougar while he was working on his cabin last week. We surprised a bear at the spring only yesterday."

She raised her head. "Well, then, we'll simply stay in the house until you return."

The silk of her hair tickled his chin, and he caught the scent of lemon and lavender, tart and clean. He needed to end this conversation and leave before he did or said something they'd both regret.

"You can't promise to remain indoors," he told her. "Even if we lay in a stock of wood and water, it might run out. Like it or not, Miss Stanway, you need me."

And she didn't like it. He could tell by the way her blue eyes narrowed, her chin firmed. This was a woman used to getting her own way.

And that could be trouble. He could only wonder: Over the next two days, which would prevail, her will or his determination?

Chapter Five

Two days. Surely she could survive two days. She'd sat longer vigils in the wards in Boston, taking breaks only for short naps, determined to cheat death. Two days was child's play.

Of course, normally, when she sat with a patient, she was either alone in the ward or a doctor or other nurse was nearby. This was the first time she'd served as a nurse in someone's home.

She found it decidedly unnerving.

For one thing, the Wallin house was anything but quiet. Levi had pounded up the stairs and thrown himself in bed on the other side of the loft. The buzz a short while later confirmed that Simon wasn't the only brother who snored. Beth crept up the stairs more quietly before slipping into a darker corner and emerging in her nightgown, then climbing into her own bed. The logs popped as the house cooled with the night. Wood settled in the small fire she'd had Drew rekindle. Something with tiny claws scampered across the roof over Catherine's head. Mournful calls echoed from the woods, as if all nature worried with the Wallins.

But worse was her awareness of Drew. He had agreed to take turns with her during the night, then left to finish some chores. She felt as if the entire house breathed a sigh of relief when he entered it again. His boots were soft on the stairs, and the boards whispered a welcome as he crossed to her side. He laid a hand on her shoulder, the pressure assuring, supportive. Then he turned and disappeared downstairs again.

Her pulse was too fast. She took a breath and leaned forward to adjust the covers over her patient again.

She had barely managed to restore her calm when he returned carrying a wooden platter and a large steaming pink-and-white china bowl with a spoon sticking from it.

"You've had nothing to eat," he reminded her. "You'll need your strength." He set the platter across her lap. On it rested a bowl of stew, a crusty loaf of bread, a bone-handled knife and a pat of creamy butter.

Catherine's stomach growled its answer. "Thank you," she said. She bowed her head and asked a blessing, then scooped up a spoonful of Beth's stew. The thick sauce warmed her almost as much as his gesture.

As she ate, he reached down, sliced off a hunk of the bread and set about eating it. Crumbs sprinkled the front of his cotton shirt, and he brushed them away, fingers long and quick. She wondered how they'd feel cradling her hand.

A hunk of venison must have gone down wrong, for she found herself coughing. He hurried to pour water from the jug by the bed into a tin cup, but she waved him back.

"I'm fine," she managed. Swallowing the last of the

stew, she set the bowl on the platter. "Thank you. That was very good. Beth is a talented cook."

"Ma taught her." He went to lean against the fireplace, the only spot in the room where he could stand completely upright. His gaze rested on the woman on the bed, who seemed to be sleeping blissfully through their quiet conversation. "She taught us all, saying a man should know how to care for himself."

Catherine couldn't argue with that. "My father had a similar philosophy. He said a woman should be able to fend for herself if needed."

"Yet he never taught you to shoot?"

He seemed generally puzzled by that. Catherine smiled. "There's not much call for hunting near Boston, at least not for food. I suppose parents try to teach their children what they need to survive in their own environment. I wouldn't expect your mother to teach you how to dance."

"There you would be wrong." Even in the dim light she could see his smile. "Pa used to play the fiddle, and Ma said if she didn't teach us boys to dance, she'd never have a partner." His smile faded. "Not that she needs one now."

Catherine had never been one to offer false hope, yet she couldn't help rushing to assure him. "We'll make sure she gets well."

Her words must have sounded as baseless to him as they did to her, for he said nothing as he pushed off from the hearth. He gathered up the dishes and disappeared down the stairs once more.

Catherine sighed. That exchange was simply a reminder of why it was better to stay focused on her task of nursing the patient, not on the emotional needs of the patient's family. She had found ways to comfort grieving loved ones before her father and brother had been killed. Now she felt hurts too keenly.

She tried to listen to Mrs. Wallin's breathing, which seemed far more regular than her own, but from downstairs came the sounds of dishes clanking, the chink of wood on metal, the splash of water. It seemed Mrs. Wallin had taught her sons to wash up, as well. Their future wives would be pleasantly surprised.

She expected him to return when he was finished, but the house fell quiet again. She added another log to the fire, then checked her patient once more. All was as it should be. The wooden chair didn't seem so hard; her body sank into it. The warmth of the room wrapped about her like a blanket. She closed her weary eyes.

Only to snap them open as someone picked her up and held her close.

"What are you doing?" she demanded as Drew's face came into focus.

He was already starting for the stairs, head ducked so that it was only a few inches from hers. "You fell asleep."

Catherine shifted in his arms. "I'm fine. Put me down. I have work to do."

Beth had sat up in bed and was regarding them wide-eyed as he started down the stairs. "Let Beth watch Ma for a while. I'll spell her shortly. We'll send for you if anything changes."

He reached the bottom of the stairs and started across the room as if she were no more than a basket of laundry destined for the line. "I can walk, sir," she informed him.

He twisted to open the door. "That you can. I've seen

you do it." He paused on the porch to nod out into the darkness, where the only light was the glow from a few stars peeking through the clouds. "But our clearing isn't a city street. There are tree roots and rocks that can trip you up in broad daylight. I know the hazards. Best you let me do the walking."

She hadn't noticed that the space was so bumpy when they'd arrived. Indeed, it had seemed surprisingly level; the grass neat and trim. Very likely the goats cropped it. Still, she didn't relish tripping over a rock and twisting her ankle. She hardly wanted to stay at Wallin Landing a moment more than necessary, and certainly not long enough to heal a sprain.

So she remained where she was, warm against his chest, cradled in his arms, as Drew ferried her across the clearing to another cabin hidden among the trees. Her legs were decidedly unsteady as he set her down on the wide front porch and swung open the door to enter ahead of her. She heard the scrape of flint as he lit a lantern.

The golden light chased the darkness to the far corners of the room, and she could see a round planked table in the center, set over a braided rug and flanked by two tall solid-backed chairs. A little small for a knight of the round table, but cozy. As if he thought so, too, Drew's cheeks were darkening again, and he seemed to be stuffing something white and lacy into the pocket of his trousers.

"There's a washstand and water jug in the corner," he said, voice gruff. "The necessity's between the two cabins."

In a moment, he'd leave her. Perhaps it was the strange surroundings or the lateness of the day, but she found herself unwilling to see him go. Catherine moved into the room, glanced at the fire simmering in the grate of the stone hearth. As if he was watching her, expecting her to find things wanting, he hurried to lay on another piece of wood.

"Should be enough to see you through the night," he said, straightening. "But I can fetch more from the woodpile if you'd like."

Was he so eager to leave her? "No need," Catherine said. "I'm sure I'll be fine. You could answer one question, though."

She thought he stiffened. "Oh? What would that be?"

"Who's Mary?"

Now she waited, some part of her fearing to hear the answer. His face sagged. "My little sister. The one who died. Ever since Ma took ill, she's been asking after her. We think maybe she's forgotten Mary's gone."

His pain cut into her. She wanted to gather him close, caress the sadness from his face.

What was she thinking?

"She's delirious," Catherine told him. "It's not uncommon with high fevers.

He nodded as if he understood, but she could see the explanation hadn't eased his mind. She should think of something else to say, something else for him to consider, if only for a moment. She glanced around the room again. Her gaze lit on the ladder rising into the loft. Oh, dear. Her hand gripped her wide blue skirts.

"Is that how you reach the sleeping area?" she asked, hoping for another answer.

"There's a loft upstairs," he said, "but the main bed's there." He pointed toward the fire.

What she'd taken for a large cupboard turned out to

be a box bed set deep in one wall. The weathered wood encircled it like the rings of a tree. Catherine wandered over and fingered the thick flannel quilt that covered the tick. Blues and reds and greens were sprinkled in different-size blocks, fitted together like a child's puzzle and stitched with yellow embroidery as carefully as her father's sutures.

"Ma made that when I turned eighteen," he explained, a solid presence behind her. "Those are pieces of every shirt she ever sewed for me. Waste not, want not."

How could she possibly sleep under something so personal? Catherine pulled back her hand and turned. "Perhaps I should stay with my patient."

He took a step away from her as if to block the door. "Beth and I can handle things. You deserve your rest." He nodded toward the bed. "She left you one of Ma's clean nightgowns, I see. If you need anything else, just holler."

Yell, and have nearly a half dozen men appear to help her? Some women would have been delighted by the prospect. She could imagine her friend Maddie crying out and then sitting back with a grin to watch the fireworks. But Catherine felt as if fine threads were weaving about her like her father's surgery silk, binding her to this place, these people.

Was she really ready to be that close to anyone again?

Drew left Catherine and returned to the main cabin so he could help Beth, bringing with him the lacy doily his sister had left on his table and depositing it on her bed. He dozed for a while on one of the beds he used to share with his brothers, rousing twice to poke Levi into silence. Beth woke him before dawn and stumbled off to bed herself. Drew leaned against the hard rocks of the hearth and watched his mother.

She was a proud woman, sure of her skills and her faith. Unlike Catherine, she'd never followed any calling but the keeping of hearth and home and the running of the family farm while his father was logging. She'd been the steadying presence behind Drew the past ten years, always ready to provide advice and comfort, a loaf of bread and a warm quilt. Sometimes he felt as if each stitch formed the word *love.*

More than one man over the years had attempted to court her. But his mother had refused to leave her claim, even after most of her sons had land of their own. He remembered the day not long after his father had died when men had come from town to try to persuade her to move in closer.

"A widowed woman with five boys and a girl?" one of them had scoffed. "You can't manage this property alone."

"I'm not alone," his mother had said, putting one arm around Drew and the other around Simon as their siblings gathered close. "If this is what the Lord wants for us, He'll make a way."

The Lord must have wanted them at Wallin Landing, for they'd been here ever since.

His mother was still sleeping when his brothers left for their work and Beth started about her chores of feeding the chickens, checking for eggs and letting the goats, horses and pigs out to pasture. Simon came upstairs long enough to assure Drew that everything else had been taken care of.

"We'll have the oxen," he murmured, glancing

around Drew as if to make sure their mother was sleeping peacefully. "And I wanted to let you know that John figured the costs for the plow. We should have enough from that spar for Captain Collings to make a good down payment. Then we can put James's field in corn and make better use of those horses he was so set on."

Drew nodded. James had convinced them to invest in the strong horses when another local farmer had given up his claim and needed to sell out. Drew had hoped to put the beasts to good use expanding the fields. Their family had run perilously short of corn and wheat the past two winters, and any profit they might have made logging had been eaten up by purchasing cornmeal and flour from town. He and his brothers were determined to lay in a greater store this year.

"Do what you can today," he told Simon. "If Ma feels better, I can come finish the job tomorrow."

Simon's face tightened, and he took another look at their mother before heading down the stairs. Though he hadn't spoken the words aloud, Drew could feel his doubts.

If Ma ever felt better.

Please, Lord, make her well!

Sometimes it seemed as if he'd been fighting off illness and injury his whole life. What he hated most was the feeling that there was nothing he could do but wait.

The house settled back into quiet. The sun rose over the lake, golden rays spearing through the windows and leaving a patchwork of color as bright as his mother's quilts across the worn wood floor. Still Drew waited. When his mother finally stirred, he straightened and strode to her side. Her gaze was more alert than he'd seen it in weeks.

"What did you do with my pretty nurse?" she asked.

Drew took her hand and clasped it in his. The skin felt warm from the covers but not as dry and hot as it had been.

"We wore her out," he said, giving his mother's hand a squeeze. "But I'll fetch her back for you shortly. In the meantime, are you hungry? Thirsty?"

She cocked her head as if considering the matter, and Drew noticed that her hair was stuck to her forehead like a row of ginger-colored lace. He put his hand to her cheek and found it cool and moist. Was it possible? Had the fever broke during the night?

"Now, why are you staring at me like that?" she asked, pulling back her hand and touching her hair. "Oh, but I must look a fright!"

Drew smiled, relief making the air sweet. "You never looked more beautiful to me, Ma. Shall I make you biscuits?"

She started to yawn and hurriedly covered her mouth with her hand. "Ask Levi. That boy makes better biscuits than the rest of you combined—light as a feather."

"He's out working," Drew told her. "You'll have to settle for my cooking instead."

She was regarding him out of the corners of her eyes, as if she knew she was about to ask something she suspected he wouldn't like. "You might ask Miss Stanway to join us for breakfast."

Not her, too! "Don't you go getting any ideas about Miss Stanway, Ma," Drew said. "She's here to nurse you."

She coughed into her hand, but the noise still sounded healthy to Drew. "Yes, of course she is. And I expect I'll need a great deal of nursing yet, probably for days." She lowered her hand and heaved a great sigh.

"I have a feeling you'll be up and about in no time," Drew said. On impulse, he bent and pressed a kiss against her cheek. Her face was a rosy pink as he started for the stairs.

Thank You, Lord! The thanksgiving was instant and nearly overwhelming. Catherine had been right. His mother was going to live. Their family was whole awhile longer.

Oh, he would have to watch Ma and his brothers while Catherine was at the Landing if he wanted to remain single, but Catherine probably wouldn't be in their lives much longer if his mother's recovery was as rapid as he hoped.

His spirits didn't rise as high as they should have at the thought.

He was halfway to his cabin when he heard the noise—the drum of horses' hooves rapidly approaching. As he pulled up, the sheriff's deputy, Hart McCormick, and several other men from Seattle galloped into the clearing, faces set and bodies tensed.

"Deputy," Drew said with a nod as they reined in around him. "Something wrong?"

McCormick tipped back his broad-brimmed black hat and narrowed his sharp gray eyes at Drew. "Could be. One of Mercer's belles went missing yesterday, and Scout Rankin tells me you might have had something to do with it."

Drew held up his hands. "There's no need for concern. Miss Stanway is here and perfectly safe."

Still Deputy McCormick glared at him, as if sizing up Drew's strength, taking note that he was unarmed. McCormick was tall and lean, with close-cropped black hair and eyes the color of a worn gun barrel.

He'd earned the reputation of being one tough character, having thrown off a rough beginning before riding down a number of outlaws in the two years he'd served as deputy. Drew didn't like his chances if the lawman decided to take him on.

Just then, one of the horses pushed forward, and Drew realized the rider was a redheaded woman. Though she wore a divided skirt so she could sit astride, the way she clutched the reins told Drew she didn't have much experience with horses.

"Then you won't mind bringing her out, now, will you?" she challenged, sharp words softened by an Irish accent.

Deputy McCormick relaxed in his seat. "Miss O'Rourke is particularly concerned about her friend."

Drew lowered his hands. "She's staying in that cabin over there. If you'll give me a moment…"

"Hold these," the redhead commanded, tossing the reins at Drew. As he caught them, she threw one leg over the horse and slid to the ground. "I'll just be fetching her myself." She stalked across the clearing, gait stiff.

"Bit of a spitfire," McCormick commented, watching her. His mouth hitched up as if he liked what he saw. "Still, there's something to be said for a woman who speaks her mind."

"Yeah," one of his posse members threw out. "Spinster."

The others laughed.

"Being uppity seems to be a pretty common failing among those Mercer gals," another commented, scratching his grizzled chin. "Doc Maynard said this Miss Stanway gave him an earful for some of his practices."

"She gave us an earful, too," Drew said, watching as Miss O'Rourke hopped up on the porch and rapped at the door. "And Ma is alive because of it."

That sobered them. McCormick touched his brim again in obvious respect. "I'm sorry to hear your mother was ailing, Wallin, but I'm glad to know she's on the mend."

The door to the cabin opened. Catherine stood in the shadows, hair tumbled about her shoulders, his quilt bundled around her. Stocking feet peeped out from below. The sight hit him square in the chest, and breathing seemed impossible. One look at her friend, and she gave a glad cry and a quick hug before pulling Miss O'Rourke inside and shutting the door.

Air found its way into Drew's lungs. What was it about Catherine that made him react this way? He'd seen pretty girls before—not many and not often it was true, but still.

"I thought you said she was stuck-up," one of the men commented with a frown to his friend. "She looks mighty nice to me."

"I heard they started calling her the Ice Queen," another agreed. "Looks as though the Wallins managed to thaw her out."

"Maybe that's why she needs a quilt," the deputy said with a warning look to his posse. "Either that or she's trying to shield herself from the criticism of people who came West themselves to escape it."

His men had the good sense to look abashed.

McCormick returned his gaze to Drew, shifting on the horse so that his gun belt brushed the saddle horn. "The way I figure it, what you do with the gal is between you and her, so long as she's in agreement. If she has no complaints, we'll be on our way."

Drew nodded, though he still didn't like his chances, for Catherine had every right to complain. She'd been trussed like a calf on the way to market, thrown in the back of a wagon, jostled for miles, threatened with marriage to his brothers and exposed to a virulent fever. Though the last was probably common in her line of work, she hadn't even been given the opportunity to prepare. If she voiced those concerns to the sheriff's deputy, Drew didn't like thinking what would happen to Levi or to him.

McCormick was watching Drew as if expecting something more, so Drew offered, "It's good to know Seattle rallies when one of its own might be in danger."

The posse nodded. Deputy McCormick leaned closer to Drew.

"The sheriff wouldn't have it any other way. He'd have been here himself except he had to investigate a report of harassment to the south of you."

"Harassment?" Drew frowned. "What kind of harassment?"

Deputy McCormick straightened. "Stock let loose in the woods, a shed burned, reports of strangers riding past. Your brother Levi wouldn't know about any of that, would he?"

Drew stiffened. "Levi's been helping with Ma. And he knows better than to start a fire out here."

McCormick glanced around the clearing. "Where is your brother this morning?"

"With Simon and the others, out working." And he wasn't about to point the direction.

The deputy scratched his chin. "I suppose that's witness enough. Besides, the sheriff thought it might be Indian trouble."

Drew shook his head. "We've never had any trouble with the Duwamish, even during the Indian Wars. They were always helpful, until these new rules ended up pushing them from their land and trying to force them to settle across the Sound."

Two of the men bristled, and Drew heard someone mutter about being an Indian lover. He ignored them. His family had always dealt fairly with the natives they'd encountered, and in turn they lived in peace along the lake. But he knew not everyone agreed with that philosophy.

Knowing it might take Catherine a bit to change—at least, it always took Ma and Beth more time to dress in the morning than it did him and his brothers—Drew invited their unexpected visitors to see to their horses. He was surprised his sister didn't come hurrying out of the barn to greet them, but she must have taken the goats to the pasture by Simon's cabin, for he caught no sign of her or the animals.

"You having any trouble with your neighbors, the Rankins?" McCormick asked as Drew watered Miss O'Rourke's horse.

"They leave us alone, we leave them alone," Drew replied.

"Funny," the deputy mused. "I heard tell young Levi had words with Scout in town the other day. I thought they were friends."

It seemed there was little the deputy failed to hear about. But before Drew could answer, McCormick tipped his hat in the direction of Drew's cabin.

Drew turned to see Catherine and her friend coming toward them. Catherine's hair was once more pinned precisely in place, her blue gown surprisingly crisp after her activities yesterday. Never had he seen such purposeful strides. Dirt kicked up behind her with each step. She hadn't confessed to his family how she'd arrived at the Landing. Was she about to tell the law in no uncertain terms the full story of her kidnapping?

Chapter Six

Catherine tried not to shiver in the early-morning chill as she approached the group. She'd thought surely the events of the day or the strange surroundings would have kept her awake last night. But the moment she'd snuggled under Drew's quilt, which hinted of the scent of fir that seemed to cling to him, she'd fallen asleep, and only Maddie's knock on the door had roused her.

"So off you go running away to live in a palace of cedar like David in the Bible," Maddie had said, twinkle in her brown eyes. "Leaving your friends a-wondering."

Catherine had hugged her tight before pulling her inside. "It's fir, not cedar. And what are you doing here? How did you find me?"

Maddie had bustled into the room, picking up Catherine's gown and undergarments where they lay over one of the tall, stiff chairs. "Didn't you think I would raise the hue and cry the moment you went missing? It took a bit of persuading to get Deputy McCormick to move himself, and then I had to beg this skirt from one of the other travelers, but we started out before dawn and followed the hint from a lad and your Doc Maynard."

She'd held out Catherine's corset, the cream-colored quilted cotton looking warm in her grip. "Come along, now, Catie, me love. There are at least three worthwhile men out there. We want you looking your best. You can tell me what happened while you dress."

Catherine didn't much care whether the men outside were stellar candidates for marriage, but she couldn't have very well gone out in Mrs. Wallin's nightgown. So Catherine had explained the situation while her friend had helped her out of the soft flannel and into her corset and gown. The dressing had taken longer than she'd expected, even with Maddie's assistance, for Catherine's body was stiff from bouncing in the wagon the day before.

"You see why I must stay," Catherine had concluded after she'd put up her hair.

At the door, Maddie had glanced out to where Drew stood in conversation with Deputy McCormick. They'd made quite a contrast, the lawman all hard angles and trim lines, the frontiersman all brawn and power.

"Oh, I see exactly why you must be staying," Maddie had assured her. "He's a bit hard to miss, standing tall as a tree as he does."

Catherine had felt her cheeks warming as she'd joined Maddie in the doorway. "This has nothing to do with Drew Wallin."

"Drew, is it now? Sure'n if you've no use for him, you won't mind me batting my eyes in his direction."

Catherine had known Maddie was just teasing. Aboard ship and since arriving in Seattle, several fellows had sidled up to the redhead, but she'd never allowed them to be more than friends. Catherine didn't know whether Maddie was waiting for the right man or whether she simply had no interest in settling down. Certainly she was one of the most industrious women Catherine had met—doing laundry for men in the boardinghouses and hotels and saving money to open her own bakery. Perhaps that was enough for her. Given Catherine's own views on marriage, it had seemed presumptive to ask.

Now they stood beside the group, and Catherine recognized several of the fellows who served as storekeepers or businessmen in the fledgling city.

"Mr. McCormick," she greeted the deputy. "Gentlemen. Please tell me you didn't come all this way on my account."

Deputy McCormick nodded to her, hands gripping his horse's reins. "Just doing our duty, ma'am. Everything all right here?"

Catherine smiled at them all as Maddie went to retrieve the reins of her horse from Drew. She saw no need to tell them about Levi's hand in her transportation. With his mother ill and work waiting to be done, Drew hardly needed more trouble. "Everything is fine. Mr. Wallin and his youngest brother came to town yesterday seeking medical assistance. I was available to help."

Deputy McCormick frowned. He had the oddest colored eyes, dark and hard, like rocks at the bottom of a stream. She fought another shiver and knew this time it had nothing to do with the cool morning air.

"You left mighty quick," he pointed out, "without a word to anyone."

Catherine caught Drew's gaze. From the way he shoved his hands in his pockets, she could tell he was struggling not to join the conversation. She shook her head slightly, trying to warn him. She appreciated his help with the deputy, but she didn't want to see him run afoul of the law.

"I'm afraid I did dash off," she confessed to Deputy McCormick. "When I hear someone is ill, I tend to act. I'm sure you wouldn't want me to delay if it was your wife or mother lying at death's door."

"No, ma'am, of course not," the deputy agreed while some of the men shifted on their feet as if Catherine's words had made them uncomfortable. "But when our womenfolk disappear like that, we tend to worry."

"Especially when there's so few of us, I'm thinking," Maddie put in, patting her horse's neck.

"I'm very sorry to have worried you," Catherine said, keeping her smile in place from long practice. If she could remain calm while delivering the news to a family of death's final decision, she certainly wasn't going to faint under the deputy's hard gaze. "I promise to let someone know if I set out on my own again."

The deputy nodded. "All right, then. We'll be off. Look out for yourself, Wallin. Ma'am." He tipped his hat to Catherine.

As the men mounted, Maddie turned to Drew. "Would you be a darling, Mr. Wallin, and help me back on this horse? Sure'n it's a wily beast just waiting to trample me."

Catherine thought Drew might cup his hands to give Maddie a leg up, but he swept her up in his arms and deposited her on the saddle.

"Well, now," Maddie said with a grin as she adjusted her seat. "That's more like it. I hope to be seeing more of you, Mr. Wallin, when you come to bring my Catie-girl back."

Drew inclined his head, but Deputy McCormick's

face darkened. "Let's ride," he barked, and his men wheeled their horses and set off, Maddie with an airy wave over her head to Catherine.

"Thank you," Drew said as the noise faded among the trees. "Levi's already received two warnings from the sheriff for reckless behavior in town. If you had told them the truth, he might have ended up in jail this time."

"I did tell the truth," Catherine informed him, taking a deep breath. Her palms were damp, and she wiped them on her skirt. "I came here to treat your mother. I thought you were going to wake me last night to tend to her."

She nearly winced as her statement came out closer to a scold. Here she'd thought herself in control of her emotions, yet the entire incident with the deputy sheriff seemed to have thrown her off balance. Or maybe it was Maddie's outrageous flirting. Was her friend actually interested in Drew Wallin? Certainly, he was a handsome figure of a man, heroic even. Perhaps he was just the sort of fellow Maddie had been waiting for. She should be delighted for Maddie, but the thought made her feel as if someone had hollowed out her stomach.

To her surprise, his smile grew, peeling away the years from his face, brightening his eyes. "There was no need to call you. You did it. Ma's well."

Her heart leaped, but immediately she chided herself. She couldn't give in to such optimism, not until she had seen the lady herself and could verify Mrs. Wallin's recovery.

A humming from the woods heralded Beth's arrival. Today she wore a dress of blue gingham the color of her eyes. Seeing Catherine and Drew, she hurried up to them.

"Why are you out here? Who's with Ma? I thought we had to keep watch over her."

"Your brother says she's much better," Catherine explained. "I was just about to confirm that." She turned for the house, with Beth and Drew close behind. She could feel their excitement, but she refused to let it influence her judgment. Her own eagerness was danger enough for that.

Once in the loft, Catherine sat beside her patient and checked Mrs. Wallin's pulse, her eyes, her breathing and her temperature. Then she sat back with a smile.

"Much better," she proclaimed. "I'd say another few days and you'll be back on your feet."

Mrs. Wallin beamed at her. "Because of you, Miss Stanway. Thank you!"

"Yes, Miss Stanway, thank you!" Beth threw herself into Catherine's arms and hugged her tight. "You gave me back my mother!"

Catherine felt tears pricking her eyes. *This is why I practice medicine, Lord—to help people. Thank You for this healing!*

Disengaging from Beth, she glanced up to meet Drew's gaze. His eyes were overly bright, and he hurriedly looked away as if determined to keep her from seeing the emotions brimming in them.

"I suppose you'll be leaving us, then," he said.

Beth leaned back, and she and her mother exchanged glances. Mrs. Wallin drew in a shaky breath. "Oh, I'm sure I won't be myself again if Miss Stanway leaves us now."

Beth took Catherine's hand. "And I was so hoping we might have time to chat, Miss Stanway."

Drew glanced back, eyes narrowing. Did he see the

manipulation as clearly as Catherine did? They needn't have bothered. She knew she had work to do before she left.

"I'll stay a while longer," she told them all, and Beth and Mrs. Wallin grinned at each other. "I want to make sure there are no complications."

Mrs. Wallin leaned back against the pillows with a satisfied nod. "Very sensible."

"And I also want to track this fever to its source," Catherine continued.

Drew frowned. "Its source?"

"I thought chills brought on sickness," Beth said, glancing between them. "You know, you stand outside in wet clothes or you bathe in cold water like the lake."

Mrs. Wallin stiffened. "I have never bathed in the lake in my life, young lady, and you know it!"

"Typhoid fever is often caused by food or water that came in contact with something it shouldn't," Catherine informed Beth. "Until we discover what made your mother sick, all of you could be in danger. I'm not leaving until I know we aren't spreading the disease any further."

She meant the comment for a warning, but the smiles on Beth and Mrs. Wallin's faces were as deep as the frown on Drew's. Just what were the ladies planning that they were so determined for Catherine to stay?

Chapter Seven

Drew didn't like the way his mother and sister were looking at each other. He didn't think they knew about Simon's idea that one of the Wallin men must marry Miss Stanway. But if the Wallin women had hit on the same notion, he was doomed.

Best to focus them on something else. "So you think our food or water is contaminated," he challenged Catherine.

For a woman who didn't wear her heart on her sleeve, she could look remarkably determined. Her chin came up, and her blue eyes flashed like lightning.

His mother was nearly as indignant. "Contaminated food?" she sputtered, ribbons on her nightcap dancing about her pale face in her agitation. "What have you all been doing on my stove?"

"Nothing, Ma!" Beth cried. "I promise! It can't be the food. We all eat the same things. You were the only one to get sick."

Catherine nodded. "Very well, but I imagine you all drink the same water, too."

"Not entirely," Drew said. "The hillside above us is

littered with springs. Simon has a pipe from one coming in to his cabin. I tapped another for the pump on the side of my cabin. Ma is the only one still drawing from the spring Pa favored. It's closest to the house."

"But it's closest to the barn, too," Beth reminded him. "That's how we water the animals. None of them got sick."

"They wouldn't," Catherine said. "Some diseases are unique to humans."

"Well, Levi and I still live here," Beth pointed out. "Why didn't we get sick?"

"Half the time Levi is out with us," Drew said. "And you did get sick a while ago."

Beth sobered.

"It seems we must examine your spring," Catherine said.

"After you eat," his mother insisted, leaning back against the head of the bed as if satisfied her cooking had been exonerated. "You can bring water from Drew's spring if you're concerned about mine, but I won't have a guest in my house or any of my children starving."

"I'll cook them something, Ma," Beth said, hopping up out of her seat. "Drew can help."

Although he didn't mind helping, he didn't like the smile that crossed his mother's face or the way she glanced at Catherine. Who knew what the two would get up to if he left them alone for too long?

"We need more wood for the fire," he said. "I'll be right back."

His mother's smile widened.

"You're in trouble," Beth said as he followed her down the stairs. "I know that look on Ma's face. She wants something, and I think it's Miss Stanway as a daughter-in-law."

"Miss Stanway might have something to say about that," Drew replied, heading for the door. He glanced back in time to see his sister shake her head.

"It doesn't matter what Miss Stanway says. It doesn't matter what you say. And Simon has the least say of all."

So she had heard his brother's outrageous demands last night. "Don't start, Beth," Drew warned.

"Oh, it's far too late," his sister predicted. "You know that when Ma makes up her mind about something, it's going to happen. If I were you, I'd talk to the Reverend Bagley about a church date." Humming to herself, she disappeared into the back room.

First his brothers and now his mother. Were they all mad? Drew stepped onto the front porch and glanced around the yard in the cool morning air. A dozen projects called for his attention, from a loose shingle on the barn roof to the field waiting for the plow. Did his family really think he had time for a wife?

Well, they could scheme all they liked. He knew what must be done. Another day to make sure Ma had recovered and to track down this sickness, and Catherine Stanway would be out of his life. All he had to do was hold firm to his convictions.

And try to forget the warmth of her cradled against his chest.

"He's a good man, you know," Mrs. Wallin said after Drew and Beth had left the room. "Proved up a hundred and sixty acres all on his own, and raised his brothers and Beth when their father died."

Catherine kept herself busy tucking the covers

around her patient's waist. "Your family is certainly to be commended, making a home in the wilderness."

Mrs. Wallin caught her hand. "But he doesn't have a home."

Catherine frowned. "He most certainly does. I slept in it last night."

Mrs. Wallin shook her head. "He has a house. That's not a home. The Bible says a man is to grow up and start his own family. How can Drew do that when he won't let go of this one?"

From somewhere deep inside her, anger pushed its way out of Catherine's mouth. "Why would you want him to let go? He's trying to protect you all. I wish my father and brother had had that much sense. Maybe I wouldn't be alone now."

She turned away from the bed and went to stand by the fire. Her breath shuddered, and she forced herself to draw in the air, then let it out slowly. What was wrong with her? Mrs. Wallin had every right to be concerned for her son's future. That was what families did—care for each other.

But why didn't my father think about me, Lord? Was it really so important that he and Nathan had to go and fight? Or was I such a termagant of a daughter and sister they couldn't wait to escape me?

She heard the bedclothes rustle, and then the creak of the floor as feet padded toward her. Turning, she found Mrs. Wallin beside her. A tall woman, she gazed down at Catherine, face twisted as if she were in pain or feeling Catherine's.

"Oh, my dear, I'm so sorry," she said. She drew Catherine close and held her gently. "It's terrible to lose a loved one. Why, it cuts the heart right out of you."

Tears burned Catherine's eyes. As if of their own volition, her arms came up and she hugged the woman closer. "It's all right," she said. "I'll be fine."

Mrs. Wallin held her out and met her gaze, her face now stern. "Of course you will. Things will never be quite the same, though. Tragedy changes a body. How long has your family been gone?"

Catherine counted the months and was surprised by the answer. "Just over a year." That seemed like such a short time when it felt as if she'd been grieving forever.

"Well, then." Mrs. Wallin squeezed her shoulders. "Give yourself more time to accustom yourself to the changes. You left everything you knew to come to a strange place, with no friends or family waiting for you. That takes some adjusting, I know. And there will always be a part of you that misses them, no matter what else happens."

She glanced up at the mantel, and Catherine saw a daguerreotype there of a sturdy-looking man. He had Drew's eyes, Simon's rock of a chin and Levi's cocky grin. Mrs. Wallin rubbed a hand down the worn silver frame, and Catherine felt her sigh.

That was entirely enough of this sentimentality. She had to remember her purpose for being here, and it wasn't to wallow in the pain of her past. She turned her patient toward the bed with a smile.

"Thank you. I needed that reminder. Now, let's get you back under the covers. Despite what I told Beth, sudden changes in temperature aren't good for someone recovering from an illness. I want you cozy again."

Mrs. Wallin allowed herself to be tucked back into bed, but the smile on her face told Catherine that the older woman was humoring her. Catherine suspected

Drew's mother was feeling far better than she let on. But for all the lady wanted to be up and back to her usual routine, Catherine didn't want her to do too much and suffer a relapse. Nor did she want the illness to affect anyone else. And that meant she had work to do.

So after a breakfast of eggs, biscuits with honey and apple cider, she directed Beth on the types of food that would help her mother convalesce—beef tea, calf's foot jelly and honeysuckle conserve. Then she convinced Drew to accompany her on a survey of the Landing.

Between the dim light last night when she'd arrived and the need to appease the deputy sheriff this morning, she hadn't taken a good look at the Wallin property until now. The main house sat facing west, with its back to the lake. Now she could see the water, sparkling through the trees in the spring sunlight. It was the same deep shade of blue as Beth's and Levi's eyes. Hills rose sharply on the three sides, thick with dense stands of deep green fir and the reddish bark of cedar.

"There's a good-size stream north of us," Drew said as if he'd noticed the direction of her gaze as they stood between his cabin and his parents'. "That's where Pa got the name for the property. The ground slopes, making it a good place to land canoes or start logs on their way to the Sound."

"But you don't drink from that stream," Catherine surmised, turning for the barn.

"Only when we're working out that way," Drew admitted, long legs moving him past her. "It's too far to carry the water for the house or the stock." The shadows of the barn swallowed up his tall frame.

Catherine followed him inside. The barn was of weathered wood, with a pitched roof of silvered cedar shingles turning green with moss. The upper part was open at each end, and as she looked, swallows darted past the triangle of sky.

Stalls and pens lined up along the packed-earth aisle, many with hinged doors allowing access to fenced pasture.

"Simon and the others took the oxen out this morning to clear away some brush," Drew told her. "And Beth turned out the goats, horses and pigs." He glanced around at the harnesses and tools hanging from the walls, the rough-hewn troughs of fresh water.

Catherine opened the lid on the large bin near a square of planked floor that somehow seemed out of place. The bin was empty, but it smelled of something dry, nutty.

"That's the grain bin," he told her. "And the threshing floor beyond it. But Simon and the others help with that. With all of us around, Ma generally doesn't need to come out here anymore. I can't see how anything in the barn could have made her sick."

He sounded puzzled again, but something else simmered behind the words. Frustration? She was certain he wanted to learn what had caused his mother's illness. Did he disapprove of Catherine's methods?

"I don't see anything dangerous in here, either," she agreed, closing the lid, "but it's wise to check all possibilities when it comes to your family's health."

He snapped a nod and stalked deeper into the barn.

Mystified, Catherine lifted her skirts out of the dirt and followed. "Really, Mr. Wallin, this search is important." She detoured around a suspicious-looking clump on the floor. "Do you want one of your brothers to sicken? Beth to grow ill?"

"Of course not." The words sounded as if they had

been bitten off. "But I've been keeping them safe for years. I don't know what's changed."

He'd stopped at the end of the barn, where another set of wide doors led out into the forest. The breeze carried the scent of damp wood and new growth. She could hear birds calling from the shadows. Yet Drew stood a silhouette against the light, neck stiff, shoulders braced.

Catherine lay a hand on his arm. "Forgive me, Mr. Wallin. I never meant to imply any of this was your fault. You cannot know everything about medical science. It's constantly changing! What we were certain of last month will be challenged as folklore tomorrow. I merely wish to help."

His hand came down on hers. "Thank you."

The two simple words, said with conviction, warmed her more than she'd thought possible. Or perhaps it was the feel of his calloused palm pressed against her skin. She couldn't help remembering the scars she'd seen yesterday. This was a man who had earned his place, whose physical efforts kept his family fed and clothed and housed. A man who took the health of his loved ones as seriously as she did as a nurse.

She traced the vein of puckered skin across the back of one hand. "How did this happen?"

He did not pull away from her touch. "A saw snapped. The end whipped free and caught me. I was just glad it missed my face."

So was she. She swallowed at the thought and dropped her hand.

He was gazing down at her, face in the shadow, hair a golden nimbus of light. She waited, expecting a word, a movement.

The touch of his lips to hers.

"Do you hear that?" he asked.

She didn't think he meant the birds outside. Now that she wasn't so focused on him, she did hear something else—a rumble and a snort that sounded somehow familiar.

Drew grabbed a long iron pole from the wall and poked it up into the hay stored loosely above their heads in the mow. Someone yelped, and a moment later, Levi's curly-haired head popped into sight.

"What are you doing up there?" Drew demanded. "I thought you were with Simon."

Levi slung a leg over the nearby ladder and clambered down to drop beside his brother and Catherine. Hay stuck out at odd angles from his curls, clung to his flannel shirt and poked from the suspenders holding up his rumpled trousers. "Simon thought you might need help with Ma."

Drew towered over him, voice deepening. "And you thought the best way to help Ma was to sleep in the hay?" He pointed out the door. "Git!"

Levi dashed out of the barn.

Drew shook his head as he and Catherine followed. "Can't turn my back for a minute."

"It was only a lark," Catherine said. "But if you're concerned, you can always find better things for him to do."

Drew cast her a glance. "Good idea. Levi! Show Miss Stanway to the spring."

Levi led her to where the ground sloped upward between the barn and the main house. A deep, stone-lined basin followed the curve of the hill; a wall of mortared stone about three feet high enclosing the water filling it. At the back of the pool, overshadowed by the firs, water bubbled, cool and clear. A wooden weir on the west side allowed the spring to overflow in a stream that ran away from the house down to the lake. Just inside the pool, a stone lip provided space for cooling food like milk and cider. Iron rings driven into the ground around it served as anchors for the ropes that held several wooden buckets for accessing the water.

Catherine picked up one of the buckets. The wooden staves were worn, the iron binding them turning red from prolonged exposure to water. "How often do you clean these?" she asked.

Levi rolled his eyes as if he thought she was being too fussy. Drew frowned as if thinking. "Since we only use them to draw fresh water, would they require cleaning?"

Catherine ran a finger around the inside of the bucket and held it up for him to see the green smearing it. "Moss will grow with damp and dark. Scrub them out at least twice a year."

He nodded, brow clearing. "I will."

How easily he believed her. It was refreshing, and she felt herself drawing in a deeper breath, her shoulders settling.

Levi was clearly less impressed. "Never heard of moss making a body ill," he scoffed.

"You never heard of keeping the windows open, either," Drew reminded him. "And Ma is better for it."

He stuck out his lower lip, as if considering the matter.

"I doubt the moss caused your mother's fever," Catherine said, "but it is a sign that things could be more sanitary." She leaned over the lip and gazed down into the dark pool. The sun filtering through the trees turned the water to amber. She sniffed the cool air.

"Does that smell odd to you?" she asked Drew, straightening.

He leaned over beside her, his broad shoulder brushing hers. She could feel the warmth radiating from him and had to fight the urge to hug him closer. He gave a perfunctorily sniff as if he doubted her senses. Then he frowned again. "I smell something. Could be from the barn. We are downwind."

"Let me take a gander." Levi stuck his head over the wall, then straightened and shrugged. "I don't smell anything."

Drew reached across to cuff him on the shoulder. "That's because you've been avoiding a bath for weeks."

"Have not!" The youth's cheeks were turning crimson. "I jump in the lake on a regular basis."

Catherine hid her smile as she peered in the pool again. "I'm sure there's an odor, and I doubt it's coming from your brother. Could something have fallen in?"

"With the lake so close, there's generally no need for an animal to risk trying to scale that wall," Drew reasoned. "But the best way to be sure is to put someone into the water." He turned to his brother. "I'll hold the rope, Levi."

"Me?" His brother scrambled back, dark blue eyes widening. "I'm not going in there."

"Surely there's some other way," Catherine protested. She could not imagine it was safe or sanitary to let the youth enter the drinking water.

Drew had pulled up one of the buckets and was untying it from the rope. "No other way I know," he said, tugging on the line as if testing its strength. "We could wave around a lantern, but if that smell's caused by firedamp, we'll only cause an explosion."

"An explosion!" Catherine cried, hands pressed to her chest.

Levi turned white. "You can't put me in there, Drew. I won't go."

Drew shrugged, coming around the wall toward his brother. "You're the logical choice. You're light enough to brace easily and strong enough to take care of yourself. Besides, you'll know what you're looking for."

Levi shook his curls off his forehead and pointed at Catherine. "She's light. Make her go."

Catherine felt a moment of panic, but Drew waved away the suggestion with one hand. "You can't send a woman in a dress into a pool that deep. The weight of her skirts would pull her down, and you'd never get her out. The idea is to fix the spring, not plug it up."

Catherine nearly choked. *That* was his reason for not putting her in the pool?

Levi wavered a moment longer, then stalked up to Drew and held up his arms. "Fine. I'll go. But you owe me."

"Is this safe?" Catherine asked as Drew knotted the rope around Levi's waist. "How deep is that pool?"

"About six feet," he told her. "He's not the best swimmer in the family, it's true, but if the rope fails and he can't reach the side easily, it will only take me an hour or so to locate Simon to help get him out."

Levi stared at him. "An hour!"

Catherine frowned at Drew. For someone so careful of his mother, he seemed to have little regard for his brother's well-being. But as Levi slung his leg over the edge of the wall, Drew winked at Catherine. What was he up to?

He braced his feet on the stones and nodded to his

brother. Levi leaned back against the rope and slowly edged into the pool. Drew played out the rope, and his brother shuddered as the cool water inched up his legs, then his torso. Catherine watched, fingers clasped, until only his curly blond head showed above the top.

"We've never had an issue with firedamp," she heard Drew murmur beside her. "I'll only keep him in a moment, but maybe he'll think before jumping into things in the future."

Catherine managed a breath and nodded. It seemed Drew Wallin knew his brother better than she'd thought.

"Report," he called to Levi.

"Moss," Levi replied, twisting in the water. The eddies around him told Catherine that Levi was moving his arms and legs to stay afloat. "And something darker over there." He bobbed toward the far side of the pool, closer to the trees.

The rope tightened beside her. Catherine glanced up and caught her breath. Drew stood, arms stiff, shoulders hard. Surely King Arthur must have looked like that when he'd pulled the sword from the stone.

"Get me out!" Levi shouted, and Drew hauled, muscles bunching. Catherine shook herself and held out her hands to grab Levi's arms and help him up onto the wall. His hands were covered in something black. At first she thought it was mud, but Levi thrust a finger under her nose, and she recoiled at the potent smell.

"Manure," he said, shaking off his hands and shaking his head at the same time. "Just a little. If there was more, it probably flushed out by now. Someone must have dumped it into the pool by mistake."

Catherine felt ill. "Surely everyone knows that isn't healthy."

"Everyone knows." Drew's words were no less forceful for their quiet. He dropped the rope and tugged his brother upright. "No one in my family would do this, mistake or otherwise. Someone tried to poison the spring. I want to know who, and I want to know why."

Chapter Eight

Drew fought down a rising temper. He'd heard tales of cattlemen and farmers fighting over grazing rights and poisoning each other's water supply, but that had been in other territories. No one he knew bore any grudge against him. Why dump manure in the spring?

"We should call back Deputy McCormick," Catherine said. "Surely this is against the law."

Drew focused on her. Her head was high, her eyes narrowed to blue chips of ice. She looked ready to fight anyone who would dare to threaten the health of her patients. Despite himself, he felt a smile forming.

"McCormick mentioned some of the other farms out this way had been harassed," Drew told her. "There may be a pattern. I'll report the matter when I take you back to town. In the meantime, we'll keep a closer eye out for strangers."

"It was probably just a mistake," Levi protested. "It's not as though we need to mount a guard or something."

Was the boy determined not to do an honest day's work? Drew forced himself to take a deep breath before answering, "If we all lend a hand, it won't be a burden on anyone."

Levi's lean face was turning red. "I never said it was a burden. But all you think about is working! Having a little fun isn't a crime, you know!"

His vehemence seemed too strong, even for his mercurial personality. Drew eyed his brother. "Do you know who did this, Levi?"

"Me?" He took a step back. "No! Of course not! I'm just upset they made more work for us." He turned and stalked off to the barn.

"Surely he wouldn't poison a spring his family uses," Catherine said, her tone unusually gentle. Drew glanced back at her to find her watching him as if to gauge his response. "He may not appreciate the importance of good health, but he must realize he'd have to drink the water, too."

There was that. But something was bothering his brother. "I doubt Levi dumped manure in the spring," he told her. "But I wouldn't be surprised if he hadn't angered some other young bucks who thought this was fair retaliation. I'll let him cool down a bit before I talk to him again. I won't tolerate this kind of nonsense."

"Agreed," she said with a nod. "In the meantime, what do you intend to do about the spring? Levi is right about one thing. Your mother became ill at least two weeks ago, so the manure was added before then. Very likely the bulk of the contamination was flushed out with the rains, but obviously some remains."

"I'll have Levi clean it out," Drew said. "We'll only draw from it for the stock until we know it's purified. We can use the pumps on my claim and Simon's for the house. It's farther to go, but they're capped. It wouldn't be easy to dump anything down them. Beth can show you how to work my pump."

She frowned at him. "Are you leaving?"

"I need to find my brothers," he said. "They'll want to know about this. I'll leave Levi in case you need an extra hand."

"I'm sure he'll be quite helpful."

He could hear her sarcasm. "He will if I have to beat it into him."

She blanched. "Please, Mr. Wallin. There's no need to strike the boy."

Did she think him a brute? Many saw his size and immediately assumed his temperament was as large.

"It's only a matter of speaking, ma'am," he replied, turning away. "I've never had to raise a hand to any of my brothers to get them to obey." With a nod, he set off for the woods.

Once he'd reached his brothers, he filled them in on the day's events. They were glad to hear that Ma was feeling better but irate that anyone would damage their main water supply. Unfortunately, no one could determine a reason.

"What about that prospector who sold you your fancy waistcoat?" Simon asked James as the brothers finished clearing away the smaller trees that might damage the spar when it fell. "Could he feel cheated?"

"I don't see why," James replied, swinging his ax into a sampling. "I paid him well enough for it. If anyone is aggrieved, it should be me." He paused a moment to lay a hand on his heart and bow his head.

Drew ignored the melodramatics. "Deputy McCormick said there's been other harassment out this way. We'll just have to keep a closer watch."

None of his brothers looked amused by the thought. Between the main farm, their own claims and the logging, they had more than enough to do.

Still, he couldn't deny a sense of peace as he returned to work for the first time since he'd started nursing his mother. There was something about the feel of the ax in his hands, the weight of its swing, the sound as it came into contact with the tree, the vibration up his arms. Although accidents could happen at any time, he knew to his sorrow, the work was predictable and productive. And when the tree was down and the land was cleared, he could see his accomplishments and knew he'd done well. He only wished raising a passel of brothers and a headstrong sister was as simple.

After Drew left, Catherine returned to the house. She agreed with him that his brother's actions were suspicious, but she hated to think that a group of boys would take matters so far as to poison a neighbor's water supply. They had to know this prank could have had dangerous repercussions.

"So what do you think?" Beth asked when Catherine rejoined her and her mother upstairs. "Was something wrong with the spring?"

Mrs. Wallin was sitting up in the bed, and the sock and needles resting in the lap of Beth's blue gingham gown told Catherine what the girl had been doing while she waited. The two women listened as Catherine explained what she and Drew had found. She purposely omitted any mention of Levi's possible involvement, but Beth hopped to her feet, face reddening, tumbling the sock to the floor.

"Oh, that Levi! I will skin him for this!"

"Elizabeth Ann Wallin," her mother scolded. "I can't believe your brother would do such a thing."

Catherine was watching Beth, whose color was only darkening. "Why do you suspect your brother, Beth?"

She bent to retrieve the sock and needles, voice muffled. "I shouldn't. Ma's right." She set her things on the chair, then caught up a bit of hair and twisted the golden strand around one finger. "It's just that he's made no bones about the fact that he thinks we should have taken a claim closer to town. He says when it's his turn, he's not choosing acreage this far out."

"And that is his decision," her mother said, voice firm though her face was pale. "Just because his brothers lined up their claims along ours doesn't mean he must."

"Yes, Ma," Beth said. "If you'll excuse me, I'll just go start the baking." She headed for the stairs.

Catherine knew she shouldn't interfere, but something about Beth's reaction told her there was more to the story. "I'll come with you," she said, following her. "I need to explain what we're doing about water now."

Mrs. Wallin wiggled deeper under the covers. "You do that. I think I'll just take a nap."

Catherine caught up with Beth at the foot of the stairs. As if Beth had guessed her purpose, she paused and lowered her voice. "I'm sorry, Miss Stanway. I should never have spoken that way about Levi. It's just that he makes me so mad! All Pa did, all Drew and the others have done to build us a home, make our own community… I hear him sneak out sometimes, going off at night when he thinks Drew and the others are asleep. He doesn't seem to value anything Drew taught him!"

"Maybe he just wants to go his own way," Catherine

said, remembering her brother with a pang. “Boys often do at his age.”

“Well, I’m glad I’m not a boy, then.” Beth started for the back of the house. “I’m not abandoning my family when I turn eighteen.”

Catherine hid a smile at the defiant tone, spoken with such authority by one who had seen so little of the world as yet. “You never know,” she told Beth as she joined the girl in the back room. “More and more professions are open to women, and Seattle will have many opportunities as it grows.”

Standing by the iron tub, which seemed to serve for both laundry and bathing, Beth grinned at her. “At least you didn’t tell me it’s a woman’s duty to wed and have babies.” She stuck up her arm and pointed to the ceiling as if calling the Lord as a witness. “By golly, young lady, don’t you know that’s how the West was won?” She dropped her arm and giggled.

“I would be the last one to tell you that you must marry,” Catherine assured her.

“Then you’re the only one.” Beth sighed. “I may cause the West to be lost, but I’ve already had my fill of cooking and cleaning for a mess of men. Now, what do I have to do differently to keep us all healthy?”

Catherine and Beth spent the rest of the day planning what needed to be done and setting it into motion. Drew and his brothers must have had chores or timber that needed cutting, for she saw nothing of them. She and Beth aired the ticks and washed the linens and hung them to dry on tree limbs around the clearing. They washed and hung out Mrs. Wallin’s nightgown and underthings, as well.

Levi helped whenever they managed to catch him,

and always with such a martyred expression on his face that Catherine wanted to send him to the corner. Unfortunately, he was past the age where such discipline worked, and she didn't have the authority in the house for that sort of thing anyway. She was merely glad Mrs. Wallin and Beth were willing to listen to her suggestions.

Beth had dinner on the stove, and the sun was dipping low when Levi brought in another load of firewood. Catherine had noticed a raised crib, sheltered under the eaves of the barn, where they must set the logs to cure.

"Will the others be coming home soon?" Catherine asked as she helped Mrs. Wallin to the table. Her patient had felt well enough that Catherine was willing to allow her to eat with the family. Just the trip down the stairs had taken its toll, however, for Mrs. Wallin's hands were shaking as she tried to sip from the cup of cool water Beth had handed her. Catherine couldn't help remembering the strength of Drew's arms as he'd carried her across the clearing last night. Surely he could help his mother back upstairs after dinner if needed.

"Oh, we have to call them," Beth said from behind the hearth. She hooked her stirring spoon over the edge of a steaming pot and headed for the back door.

"They're close enough to hear us?" Catherine asked with a frown.

Levi grinned. "In a matter of speaking."

"It's something their pa dreamed up," Mrs. Wallin explained. "Levi, go fetch Miss Stanway the plates we use for dinner. None of that tin on my table."

Levi was returning with some delicate-looking pink-and-white-patterned dishes from the sideboard when a gun roared outside. Catherine nearly jumped out of her skin and found her own hands shaking as the gun barked again. Levi started laughing, but a look from his mother silenced him.

"Two shots means you're needed at home," Mrs. Wallin told Catherine. "One shot means come a-running, now."

Beth poked her head in the door. "They should be here shortly."

She was right. Catherine had barely set the last china plate on the table when boots thudded across the boardwalk of the house. John was the first through the door. His face was smeared with dirt, his red plaid shirt darkened by sweat. His smile brightened when he saw their mother, and he went to peck her cheek before taking a seat farther down the table. James, an elegant silver-shot waistcoat wrapped around his lean frame, had a similar reaction, though he went to wash his hands before joining them.

Simon approached his mother more cautiously. "Should you be up?" he asked her, his gaze seeking Catherine's as if for confirmation.

"Nurse Stanway approved it," his mother assured him with a smile to Catherine. "Besides, having my family around me is the best medicine, if you ask me."

Catherine didn't meet her gaze. It was the best medicine in her mind, too, although she thought her father might have once argued the matter.

Drew was the last one through the door. His damp hair clung to his head as if he'd dunked it under the pump. His face was clean, though an evening's stubble lay like gold across his jaw. He took his seat opposite his mother at the foot of the table, then bowed his head and asked the blessing. Male voices punctuated by Beth's and Mrs. Wallin's sopranos rumbled the amen.

Catherine wasn't sure what to expect from a family of rough loggers, but the Wallins were polite in their eating. Platters and plates passed in orderly fashion up and down the table and, except for an occasional lunge for a particular goody, everyone took turns serving themselves. There was ham, molasses clinging to the edges; mashed potatoes with salty gravy; biscuits and carrots. Though the fare was plain and simple, she couldn't remember enjoying a meal more.

As they ate, she monitored Mrs. Wallin. The lady partook sparingly, but her color was good and her eyes sparkled at the stories her sons were telling of their day in the timber.

"John was nearly carried away today," James reported, helping himself to another biscuit.

John rolled his eyes, but his mother smiled. "Do tell."

"Was it a bear?" Levi demanded, fork stilled a moment in his hand. "I saw some fearful tracks down by the lake earlier."

"Not a bear," James said. "And no cougar, either. It seems fair John surprised an owl up in the tree and the beast nearly took his head off. I figured that, seeing he was so wise, our friend the owl thought to carry him off for its own."

His brothers chuckled, and Mrs. Wallin shook her head at his jest. John leveled his spoon at his brother.

"If you'd bother to open a book once in a while, you might be just as wise. Besides, at least I caught a few quills for writing later." He nodded to Beth. "I'll give you one."

"Thank you!" Beth beamed at him.

The stories continued over a dried-apple pie that seemed to disappear in one bite. But Catherine noticed she wasn't the only one watching her patient. Every time she glanced in Drew's direction, he was eying his mother.

Indeed, he didn't enter into the teasing with his family. He seemed to stand aside, like a massive oak, shielding them from any harm. Although his protection was noble, she couldn't help wondering whether it was a lonely vigil.

"What about a game tonight?" Levi asked, slinging a leg over the bench where he, James and John were sitting.

"Kitty in the Corner," Beth said with a clap of her hands before reaching for the empty pie plate.

Levi made a face, but Drew spoke up, hands cradling his tankard of cider. "We should have music tonight in honor of Ma coming down to dinner."

This time when Mrs. Wallin smiled, Catherine could see the effort it took. "Perhaps one tune. Simon, would you play for us?"

Simon climbed off the opposite bench from beside Catherine. "Whatever you want, Ma. Just give me a moment to fetch my fiddle."

Drew stood and came around the table to lift his mother. "Miss Stanway," he said, gazing at Catherine over his mother's shoulder, "please join us. The rest of you, clear up."

With good-natured grumbling, his brothers rose to help.

A short while later they were all seated around the hearth. Mrs. Wallin had settled so contentedly in the bentwood rocker that the dark wood seemed curved to her frame. Beth sat at her feet, legs curled up under her gingham skirts. Levi, James and John lounged on the rug before the fire. Catherine felt like a queen seated on one of the ladder-backed chairs. Drew braced his shoulders against the log wall and crossed his arms over his chest. Catherine could feel his gaze roaming over his family; her cheeks warmed when she felt it resting on her.

She told herself to focus on Simon, who had moved to stand before the fire. He held a well-polished violin and bow. Since arriving in Seattle, she'd heard a number of fellows scrape out a tune with many a protest from the instrument and prepared herself for a similar performance.

"Something gentle, I think," Mrs. Wallin said, leaning back in her chair. "Something to calm the spirit."

"Gentle it is." Simon put his bow to the strings and out drifted a lilting song. The notes danced and skipped about the room, like young lambs in the spring. Catherine felt a smile forming.

Mrs. Wallin was smiling, too, as were most of her sons. Beth had her lips pressed close together as if to keep from laughing, but Levi went so far as to snicker.

Drew pushed off from the wall. "Very funny, Simon. Try something else."

Simon inclined his head, and the tune changed. It was slow, serious, nearly mournful. Beth frowned as if she had never heard it before. Mrs. Wallin sighed and seemed to hunch in her chair.

The sounds spoke to Catherine of loves lost and friends parted, yet hope rising through it all, whispering of new life, fulfilled purpose. Around her, the men quieted and stilled. It was as if the very forest was holding its breath and listening.

Simon urged one final note from his violin and lowered it.

Mrs. Wallin managed a smile. "Well done, Simon. You surely inherited that skill from your father. He'd be proud."

Simon shrugged as he set down the instrument, but Catherine could see the faintest of pink in his lean cheeks.

Mrs. Wallin rose then, saying good-night to her family. Catherine watched as each of her children went to kiss her or give her a hug, wishing her sweet dreams, promising they'd see her in the morning. The love glowed around them as surely as the light from the lamp. Catherine felt as if she stood in a circle of darkness.

Then Drew looked her way, and the glow seemed to expand, to encourage her closer.

She could feel her heart responding. Would it be so wrong to give in to its urging?

Chapter Nine

Drew moved to Catherine's side. He didn't think she knew what his brother had just done with his playing, but for a moment she had looked almost stricken. Once more, he'd wanted to gather her close. He had to settle for helping her instead.

"Let me," he said when she took his mother's arm to assist Ma up the stairs. He lifted his mother and carried her up. Catherine and Beth followed.

"That Simon," Beth said with a tsk. "I hope he didn't offend you, Miss Stanway."

Drew tensed, but Catherine's voice held its usual composure. "Not at all," she assured Beth as they reached the top of the stairs. "He plays beautifully."

Drew couldn't help himself. "He ought to pay more attention to his selection than his tuning." He set his mother down on the bed and stepped back to give her room to settle herself. He didn't like her pallor. It was obvious to him she wasn't as well as she wanted them to think.

But despite her evident weariness, her eyes were bright. "Why, what do you mean, Andrew?" she asked innocently. "I like to hear the songs from the old country. I thought the wedding march and the christening song fine selections."

Fine selections for a man who was courting. He wasn't. Drew bit back an answer and turned to Catherine before she could question his mother. "I'll take first watch tonight."

She raised her head, as if he'd challenged her capabilities. "Nonsense. You've labored hard all day. My place is at your mother's side."

So was his. But even as he opened his mouth to say as much, he felt weariness tugging at his sleeve, urging him to take the opportunity to rest.

Beth settled the matter for him. "No, I'll watch first," she insisted. "I'm not sleepy. You and Drew have a lot to talk about, I'm sure."

There they went again. He could see the way his mother and sister exchanged glances. So could Catherine if the set of her mouth was any indication.

Oh, no! He wasn't about to let himself focus on her lips again tonight.

"Miss Stanway has had a long day, as well," he informed his sister. He turned to Catherine. "If you're ready to retire, I'll walk you to the cabin."

"Surely there's no need, Mr. Wallin," she protested. "I believe I know the way by now."

"Oh, but Miss Stanway," Beth interrupted, "the moon's out tonight. There's nothing finer than a stroll in the moonlight."

Catherine did not seem to agree. Indeed, she was turning nearly as pale as Ma in the firelight.

He put a hand to her elbow. "Are you all right?"

She pulled away from his touch. "Fine. Just tired, as

you noted. I'll see if one of your brothers can walk me to the cabin. I'll be expecting your knock after midnight, Miss Wallin."

She turned and descended the stairs as if a bear was at her heels. With his mother and sister glaring at him, he knew just how she felt.

John agreed to escort Catherine across to the other cabin. She felt as if she was running away, but the idea of strolling in the moonlight with Drew had raised such a longing inside her that she'd known retreat was her best choice. She was merely glad John showed no interest in the silvery light bathing them.

"I find your approach to healthful living to be inspiring, Miss Stanway," he said as they neared the cabin. "Especially the different foodstuffs you advised for Ma." He opened the door and peered in. Did he think someone else had wandered into the house while she was out?

"Perhaps you can suggest a book on the subject," he said, returning his gaze to hers. "I hear Mrs. Howard has started a lending library. I may be able to persuade her to order a book for me."

"My father was rather fond of *Culpeper's Complete Herbal*," Catherine told him. "I'll see if I can find a copy for you."

He nodded his thanks, made sure the fire and lamp were burning and left her.

Despite her reaction to Drew, once more sleep came easily, the air so cool and crisp she could almost taste it. A few hours later Beth woke her as promised, rousing Catherine from a hazy dream in which she ran through the woods, searching for something she couldn't name.

"Though I'm not sure you're needed, as Ma's sleeping just fine," the girl reported as she walked Catherine back across the clearing. Both the trip with John and now with Beth had gone remarkably smoothly. Had Drew really needed to carry her the previous night?

But as Catherine settled herself in the chair next to Mrs. Wallin, she almost wished she had stayed in bed. There was nothing to keep her mind from the memories that crept up on her like a woodland mouse.

Her father teaching her brother to ride.

Nathan so proud in the uniform she'd helped sew for him.

Her standing by their gravestones, lined up clean and bright next to the church.

She rose and stoked the fire, then traveled to the far window and peered out. The moon was riding high; she could see a reflection of silver on the lake, brightening the shore. For a moment, she thought she saw a shadow slipping along below the house, but she blinked to focus her weary eyes and it was gone.

Drew or his brothers must have found food elsewhere, for no one disturbed them. The sun had already risen when she yawned and reached for the water bucket. Drew had left them plenty of wood, but she thought Beth might need most of the water for breakfast. Perhaps she could ask Levi to fill this bucket for her so she could help Mrs. Wallin wash up.

Unfortunately, she found his bed empty, seemingly undisturbed from last night. Well, she'd simply have to fend for herself. She took the bucket downstairs, intending to fill it from Drew's pump. She stepped out on the porch.

And froze.

There were men everywhere. Some had curled up along the boardwalk of the house, heads pillowed on their bent knees. Others camped under the eaves of the barn. All lay still, the silence broken by the occasional snore.

What had happened? Why were they here? Had she been wrong about Mrs. Wallin's illness? Was this the start of an epidemic?

She dropped the bucket and ran into the yard. Crouching over the closest fellow, she felt for a pulse at his wrist. It was beating strongly.

His eyes popped open, a bleary blue in his grizzled face. "Glory be, it's true! There *is* a woman in the woods."

Catherine was so surprised she fell back on her skirts. Even as he scrambled to his feet, other hands grabbed her under her arms and hauled her upright.

"There now, ma'am," a man dressed in fur skins said with a smile that revealed several missing teeth. The burned smell of badly tanned leather coiled around her before he released her. "Don't you mind Old Joe. He don't got the manners of a flea."

"But I do." Another man in a fine wool suit, starched collar lifting his shaven chin, pushed forward. He whisked out a snowy white handkerchief and attempted to dust off her skirts. "There you go, missy. All set to marry me."

"Marry you!" Catherine sputtered, shaking out her skirts.

Old Joe shoved him back into the muddy yard. "Hey, I saw her first!"

"But I got here before any of you lot," declared the man in fur. "I paid Mercer a pretty penny for a bride, and none of them hoity-toity misses in town will listen to me. By rights, this one is mine."

He shouldered aside Old Joe, who pushed him right back. The two wrestled to the ground, grappling, mud squelching with each grunt. What were they doing? They couldn't be fighting over her! Even the chickens fluttered about in their coop in protest.

She backed away from the struggling men as the rest of the strangers in the clearing roused at the sounds of raised voices and began standing. As a crowd, they shambled toward her, gazes as bright as if she were a cool drink of water on a hot day.

"Stop, right now!" she ordered them, pointing an imperious finger. "I'm marrying no one."

Old Joe managed to fend off his comrade and struggled to his feet. Wiping muck from his face, he turned toward her with a determined glint in his eyes. "Course you are. That's what you Mercer gals came for. I couldn't get into town before most of them was spoken for, but when I heard one was here with the Wallin boys I figured I stood as good a chance as any of them."

That seemed to be everyone's opinion, for they were all nodding and smiling as they converged on her, arms outstretched as if to shake her hand or grab her closer. Heart pounding, she lifted her skirts and dashed for the boardwalk.

"Won't do no good to run," one shouted after her. "You'll only get caught and brought back."

Her breath was what was caught. All this because they wanted a wife? Had they no moral grounding, no sense of propriety? She felt like the baby in the tale of Solomon's wisdom, about to be cleaved in two to settle a dispute.

She couldn't run into the house and expose Beth and Mrs. Wallin to these men. Who knew where Levi might be or whether he'd be any use at all. If Drew and his other brothers hadn't heard the commotion by now, they must already be out in the trees. They had no way of knowing an army was besieging their little castle on the lake.

And then she remembered. She reached the back door a good few yards before any of the men and snatched up the rifle hanging from a hook. She'd never fired a gun in her life, but it seemed obvious what she should do. Whirling away from the door, she held it out and put her finger in the little loop at the base of the barrel.

The men following her skidded to a stop. One put up his hands as if surrendering.

"Now, you just set that down, little lady," Old Joe said, taking a cautious step closer, eyes narrowing. "We wouldn't want anyone to get hurt."

"She don't know what she's doing," another muttered, with an elbow in the side of the man next to him. "Look at how her hands are shaking."

Catherine could feel it as well, and she could see it in the way the barrel bobbed. *Help me, Lord!*

She stiffened her spine and glared at the mob surrounding her. If they wanted her for a wife, they should know what they were getting.

"I may be shaking, sir," she told Old Joe, "but I know exactly what I'm doing." She raised the gun and fired.

Chapter Ten

Drew heard the shot echoing through the woods and lowered his ax. Simon must have heard it as well, for he paused, too. The two of them and James had been working behind Simon's cabin, cutting away some of the brush that had sprung up in the spring rains before heading out deeper into the woods for the fir they'd chosen for Captain Collings's spar. John and Levi were out notching the tree in preparation for cutting it down.

"Was Beth planning a big breakfast?" James asked, venturing closer from where he'd been dragging the brush into a pile. He must have been expecting the work to be light, for he'd elected to wear the silver-shot waistcoat of which he was inordinately proud.

Now they all listened, tensed, waiting for the second shot that would assure them all was well.

No shot came.

Drew ran.

His brothers were right behind him, axes down and at the ready. They weren't far from the clearing, but each step seemed a mile. Had a cougar wandered too close and threatened the stock? Had the enemy who'd poisoned the spring returned for more? Had their mother taken a turn for the worse? Was Catherine in danger?

He careened into the clearing and skidded to a stop at the sight of more than a dozen men surrounding the main house. Some were peering in the lower windows. Others were pounding at the back door. One was trying to climb up onto the roof.

"Hey!" Simon shouted, the first one out of the woods behind him. "What do you think you're doing?"

The men at the rear of the crowd glanced the brothers' way, and the fellow on the eaves dropped to the ground. Two turned and ran off into the woods. James made to follow, but Drew called him back.

"No! We need you here. You and Simon take the right. I'll take the left. Use your axes only if you must and handle for the blade."

With grim nods, his brothers started forward.

More men peeled off as they approached. Some looked apologetic; others glared belligerently. But no one raised a hand or stammered an explanation.

By the time Drew reached the back door, only a few remained. One was begging at the panel.

"Oh, come now, missy! You can't hide in there forever. We're all fine fellows. Just tell us which you prefer, and the rest of us will go home peaceful-like."

Drew frowned at the statement, but Simon evidently understood its meaning, for he lowered his ax as he joined Drew on the porch.

"You're too late, boys," he said, smile cocky. "We already decided she's marrying one of us."

The man at the front turned to him with a frown, but the door of the house jerked open. The remaining men scattered from the fury on Catherine Stanway's face.

She marched out onto the porch like a colonel leading a battalion into battle.

"Oh, *you* decided, did you?" she said to Simon. "Just like that. No need to consult the lady in question. You're as bad as this bunch!"

His brother was paling, but he had the good sense not to argue with her.

Drew stared around him in amazement. "You all came here to court Miss Stanway?"

"No, siree." A prospector Drew knew was called Old Joe stretched his suspenders as if he were quite proud of himself. "I didn't come to court. I came to marry."

"You came to make a fool of yourself." Catherine leveled her stare at him. As his head dropped, she met each gaze in turn. Most lowered, too, or glanced away.

"Where I was raised," she said, voice as crisp as a winter's afternoon, "a gentleman courts a lady, and they mutually agree that marriage is the best course. I will not be coerced or bullied into marrying. And anyone who attempts to force his way into my affections will rue the day he was born."

Drew raised his brows. Simon took a firmer grip on his ax as if expecting her to pounce on him any moment. From the back of the crowd, James grinned at her.

"Well, she's a shrew," someone muttered. "Think I'll take my chances with one of them tamer ones in town."

Several others nodded, backing away or turning.

Enough was enough. Drew pushed his way to the front and faced the last of her suitors. "You heard the lady. Clear off. If you've a mind to marry, you'll have to find another partner."

His brothers joined him, lining up beside Catherine,

and more men left, shaking their heads and grumbling. Soon only two remained.

One approached, cap in hand. He was a short man with a thick mustache, highly waxed, and a precise part down the center of his dark hair. Drew recognized him from town.

"Miss Stanway," he said, "I'm Jonas Cooper. I work for Mr. Yesler at the mill. He'll vouch that I'm a tidy, sober man. I attend church every Sunday, and I tithe ten percent to the poor. I've had some education, and I've managed to put money aside for a house in town. I don't cuss, but I do enjoy a fine cigar from time to time. I'd be honored if you'd consider allowing me to court you properly."

Drew's fingers tightened on the ax. Catherine had every right to choose a fine man, and Cooper was about as upstanding as they came. Yet Drew felt a sudden urge to go dunk the fellow's perfectly combed hair in the lake.

Not to be outdone, the other man swept in front of Cooper. Drew had never seen him before. He had black hair, a neat goatee and a definite twinkle in his dark eyes. James was already eyeing his coat, which was trimmed with velvet. Instead of a handkerchief at his throat, he wore a fancy cravat held in place by a gold stickpin mounted with a green stone that looked suspiciously like an emerald.

"Nay, fair maiden," he said, voice hinting of a foreign shore, "consider my suit instead. I'm Gulliver Ward. I made my fortune in the gold fields of California, and I'm set to build a playhouse in Seattle, where only the finest theatricals will be performed. My wife will be gowned in silks and satins and fed on oysters and caviar. She will be one of Seattle's first ladies, when the money starts coming in, of course. With your beauty and my wit, no door would be closed to us. Allow me to win your heart."

Drew stared at him. What was he doing, laying his life at her feet? He'd never even met her!

"Out!" he shouted, raising the handle of his ax. "You have five minutes to get off my land. James, escort these fine fellows."

His brother started forward. So did Catherine, but this time her fury was turned on Drew, and he found himself backing away from it.

"And there you go, Mr. Wallin," she said, eyes sparking fire, "deciding my future just as surely as the rest of these men. *I* will decide who I court, if I court. Have I made myself clear?"

Drew nodded. "Clear enough. But may I remind you that you shot the rifle. I thought you wanted my help."

She took a deep breath as if to calm herself. "I did. But I am quite capable of making my own decisions." She turned to the two men. Drew steeled himself to hear her answer. If she accepted that gussied-up Ward, he thought he'd have to go soak his own head in the lake.

"Mr. Cooper," she said, voice as precise and calm as it usually was when she spoke about clinical matters, "I appreciate your thoughtful assessment of your worth as a matrimonial candidate. Allow me to reciprocate. I am headstrong, opinionated and outspoken. We would not suit. I suggest you look more closely at the ladies still in Seattle."

Drew felt as if the air was sweeter as Mr. Cooper stared at her in surprise. Catherine turned to her other suitor.

"Mr. Ward, you certainly have a way with words. I predict you will go far."

Drew couldn't help it. He took a step closer to the fellow, but Ward's gaze did not waver from Catherine's.

"I'm glad we are of a common mind, my dear," he said, inclining his head. "Allow me to escort you away from this rustic hovel. You shine like a diamond even here, but I know you will positively glow in a more suitable setting."

Drew could feel his teeth grating on each other; he was surprised Catherine couldn't hear them. Simon was smacking the handle of his ax into his palm as if he couldn't wait for an excuse to use it.

"You are too kind," Catherine said with a smile that raised gooseflesh along Drew's arms. "But I have work here. You might look up my friend Miss O'Rourke in Seattle. She has a particular fondness for silks and satins. I do caution you, however, that she may be just as loath to spend her life as a decoration for a man's arm. Good day." She turned and entered the house, closing the door decisively behind her.

Drew wanted to howl at the sky in triumph. She'd turned them down!

Cooper had a harder time believing it, for he shook his head. "They said she was cold, but I wouldn't believe it. You had better think twice before taking that one to wife, Wallin."

"You, sir, are blind," Ward said, stepping down from the porch. "A man can go far with the right woman at his side. I'd heard Miss Stanway was the best of the lot."

"How did you know she was here?" Simon asked, lowering his ax.

"'Twas a tale told over a friendly hand of cards," Ward assured him. "When a lady is so lovely, word will get around. And the fact that she was willing to sojourn with you all indicated her taste in men might not be overly finicky."

Simon frowned. "Did you just insult us?"

"Not with that accent," James joked.

Ward swept them a bow. "I meant no harm, gentlemen. My own past is no less humble. That hasn't stopped me from reaching high, even in a bride." He glanced at the door and sighed. "Ah, well. Back to the city for this lad. Farewell, gentlemen." He turned and strolled out into the woods, where Drew assumed he must have a horse waiting.

"Reprobate," Cooper said with a shake of his head, as if he hadn't also just tried to marry Catherine at first sight like the fancy Ward. He turned to Drew. "Sorry to have troubled you. Mr. Yesler sends his regards and hopes you will have more timber for him soon."

"Maybe we would," Simon said, "if we weren't so busy defending what is ours."

Cooper reddened. Stammering another apology, he, too, headed for the trees.

"I'll just make sure they've all gone," James said, "and ask that Ward fellow where he purchased his coat." He set out toward the edge of the clearing.

Simon shook his head. "I warned you, Drew. If you won't marry Miss Stanway, someone else will."

"You heard her," Drew snapped. "She refused to marry any of them."

"So she said," Simon agreed. "But what I want to know is why she looked at you every time she said it."

Beth had come down from upstairs and stood by the stove as Catherine closed the door behind her, hands still shaking. The girl's eyes were wide in her round face, her fingers twisting at the material of her pink gingham gown.

"Who were those men?" she cried. "Was that Simon I saw outside? Where are Drew and the others? Should I fetch a rifle?"

Catherine only felt confident answering the last question. "No need for the gun. I think the other men have gone. I'm sorry if I frightened you when I fired."

Beth took a step closer and put out a hand as if she needed to be certain Catherine was safe. "When someone fires one shot around here, we notice. What happened?"

The chair by the hearth beckoned, but Catherine couldn't sit, not when her heart was hammering as furiously as her temper. She had to smother these emotions. She paced to the stove, a cast-iron series of steps into the fireplace with a fat-bellied oven in the center near the fire and burners on top. Reaching above it, she pulled down a copper teakettle from a hook on the wall, talking as she worked. "We had company this morning, a great deal of company. And they were not the sort of men I wanted to introduce to you."

As if she disagreed with Catherine, Beth scrambled to the window and peered out, blond hair brushing the pane. "I don't see anyone. Were they the ones who poisoned the spring?"

About to lift the bucket of water by the stove, Catherine stilled. Was it possible? Whoever had thrown manure into the Wallin's pool had been bent on making trouble. Was this simply more of the same?

But no, the water had been contaminated before Mrs. Wallin had fallen ill, which was long before Catherine had arrived. If those men were truly here because of her, they could have had nothing to do with the spring.

"I don't think so," Catherine said, pouring water into the teakettle.

Beth wheeled away from the window. "Oh, good! Drew's coming in. Maybe he'll have answers."

Catherine's fingers tightened on the wooden handle of the kettle as the door opened. Although she was grateful Drew and his brothers had come running at her shot for help, she didn't appreciate the way they'd presumed to know her mind. Like her neighbors in Sudbury, they seemed certain her only course was marriage. Had she gained nothing by traveling across the country?

Drew came in and shut the door behind him. His mouth was set in a firm line, and his eyes were narrowed as if he wasn't sure of his reception.

In truth, she wasn't sure how to receive him, either. She busied herself setting the teakettle on the stove. The movement was stiff enough that metal clanked on metal.

"What was all that?" Beth demanded as he came into the room, boots thudding against the worn boards of the floor. "Who were those men?"

"Apparently a pack of fools," he replied. He crossed to Catherine's side and lowered his head and his voice.

"Forgive me if I offended you," he murmured. "I just didn't like the idea of those men pushing themselves on you."

Neither had she. In truth, she'd panicked, something she'd always thought beneath her. She was an intelligent, well-educated, skilled woman. She'd never been in a situation she couldn't master, until her father and brother had died. Even then, she'd fallen back on reason and logic, walling off all the emotions that troubled her.

But those men had demanded that she marry one of them, as if she were no more than a commodity. How did reason prevail?

"They have no excuse for their behavior," she said, pulling down the tea canister from the shelf at the top of the sideboard along one wall. Her hand was still shaking as she scooped up some of the leaves, and she forced her fingers to still. "Wilderness or big city, there are conventions on how one goes courting."

"Courting?" Beth ventured closer, head cocked. "You mean all those men came here for you, Miss Stanway?"

"As I said, they are a pack of fools," Drew answered. He caught Catherine's hand and held it as if to stop her trembling. "You were wise to call us. I never dreamed something like this would happen. I heard there was a lot of nonsense when the Mercer belles had first arrived, but I'd thought that had died down by now."

Catherine shuddered, remembering. "This sort of thing followed us the entire trip. From Brazil to Chile to San Francisco, men flocked out to greet us as if they'd never seen a woman before. When we arrived in Seattle, men lined the shore, claiming they'd paid our passage to be their brides."

"Oh," Beth said, obviously fascinated to the point her usual banter failed her.

"I paid my own passage," Catherine informed her. "As did most of the ladies aboard. It certainly isn't our fault Mr. Mercer made promises he couldn't keep. I won't be held accountable for that man's larceny. But what I don't understand is how those men knew I was here."

"That fellow Ward said something about a card game," Drew told her, his hand still cradling hers. "Perhaps McCormick reported on your whereabouts when he returned to town."

Possibly, but most of the men seemed to have come from the area, not Seattle. She hadn't seen the smoke from a single homestead when she'd ridden north with Drew. Where had these men come from?

"Deputy McCormick was here?" Beth cried, turning pink. "Why didn't someone tell me? Oh, I miss all the excitement!"

"Be thankful for that," Catherine said. She knew she should pull back her hand and finish preparing tea, but the warmth of Drew's touch spread through her body, relaxing tense muscles and calming frazzled nerves. She'd never thought she'd be one to need a man to feel safe, but she could not deny that his presence was unaccountably comforting.

"It doesn't matter," he said. "What's done is done. James and Simon will make sure those men leave, but I'll stay nearby until you've returned to Seattle. You have no need to fear."

Fear? That emotion had long since fled. Catherine forced her fingers out of his. "It wasn't fear that made me so angry. It was your brother's statement that you've all decided one of you is going to marry me. I heard you talking with your brothers the other night. You didn't disagree, then or now."

Color was creeping into his cheeks, like the sun rising over a mountain. "Simon can speak all the nonsense he likes. He can't tell anyone how to feel."

She drew in the first deep breath since she'd seen those men in the clearing. "No, he can't. Nor can he dictate my actions. I think I've made myself clear. I'm not planning on marrying. I have a calling, a vocation, and certainly one Seattle sorely needs. I intended to stay another day, but if you all can't understand my position, then perhaps I should leave now."

He met her gaze, and this time she had no doubt the emotion flickering in that expanse of blue-green was regret. She felt it, too, just as she felt herself leaning toward him, as if her body vied with her mind as to where she belonged.

Beth spoke before he did. "No, you can't go, Miss Stanway. Not until Ma's well."

"Your mother is on the mend, Beth," Catherine said, drawing back though her gaze refused to leave his. "We've determined the cause of the illness, and your brother has already isolated it. There's nothing more for me to do here."

She waited for him to argue. She wasn't sure why she expected it. Some part of her believed him when he'd said he didn't wish to wed, either. If he truly did intend to court her or marry her to one of his brothers, he ought to protest her leaving. And if he actually cared about her…

She shut that thought away. She had never been one of those girls who collected beaux like frosted candies, turning this one aside when that one struck her fancy. She didn't want Drew to care about her.

Because that meant she'd have to care about him more than she already did.

Chapter Eleven

She was determined to leave. Drew could see the challenge in those cool blue eyes. She'd had her fill of his family, and who could blame her? Between Simon's demands and Beth and Ma's collusion, Catherine had to feel surrounded. And their unexpected visitors this morning had only made matters worse.

Still, he ought to argue. Ma was a great deal better, but who was to say she wouldn't have a relapse? And he would have liked to sit by the fire with Catherine, quiz her on what more he could do to keep his family healthy, hold her hand, cuddle her close.

What was he thinking? Maybe it really was time for her to go.

He snapped a nod, breaking their gazes at last. "I'll hitch the team to the wagon and we can take you back to Seattle right now."

She stepped away from him as if he'd ordered her to go. "Very well. I'll check on my patient one last time." She picked up her skirts and swept from the room.

Her patient, she said, as if Ma were no more than one of the stock, an ax that needed sharpening. Ma and his brothers clearly meant nothing to her. They were his responsibility only.

The kettle began to hiss. Beth went to lift it off the stove.

"Well, you made a great hash of that," she said, disgust evident in each syllable. "You need lessons in courting."

Drew shook his head and turned for the back door. "I'm not courting."

"Not like that, you aren't!" She dropped the kettle on the sideboard with a clatter, ran after him and grabbed his arm before he could open the door. "For pity's sake, Drew! You can do better. You always told us if we set our minds to something, we should keep trying until we won it."

Perhaps that was the problem. He couldn't set his mind to courting Catherine, despite his family's urging or the murmur of his heart. As much as he had taken an instant dislike to that Ward fellow, Drew could not argue that Catherine seemed destined for greater things than Wallin Landing.

From her fancy dress to her proper ways, Catherine seemed cultured. Certainly she was better educated than most people he knew, even the ever-studious John. She ought to be somewhere she could use those skills, not just doctoring his family. That was his job.

"Leave be, Beth," he told his sister. "This is for the best."

She released him with a scowl. "Whose best? Not yours. Not ours."

"No," Drew said, yanking open the door. "Hers. Tell her I'll have the team out front when she's ready." He left before his sister could launch into the tirade he saw building in her eyes as sure as the steam from the hot teakettle.

Simon and James were still out in the woods as Drew stalked across the clearing, but he heard a cheery whistle coming from the opposite direction. Not another would-be suitor! He almost pitied the fellow, for Drew was in no mood to be conciliatory. Turning, he planted his feet and brought up both fists.

John strode out of the trees, ax over one shoulder and rifle in the other hand. Spying Drew, he stopped and dropped his ax. "What have I done?"

Drew lowered his fists and narrowed his stance. "Nothing. We had some excitement this morning."

"I thought I heard a shot!" He hurried to Drew's side. "I'm sorry, Drew! I was so far out I couldn't be sure. And I knew Levi was headed this way, so I figured he'd come back for me if I was needed."

Drew frowned. "You sent Levi home?"

John nodded. "Early this morning. The dunderhead forgot the wedges. Honestly, Drew, sometimes I wonder whether we dropped that boy on his head a few too many times when he was a baby."

"We never dropped him," Drew said. "We wouldn't have dared. He was Ma's favorite until Beth came along."

"Sometimes I think he's still Ma's favorite," John said, no rancor in his tone. "That's the only reason I can see for why she wants him around so much. I take it he was too busy helping you to bring back those wedges."

"He never returned to the Landing that I saw," Drew replied.

Now John frowned. "Did you check the barn? It's his favorite place to nap."

So Drew had discovered yesterday. "If he slept through the chaos this morning, I'll make sure he doesn't sleep tonight," Drew promised, turning for the barn.

John paced him, and Drew took the opportunity to explain what had happened with Catherine's surprise callers.

John whistled as they came into the barn. "It seems Simon was right. She is valuable."

"Her value has nothing to do with the fact that men rush to court her," Drew said. His tone must have been hotter than he intended, for the chickens flew out of their roost at the sound.

John set the ax and rifle by the door. "Oh, I wouldn't say that. I understand a woman's allure is an important part of what she can accomplish. Look at Helen of Troy."

"Never met her," Drew said. He grabbed the iron pole and poked it up into the straw. "Hey! Levi! Wake up!"

No curly-haired head appeared.

"Am I the only one who reads in this family?" John complained, climbing the ladder to make sure his brother wasn't up in the haymow. His voice drifted down to Drew. "Helen of Troy was a beautiful woman in ancient Greece. Thousands of men sailed to her rescue when she was stolen away."

Drew shook his head. "That's a story."

"That's a legend," John corrected him. "There's a difference." He craned his neck to glance around the loft, then looked down at Drew. "Empty."

Drew's sigh was forceful enough to set the chickens to clucking again. "This is ridiculous. He knows we have work to do."

John hopped down beside him. "He's a loafer, but I've never known him to abandon us in the middle of a job."

The barn seemed darker. "Something's happened, then," Drew said. "Find Simon and James. We're going hunting."

John went for his rifle.

Catherine stepped out on the porch, Beth at her heels. Neither Wallin lady had taken her decision to leave well.

"I'm not convinced of my recovery," Mrs. Wallin had said, going so far as to cough into an embroidered handkerchief. "What if the fever comes back?"

"Beth knows what I did for you," Catherine had assured her, refusing to sit on the quilt-covered bed beside her patient lest Mrs. Wallin hug her close. "She has the skills to be a fine nurse."

Beth had shaken her head so violently her hair had come undone and spilled about her shoulders. "No! I don't know half of what you do, Miss Stanway. Please don't go."

"It's for the best," Catherine had made herself say. "I have other patients in town who need me."

Mrs. Wallin had caught her hand. "Ah, but do you need them?"

Catherine couldn't seem to look away from those kind green eyes. Of course she didn't need any specific patient. That was not a nurse's role. A friend of her father's had once commented that a doctor's goal was to work himself out of a job by making his patients well. Unfortunately, she'd found there were always more sick or injured people.

She'd set Mrs. Wallin's hand down on the covers and

pulled back her own. "Truly, I must go. Send word if you need help later. I'll see that someone comes out."

Mrs. Wallin's face had crumpled, but Catherine had turned and walked away. She knew how to comfort those who had been cut or bruised; she knew how to bring down a fever. She didn't know how to heal a wound she was feeling herself.

Now she stood beside Beth, surveying the clearing. The goats were munching in the closest pasture, horses and oxen farther out. She could hear the chickens clucking and the grunt of a satisfied pig. There wasn't a wagon in sight.

"They're clumsy, my brothers," Beth murmured, rubbing a hand up the sleeve of her gown. "They don't do what they should, and they say what they shouldn't. But they're nice when you get used to them."

"I'm sure that's true," Catherine replied. The problem was, she wasn't willing to get used to them. This family, this place, was already growing in her heart, like a seed planted in fertile soil. If she didn't weed out these feelings now, they would only overpower her just as they had when her father and Nathan had died.

Beth, however, was warming to her theme. "Take Drew," she said, pushing her hair back from her face. "Everyone says he's just like Pa, always working, always trying to make things better for us. He spent last winter carving me a hope chest. Roses on vines. Would another fellow even have thought of that?"

"Very likely not," Catherine had to admit. It was a kind thing for Drew to have done, an acknowledgment of impending womanhood in a predominantly male household. At times, she'd thought Nathan and her father would have found it decidedly more convenient if she'd been born a male.

If she'd been male, perhaps they'd have listened to her and stayed home. If nothing else, she might have fought beside them.

Just then Simon and James came striding out of the woods, John beside them. She'd never seen their faces so set. Even the ever-teasing James was frowning. Were they about to lecture her, too?

She raised her head, determined that logic would prevail this time, but they merely nodded to her and Beth before converging on the door of the barn. Drew came out, and four heads, ranging from coppery red to golden brown, bent together.

"What are they up to?" Beth wondered, speaking Catherine's thoughts aloud.

Whatever it was, they seemed to have reached an agreement, for Simon and James headed in one direction, and Drew and John crossed the clearing to the porch.

"Forgive me, Miss Stanway," Drew said, "but our trip to Seattle will have to wait. Levi's gone missing."

Beth clamped her mouth shut as if she couldn't find the words, but Catherine's heart skipped a beat. "Missing? I thought his bed didn't look slept in."

"He didn't sleep in the house last night?" Drew glanced at his brother. "Was he bunking with James?"

John shook his head. Though Catherine knew he was a lean fellow, he seemed all the smaller compared to Drew's brawn, or perhaps it was his concern for his brother that made him look so tense.

"He didn't sleep in Simon's cabin, either," he replied. "But he was in the barn when I went to fetch the ax this morning, and he came with me to the tree. I sent him back to the house for some tools, but he never returned."

"Surely if he'd reached the Landing he would have come to help us," Catherine reasoned, growing colder every minute. "Something must have happened along the way."

The look on Drew's face told her he agreed with her.

"He's probably just loafing off somewhere," John assured her.

Beth nodded. "You'll find him eating the honey from a comb behind some bush."

"Very likely," Drew said.

Catherine didn't believe him. An assurance was building inside her. Levi wasn't trying to avoid work this time. Just as when her brother had met unexpected cannon fire, something had gone wrong. But this time, she had the power to fix it.

"Take Pa's rifle, and stay in the house," Drew was telling Beth. "We'll send word as soon as we know anything."

"All right," Beth agreed. "Be careful."

Drew nodded, then stepped back from the porch. His gaze lingered on Catherine as if he thought it might be the last time he'd see her.

The look propelled her to his side. "Take me with you."

Chapter Twelve

Catherine was certain Drew would refuse her request. His brows were drawn down, and the muscle under her hand was unyielding. Still, his voice when he spoke was as gentle as a caress.

"If there's something dangerous enough in the woods to take out a seasoned young man like Levi," he said, "I don't want it anywhere near you."

How could she argue with that? Besides, he had to wonder why she'd changed her mind. One moment she had been ready to walk out of their lives, the next she was determined to ride to the rescue.

"I appreciate your concern," she said. "But my thoughts right now are for your brother. If he's hurt, I can help."

"If he's hurt," Beth put in, "she can do more than help. She might save his life."

Drew's head came up. She should have known that, where his family was concerned, the more help, the better.

"Very well," he agreed. "Simon and James are circling along the lake in case Levi decided to take a swim instead of working. John and I are tracking back through the trees. This way."

She fell into step beside him. Though her heart was beating rapidly at the thought of Levi in danger, she forced herself to walk as calmly as if they were strolling to church on a sunny Sunday morning. She would not allow her inexperience with the wilderness to hinder their search.

Unfortunately, it was tough going almost immediately. He and his brothers had apparently hacked a path to the tree they hoped to fell, but they had hardly designed it to accommodate a lady in full skirts. Drew and John had to slow to help her over logs and push back encroaching limbs. All the while her mind kept bringing up the picture of Drew's brother lying on the ground, life ebbing.

Not Levi, Lord! He's so young. He doesn't even understand how life works yet.

"And you're confident this is his most likely route?" Catherine asked as she ducked under a low-hanging branch.

"It is the shortest way from the tree to the Landing," Drew replied, spreading a clump of saplings that had been reaching out to clutch at her sleeve.

"Not that he's ever been known to favor the shortest route," John said. He took his ax to an encroaching shrub. "Levi has always had his own way of doing things. Drew, remember when he announced he wanted to be called Matthew on account of it being more biblical?"

Drew slapped a fly off his cheek and smiled at the memory. "He renamed us all. Simon wasn't too fond of being dubbed Cephas."

"Cephas?" Catherine tugged her skirts out of the grip of a thorny blackberry vine. "Why Cephas?"

"Pa named us for the first disciples," John explained. "By order of their calling. Andrew, Simon…"

"James, John and Levi," she finished. "Very clever."

Drew frowned as if he thought his father had taken the matter too seriously, but John grinned as he used his ax handle to push back a set of brambles. "James always says we should be glad Beth was born, or we might have ended up with a Judas Iscariot, and no child should have to be saddled with that name."

Despite her fears, Catherine felt laughter bubbling up. By the similar smile on Drew's face, the sound had warmed him, as well.

Ahead, something rustled in the bushes. John dropped the ax and aimed the rifle. Before Catherine could think, Drew had shifted around her, blocking her path. He was like a sturdy stone wall between her and the danger.

"Oh!" a higher-pitched male voice exclaimed. "Didn't know you were in the woods this morning."

Drew relaxed his stance enough that she could peer around him. Half tangled in blackberry vines was a youth about Levi's age. In other circumstances, she might have wondered at the state of his worn, wrinkled and stained shirt and trousers and the matted thatch of his brown hair, but what caught her attention now was the blood tricking from his crooked nose.

She pushed past Drew. "You appear to have broken your nose, sir. I'm a nurse. Let me help."

He took a step back, vines snagging his sleeve and fingers going to his nostrils. "It ain't broke. It just naturally looks that way."

Catherine didn't believe him. She'd seen any number of noses through the years, and that lump near the bridge and the sideways cant were decided clues that something was wrong. She was only surprised there was no sign of swelling.

"Miss Stanway," Drew said, voice a warm rumble behind her, "meet Scout Rankin. His pa has the closest claim to ours to the south. And he doesn't look any different to me than he did the last time I saw him."

So the break had to be old. Then why the blood? As if to remove any trace, Scout rubbed his nostrils with the back of one hand and sniffed. "Nice to meet you, ma'am. I'd best be going."

He started to ease around John, but Drew put out a hand to stop him. "What are you doing up this way, Scout?"

"And does it happen to have anything to do with Levi?" John added.

Scout froze like a squirrel started by a carriage, brown eyes wide. "Levi? Are you all looking for Levi?"

"We are," Catherine told him. "Do you know where he is?"

His hands were starting to shake. He must have noticed her watching him, for he shoved them behind him. "Saw him up by that tree you all are working on," he said, gaze avoiding hers. "If you find him, tell him I sent you that way."

It was an odd thing to say, but he darted past Drew, branches clutching at his clothes, and dived into the bush for all the world as if he expected the Wallins to hold him captive otherwise.

"Is there some disagreement between your family and his?" Catherine asked Drew.

He shook his head, but more at Scout's behavior than at her question, she thought. "Not that I know of," he answered.

"They're not the friendliest sorts," John said, lifting the ax once more. "Ma tried to be hospitable when they first took over the claim a few years ago. Scout used to come up for lessons in reading and arithmetic. It doesn't seem to have done much good." He, too, shook his head as he turned toward the path once more.

Catherine fell in behind him. She had her suspicions as to why Scout Rankin might have trouble learning, but she could not voice them without more evidence. Given where Scout and the Wallins lived, any number of accidents might explain why a child would receive a broken nose in the past and a bloody nose now.

But so could something other than an accident, such as a beating. She made herself a promise to find a way to look in on the boy in the future once they had Levi home safe and sound.

Drew pushed back a clump of wild grapes to allow Catherine to move ahead. Perhaps it was the cock of her head, the filtered sunlight sparkling off her pale hair. Perhaps it was the fact that she'd grown silent, the only sound the swish of her blue skirts against the rough path. Either way, something about their meeting with Scout seemed to have troubled her.

It troubled him, too. There was no reason for Scout to be on their land so far from the house. And he'd seemed surprised to find them in the woods, when some set of his brothers could always be expected out among the trees any day but Sunday. Then again, Scout had known right where to find Levi. What were those two up to?

"And here we are," John announced, lifting a branch out of the way for Catherine. Ahead lay the area Drew and his brothers had cleared in preparation for removing the graceful fir destined for the deck of the *Merry Maid*. The tree reached for the sky, the floor surrounding it covered in a thick carpet of shed needles and dotted with the leafy fronds of ferns.

Drew didn't spot Levi right away, but Simon and James must have made good time along the lake, for they had beaten Drew and the others to the tree. James was crouched near the base, and Drew sucked in a breath when he realized Levi lay still on the ground next to him.

Simon came to meet them at the edge of the cleared area. His face told Drew the news before he spoke.

"He must have missed John on the way back," Simon said. "It looks like he went up the tree to clear some branches. You know how he is about widow-makers, Drew."

The words felt like a punch in the gut to Drew. He knew how Levi felt about the broken branches higher up. Every Wallin understood that a loose branch had killed their father.

"How bad?" Drew asked.

Simon was paling. "He isn't conscious."

Drew felt ill.

"It may have been the jar from hitting the ground," Catherine said. "I won't know until I examine him."

She stood beside him, head up and one hand fisted in her skirts as if to give her freer movement. All he could do was nod.

Simon reached out and took her free hand. "Thank you, Miss Stanway. This way."

Levi was spread out not far from the base of the fir. Either James or Simon must have pulled a branch off him, for it was bent off to one side. Their brother's shirt and trousers were rumpled, as if he'd hit a few branches as he fell, and his pale face was bruised and swelling. Beside him, James met Drew's gaze, his usual humor fled. John went to his other side as Catherine knelt next to Levi, skirts belling out among the needles.

Drew could see her head turning as she surveyed his brother's form. As if Levi felt the look, his eyes opened. He stared at the branches overhead, then focused on Catherine.

"How'd you get here?"

James leaned back with a chuckle that was all relief. "You kidnapped her, remember?"

Catherine ignored him. "You seem to have met with an accident, Mr. Wallin. Should we be concerned?"

To Drew's surprise, Levi's face darkened. "No, ma'am. I'm sure I'll be fine." He started to lever himself up with his elbows, then gasped and dropped back onto the ground, eyes tearing.

"Easy," Simon advised. "Looks as though you fell out of the tree going after a widow-maker."

"The tree?" Levi blinked as if recognizing the branches above him for the first time. "The tree. Right. I fell out of the tree." He turned his head and met Drew's gaze. "Don't be mad, Drew." He coughed, and blood trickled out of his mouth.

"We'll talk about it later," Drew said, throat tight. "Right now, we need to get you home."

"No." Catherine put a hand on Drew's arm as if to hold him in place. "First we need to know exactly what we're dealing with."

She didn't wait for Drew to respond, turning instead to his brother. "I'm going to ask you some questions, Levi, and then I'm going to touch you. I want you to tell me what you feel."

His gaze darted between her and Drew, as if he sought permission.

"Do as she says," Drew told him.

"Just think what a lucky fellow you are," James said,

his usual teasing tone strained. "Lying there while a pretty lady gives you all her attentions."

Levi managed a weak smile.

Catherine set her hand carefully on his chest. "Can you breathe? Swallow as good as usual?"

Drew could see Levi's Adam's apple bob as if he was testing. "Yes."

Relief washed over Drew, but he knew he could not trust it, not yet.

"That's good," Catherine encouraged the boy. "Does anything hurt a lot?"

He sighed as if too much hurt. "I can't rightly tell. Everything is sort of sore right now."

"Well," James said with a grin, "that does tend to happen when you fall out of a tree. A shame you didn't just land on your head. That's hard enough to absorb anything."

Levi glared at him.

Catherine's smile was prim. "Perhaps we should test your brother's theory, Mr. Wallin. I have a feeling your legs are more sturdy than he thinks." She rested her hand on his right thigh. "Can you feel that?"

Levi nodded. "Yes, ma'am."

Thank You, Lord! Surely the fact that his brother could feel sensation in his leg was good news. Yet Drew's body couldn't seem to relax. He watched as Catherine moved her hand to Levi's knee.

"Here?" she asked, watching him.

"Yes." Levi's face was brightening. He wiggled on the ground as if he thought he could jump right up, then sucked in a breath and blanched. Drew felt as if he was the one who'd fallen.

"Where does it hurt?" Catherine asked.

"Left leg," he grit out. "Below the knee."

Gingerly, she reached across him and touched his calf. Levi jerked.

"Hold him down," she ordered Drew.

How could she be so calm? Drew blinked sweat out of his eyes, though the day was still cool. His stomach was a knot; his hands shook. While James kept an eye out for trouble, all merriment gone, Simon held Levi's shoulders and John leaned over his brother's hips. Drew grasped Levi's ankles, anchoring him to the ground.

Catherine never hesitated. Levi grunted as her hands passed down his leg and over his ankle-high boot. "The leg's broken," she reported as if relaying the expected weather for the day. "I can feel the crack, but I see no blood, so I don't think it's come through the skin. Still, I need to set it and splint it before we move him anywhere."

"Drew," James murmured.

He wasn't sure why James would protest, and he wasn't in the mood for one of his brother's jests. Drew released Levi and leaned back. "I'll find sticks for a splint. John, help Miss Stanway."

"Drew." James said his name more forcefully this time. Glancing toward him, Drew saw that his brother's face was nearly as white as Levi's.

"What is it?" Drew demanded as Simon, John and Catherine frowned at James.

"Cougar," James said as if the word would barely leave his lips. "In the tree over your right shoulder. And he looks annoyed we're about to deprive him of a meal."

Chapter Thirteen

Catherine saw the blood drain from Drew's face as she stiffened. The big catamounts were the stuff of legend in town. Men talked in hushed tones of the nine-foot-long monster an early pioneer had shot. Massive footprints were still seen along the edges of the community. Cougars devoured stray calves and colts, and they sometimes stalked people. Maybe this one had heard Levi's fall and come to investigate.

"Won't it be frightened by so many people?" she murmured to Drew.

"Bears run from noise," Drew said, back straight and hands stilled. "Nothing scares a cougar intent on prey." He glanced at Simon, James and John. "Whatever happens, we protect Catherine and Levi. Agreed?"

Catherine knew she should protest. He had his family to consider. But she could feel her legs starting to tremble, and she knew she'd never be able to outrun the big cat in her skirts.

Simon and John nodded, faces determined.

"I would love to be included on that list," James said. "But agreed."

"What do we do?" Catherine said. "We can't run with Levi in this condition."

Levi glanced among his brothers. "Leave me. I'm the least important person in the family. All I do is cause trouble."

Drew jerked as if the youth had struck him. "No one is running. We go together or not at all."

"Besides, running would only encourage it," James said cheerfully.

"But if you leave me behind, it won't follow you," Levi protested.

Had he hit his head on the way down so he didn't know what he was suggesting? The idea of abandoning the boy raised bile in her throat.

"That is entirely enough of that sort of talk," Catherine told him. "No one is leaving anyone, not even for a splint." Still, she had to do something. She had no doubt Drew could carry his brother, but jostling that leg could turn a simple fracture into a compound one. There had to be something nearer to hand that she could use, something stiff enough, firm enough.

She eyed James. "Mr. Wallin, remove your waistcoat."

James glanced down at the garment that covered his cotton shirt. Catherine suspected it was made from heavy brocade and probably lined with satin. It was certainly stiff enough to stand on its own, and the firmest piece of fabric among them.

James fingered the collar. "I paid a pretty price for this."

"Is it worth more than your brother's life?" she challenged.

He began loosening the silver buttons.

Drew's head was turned as he watched the carnivore. "It hasn't moved. What do you have in mind, Catherine?"

Did he realize he'd used her first name twice now? Every time he said it, she felt as if he'd run his hand against her cheek in a caress.

"We'll wrap the waistcoat around Levi's leg and use the laces from his boot to secure it. Then one of you can carry him on your back while the others protect us from the cougar."

She waited for him to disagree with her plan. What did she know about surviving in the wilderness? But he merely nodded and rose. "I'll carry Levi. James and Simon, keep your rifles at the ready. John, the ax is yours."

The plan made, they set to work. John unlaced Levi's boot, fingers moving with quick efficiency. Levi clamped his lips shut as if to hold back sharp words as Catherine tied up his leg. Then she and John helped him climb to his good foot, and they hefted him onto Drew's back. Above them, dark clouds obscured the blue of the sky as if in sympathy with their plight.

"Try not to jiggle him," she told Drew as he adjusted his hold on his brother. "We don't want to make the break worse."

"Oh, I don't know," James said, gaze on the tree where he'd spotted the cougar. "A little hobble might give him character."

Behind them came a soft thud. James stiffened. "It's jumped down."

For the first time, Catherine looked toward the brush at the edge of the clearing. Through the thicket of bracken and blackberries, she made out the shape of something long, sinuous and tawny. Baleful amber eyes met hers, unblinking. It was as if she were being evaluated for her best parts.

"Walk," Drew advised. "John, lead the way. Simon, take the rear. James, keep an eye on that cat."

"The blond Cat or the tawny one?" James quipped, but Catherine could feel him behind her as John started for the trees.

He hacked away a bit more of the brush as he went, trying to make a path for the others. Simon remained between the rest of them and the cougar, James at his side. Drew used his shoulders to widen the path and carry Levi through, Catherine right behind him.

"I'm sorry, Drew," Levi said, clinging to his brother's shoulders as his feet stuck out on either side. "It's all my fault. I should never have left John."

"No, you shouldn't have," Drew agreed, stepping over a log. "You know we agreed no one would go up a tree alone. You should have waited until someone else was near in case you needed help."

"We don't make the rules to annoy you, you know," James added from behind Catherine. "Though that is a nice benefit."

Catherine wanted to smile, but she felt as if those fiery eyes were watching her every move. She chanced a look back around James and Simon and saw the cougar slipping from sunlight into shadow, tail looped up behind its body, less than twenty feet back.

She spun forward again. "It's following us."

"That it is," James replied. "Sorry, I assumed everyone knew that." He reached out to lift a branch so that Catherine could cross under it.

"It will follow until it sees whether we'll give it an opportunity to strike," Simon said.

Drew hitched Levi up, and his brother grimaced.

"Cougars tend to pick off strays," Drew explained to Catherine. "We won't allow that. We stay together."

Catherine nodded, drawing in a breath. She couldn't help moving a little closer to him. Drew's strength seemed to radiate out from him as they walked, his steps firm and back barely bent under Levi's weight. His gaze was focused ahead, as if he was determined to make the Landing at all costs. Once again, he reminded her of a knight, intent on his noble quest, determined to prevail.

"Still a good fifteen feet back," James reported. He started whistling as if he hadn't a care in the world. Rain began to fall, pattering down softly on the boughs over their heads.

Catherine wished she could be so calm as to whistle. She'd faced with equanimity mothers crying in fear as their babies struggled to be born, men with wounds spurting blood. That was her profession, her duty. This was something else entirely. The thought of that big cat leaping on Drew or his brothers made her chest hurt. She couldn't seem to stop the panic from rising.

Was this how Nathan felt when he heard the roar of the cannon, Lord? I hate being so helpless! There must be something I can do!

"You know what might help?" James asked, pausing in his whistling. "Singing. You can sing, can't you, Miss Stanway?"

Catherine swallowed. At the moment she barely trusted herself to speak. "I'm not sure now is the time, Mr. Wallin."

"The best thing with a cougar," John told her, glancing back over his shoulder, "is to act as if you are not prey. I must admit I've never known prey to sing." He swung the ax and hacked off the top of a fern as if to prove to the big cat he meant business.

Catherine couldn't help glancing back again. There was no sign of the cougar, but she felt as if something was watching her, waiting for her to fall, to fail. She turned front and raised her head.

"Do you know 'Wait for the Wagon,' Mr. Wallin?" she asked.

"That I do," James replied. His baritone burst out, strong and sure. "'Will you come with me, my Catherine dear, to yon blue mountain free?'"

"It's Phillis, not Catherine," Levi complained, but John's voice joined his brother's.

"'Where blossoms smell the sweetest, come rove along with me.'"

Now Drew's bass and Simon's tenor chimed in, as well.

"'It's ev'ry Sunday morning, when I am by your side. We'll jump into the wagon, and all take a ride.'"

Their confidence was contagious. Catherine found herself joining in the chorus, her higher voice melding with their deeper ones, the rain drumming a counterpoint.

"'Wait for the wagon, wait for the wagon, wait for the wagon, and we'll all take a ride.'"

They sang the song through three more times before she saw the brighter light of the clearing at Wallin Landing ahead through the trees. Beside her, Drew sucked in a breath. His hair was damp against his forehead, turning the gold to brown. She didn't think it was just from the rain, for his face was darkening, as well.

"Holler," he said as if the song had taken the last of his strength.

"You-halloo!" John obliged. "Beth, bring Pa's rifle! Cougar!"

The horses must have sensed the cat's presence, because now Catherine could hear the frightened neighs coming from the field.

Beth met them at the edge of the wood, cloak wrapped about her, hood surrounding her worried face. "What's happened? Did it get Levi?"

James answered for Drew. "Alas, no. He fell out of a tree. The cougar is stalking us."

Simon turned, cocked the gun and swept the path. "We're ready. James, stay with me."

"Right." With a nod to Catherine, James dropped back.

John stepped closer to Drew. "Can I help?"

"Just…steer…me…to the porch," Drew said, panting. Catherine took one elbow and John the other, and together they managed to reach the broad boards with Beth hurrying along beside them. John helped Levi down, and he and Beth assisted the youth into the house. Drew bent a moment and gulped in air.

Catherine put a hand on his damp back. "Are you all right?"

He nodded, straightening. Catherine knew she should tend to Levi, but her concern at the moment was more for the man standing in front of her.

"That was heroic," she said. "You may well have saved your brother's life."

Instead of smiling at the praise, he shuddered, the muscles rippling under her hand. "That's one, at least. Do you need my help with him?"

Catherine lowered her hand. "Beth can help me. You should rest. You're in no condition to fight off a cougar."

He pushed away from the porch. "I'll be fine. Watch over Levi." He lifted the ax he'd left behind when they'd set out earlier and started after his brothers.

As the rain turned to mist, Drew followed James, John and Simon a little ways into the woods. His back ached and water ran down his face, but his breath grew stronger with every step. Once more thanksgiving raised his spirits and lifted his head.

Thank You, Lord.

"Any sign of it?" he asked when he caught up with his brothers.

Simon nodded into the bush. "It came close enough to get the scent of the stock, then headed off toward the lake."

"No doubt it was our singing," James said. "All we needed was Simon on his fiddle, and we could well have frightened it over the mountains to Walla Walla."

Simon shook his head.

"We're safe for the moment, at any rate," Drew said with a warning look to his irrepressible brother. "With any luck, it will find easier prey along the water and forget about us. But just in case, we'll leave someone at the Landing for a while to protect the stock."

"And our little Cat," James agreed as they turned for home. "She seems to attract any number of predators."

"That's enough," Drew said.

James danced out of reach as if he expected Drew to try to cuff him. "Are we a bit concerned for Miss Stanway? Methinks the gent is smitten."

What sane man wouldn't be? If it had been Beth out in the woods, Drew would likely have had to carry her back, too. Even his mother had been known to freeze at the sight of a bear or a cougar. But Catherine had been all business, focusing on how to bring Levi home. She'd sung that song as if she'd been standing in service on a Sunday, best bonnet on her head, prayer book in her hands. Some men might quibble about her unflappable nature, but Drew could only be thankful for it.

"Miss Stanway deserves our respect," he said as they neared the house. "I won't have her teased or bullied."

"Miss Stanway, eh?" James jumped up onto the porch ahead of Drew. "I was certain I heard you call her Catherine in the woods. No doubt it was the strain of the moment."

"No doubt," Drew returned, hearing his voice deepen.

John shook his head. "Now you went and made him mad, James."

"I'm not mad," Drew growled.

"Yes, you are," Simon corrected him. "I wasn't ten before I understood what that set face meant. The problem with having brothers is that we know you too well."

"The problem with having brothers," Drew countered, "is that you all talk too much."

John didn't follow him onto the porch. "I'll take first watch, Drew. Send someone out to tell me how Levi's doing." He loped toward the barn.

With a chuckle, James shouldered his way into the house.

Simon caught Drew's arm before he could follow. "A moment. You may not like talking, but I need an answer."

Drew nodded, pausing on the porch. Simon glanced in the door, then shut it carefully behind James. Drew felt his wet scalp tingle in foreboding. "What's wrong?"

"Nothing." Simon leaned his rifle against the wall

of the house. "I told you the other night that the best thing for this family would be for one of us to marry Miss Stanway. From what I can see, this episode only proves that."

Drew shook water off his face. "We had this conversation this morning. Why do you persist?"

"Because we need her!" Simon's eyes narrowed as his gaze bore down on Drew. "Why can't you see that?" Though they had disagreed on any number of topics over the years, he generally deferred to Drew in the end. Not this time, Drew thought.

He glanced in the window, watching as Catherine carefully unwrapped James's prized waistcoat from Levi's leg. "I can see it. But she isn't a heifer needed to build the stock or a new plow to open more acreage. She's a person, Simon. She has wishes and needs, too. She won't be content to stay out here."

"Maybe she just hasn't heard an offer she likes," Simon countered. "So I'll ask you straight out—are you going to court her?"

Something leaped inside him at the thought. He could imagine walks along the lake, sitting on the porch holding hands under the stars, her head on his shoulder by the fire at night as he listened to her tell him all that was in her heart. He could build her a dispensary where she could treat any who came to her for care. He could see himself at the head of the table, her at the foot, and ranged between children with her beautiful hair and stunning smile.

But those were crazy thoughts. If she stayed, there'd be more days like this, worse days, living in terror that something would yank her out of his arms, send her to the grave and leave him powerless, broken. That thought, more than any of the others, set his gut to churning. Catherine might praise his strength, and his brothers might rely on his arm to swing an ax, but when it came to losing someone he loved, he feared even his strength would fail.

"No, I won't court Miss Stanway," Drew said to his brother. "I have enough to do around here without looking out for a wife."

Simon was watching him as if doubting his word. "Then you won't mind if I give it a try."

His hands fisted, but he forced his fingers to relax. "You do what you must, Simon. You always have."

Simon shook his head. "You have an odd way of encouraging people, brother. But you're right. I tend to look at the practical side of things. There are too many opportunities for us to get hurt or sick out here, and it takes too long to bring people to town for tending. We need a doctor or nurse. I doubt we can hire one, so I plan on marrying one, whether you like it or not."

Chapter Fourteen

It was nearly dinner before Catherine had Levi settled. First she and the others had to dry themselves from the rain. Although she had toweled off her hair with a cloth Mrs. Wallin provided, the only way to dry her dress was to stand and turn in front of the hearth like a chicken on a spit, careful not to get too close lest a stray spark catch her skirts on fire.

She used the time to direct James how to shave kindling to her specifications for Levi's splint and to send Beth for the other supplies she'd need. Then she splinted the leg properly and added a stick at the end that could be twisted as needed to provide traction.

Levi generally cooperated with few protests, and Beth peppered her with questions. But by far the most helpful was Drew. Once she had Levi positioned on one of the benches near the table, he sat at his brother's head, hands braced on Levi's shoulders as both a warning not to move and a deterrent when the youth had second thoughts.

"You'd make a fine nurse," Catherine commented at one point when she'd finished setting the bone.

"I'll leave that to the professional," Drew answered, but his smile warmed her more than his words.

When she finished, Levi gave the splinted leg a wiggle, then yelped at the pain the movement must have caused. "How long do I have to wear this?"

"Weeks if you're careful," Catherine said, rising and shaking out her skirts. "Months if you're not. Despite what your brother said about hobbling, limping for the rest of your life is best avoided if possible."

The boy grumbled, but his pallor told Catherine that some part of him would heed her warning.

Mrs. Wallin had been sitting nearby. Now she shifted to be next to her youngest son. "You listen to Miss Stanway, Levi. And to your brothers, as well. What would you have done if they hadn't come back for you?"

"Died and rotted," James said cheerfully, and Beth smacked him on the shoulder with one hand.

Catherine drew back, watching as James and Beth teased Levi until the youth's cheeks bloomed red. John had returned to the house a while ago, with Simon out spelling him on watch. He, too, joined in the fun.

Catherine wished she could joke about it, but the entire time she'd been working on Levi, her family had kept intruding on her thoughts. What if someone had gone back for Nathan on the battlefield? Would he be alive today? Where were the men her father had tended when the medical tent had been shelled? Had none of them gone to see if he could be saved?

Levi's wounds weren't as serious, and for that she was thankful. But something about his injuries nagged at her, and she wasn't sure why.

Drew rose and came to where she stood by the stairs.

"I didn't want to ask you in front of Levi," he murmured, "but I need to know. How bad is it?"

"It was a simple fracture," Catherine assured him. "From the lack of swelling, I'd say nothing was damaged internally, and externally, as you saw, he's fine."

Drew nodded, but she wasn't sure he accepted her explanation.

"I know from experience as well as education," she told him. "I've seen someone fall out of a tree before."

His eyes widened.

"Oh, he wasn't up as high as Levi, I'm sure," she said with a smile. "But my brother, Nathan, climbed a sycamore in our yard once, going after a wayward kite. He managed to free the kite, but he lost his balance on the way down and tumbled out." She shook her head, remembering.

"Did he break anything?" Drew asked, watching her as if the story had given him hope.

"No, but you should have seen his face and hands. Scratches everywhere! One took stitching up. Oh!" She stared at Levi.

Drew had stiffened at her explanation. "Forgive me. I didn't mean to bring up bad memories."

"It's not that." Catherine shook her head to clear it as Levi ducked under James's hand to avoid his brother's teasing. "I've been trying to determine why your brother's injuries trouble me, and I think I know why." She turned to Drew. "There isn't a scratch on him."

Drew frowned, glancing between her and Levi. "He looks pretty beat up to me."

"He is, but that's my point. Falling through a tree, you don't generally think to protect your face, and if you did, the backs of your hands would bear the brunt of the damage. Levi's face and hands are clear."

"Perhaps he hit his chest instead. He coughed blood. Did he break a rib?"

Catherine shook her head. "He isn't any more sore there than anywhere else. And the blood in his mouth came from a split lip."

Drew cocked his head. "There's that bruise around his eye."

"Indeed," Catherine replied. She glanced at Drew. "Exactly as if someone had struck him."

Drew's shoulders tightened, raising him higher above her. "You think someone beat him? Broke his leg?"

She knew it sounded far-fetched. Why would anyone be so cruel? Besides, Levi had confessed to climbing the tree. Yet she also had had suspicions about Scout. Could the two have been fighting?

"I don't know," Catherine admitted. "But I'd talk to him about the matter if I were you."

He growled something under his breath about that being his life's work, and she thought it best not to ask him to repeat himself.

Beth hopped up just then and hurried toward the back room and the stove. A moment later, she was in the doorway, beckoning John to help. Simon came in the door and set down his rifle before wandering over to Catherine and Drew. She thought he might ask about his brother's situation, but instead he pulled a little leather-bound book from his coat pocket.

"My father was partial to poetry, Miss Stanway," he said, offering the book to her with a smile that didn't quite light his green eyes. "I wonder, would you be willing to join me in a reading for the family tonight?"

She glanced at the title, picked out in worn gold on the slim volume: *The Courtship of Miles Standish.* "My father was partial to Longfellow as well, Mr. Wallin. I'd be delighted to help."

"Please," he said, eyes lighting at last, "call me Simon. It's far too confusing to have all of us be Mr. Wallin."

Drew shifted beside her, calling her attention to the difference between him and his brother. Though Simon was a match for him in height, Drew's younger brother was more slender, a willow to Drew's cedar.

"Very well," Catherine said. "Is there a particular part you'd like us to read tonight?"

"Try page thirty-three," Simon said. With a nod to Drew, he strolled back to Levi's side.

"Poetry," Drew muttered under his breath, as if the very idea was ridiculous.

Catherine frowned at him. "Do you have something against lyrical language, Mr. Wallin?"

He shook himself. "Forgive me, Catherine. This argument is between Simon and me. We both have the same goal, to keep this family safe. We just disagree on how to go about it. If you'll excuse me, I need to go check that the barn is closed up properly."

Catherine nodded, and he strode out the door without another look to his brother. She couldn't help noticing, however, that Simon watched him go.

Curious, she opened the book's well-worn pages to the section Simon had indicated. The Pilgrim hero John Alden had just called upon the lovely Miss Priscilla Mullins on behalf of the colony leader, Miles Standish, and the young lady was protesting that if Mr. Standish was too busy to court her, he was likely too busy to be married to her. This was what Drew's brother wanted her to read?

"Excuse me, Miss Stanway." She looked up to find that John had finished helping Beth and stood beside Catherine. She snapped the book shut and met his gaze.

"Yes, Mr. Wallin? What did you need?"

"Perhaps you could call me John," he said with a soft smile. The closest in age to Levi, she could see that he resembled his mother the most, for his straight, thick, neatly cut hair was a reddish-gold, and his eyes were the greenest of all the brothers. "I merely wanted to thank you for your excellent work on Levi's leg. I've always been fascinated by the human body's ability to heal after great trauma. Is there some secret to how you treat a break like that?"

He looked so earnest, eyes intent on her face, wiry body poised forward, that Catherine found herself prosing on about fractures and sutures and dressings. He asked probing questions, offered suggestions from things he'd read and praised her knowledge so much that she was in an uncommonly good mood when Beth called them all to dinner.

John offered her his arm to escort her to the table. Simon pulled out the chair Drew normally sat in for her, and James presented her with a bouquet of wild flowers, which earned him a glare from Simon.

"There's no need to thank me," Catherine told them as Beth and Mrs. Wallin took their seats at the table. "I was only doing my duty in helping your brother."

"But with considerable style," James assured her as he sat. He elbowed Levi, who had been propped up next to him on the bench, leg straightened out before him. "Isn't that right, Levi?"

Not waiting for the blessing to be said, Levi spooned a mass of mashed potatoes onto his plate and shrugged. "I suppose."

James shook his head.

Catherine glanced to the window overlooking the yard. "Isn't your eldest brother going to eat?"

"Drew's busy with the stock," John said, seating himself on the bench nearest her and pushing Simon father down as he did so. "We can send something out to him when we're done."

"If there's anything left," James agreed, reaching for a biscuit.

"Boys," their mother chided. "Just because I'm not up to taking him a plate doesn't mean one of you can't do it."

Catherine found herself on her feet before she'd thought better of it. "I'll go."

Immediately Simon was on his feet, as well. "Allow me, Catherine."

James stood so quickly he set the bench to rocking, raising a protest from Levi. "I probably owe him the next shift. I'll go, as a favor to you, Cat."

They were all entirely too thankful for her intervention with Levi. "Catherine," she corrected him. "And truly, gentlemen, there is no need. You've worked hard most of the day. It will only take me a moment."

"I insist," Simon said, grabbing Drew's plate and throwing on a biscuit. "We can't impose on a guest."

"Quite right, Simon," James said, lowering himself back onto the bench. "I'll just stay here and keep Catherine company."

"Catherine isn't the only one at this table, you know,"

Beth put in. Her mother patted her hand as if to quiet her, a smile hovering about her mouth.

John nodded. "She's right. You both can go out and help Drew. I've already taken my shift, and I'm perfectly capable of keeping Catherine company."

What was wrong with them? Now all three were glaring at each other, while Beth shook her head and Mrs. Wallin's smile broadened. Levi kept shoveling food into his mouth as if he suspected someone would take his plate next.

"We'll all go," Simon announced, lobbing on a dollop of mashed potatoes and splashing it with gravy.

James rose once more. "Fine," he said, grabbing a cup.

"Fine," John agreed, snatching up a fork. They bumped each other's shoulders on the way out the door.

Mrs. Wallin laughed. "How nice to see my sons so helpful. Would you care to say the blessing, Levi? I believe you have the most to be thankful for."

Levi dropped his fork, face reddening, then bowed his head and clasped his hands.

Catherine bowed her head as well, listening to his simple prayer of thanks for the food and the family around them. She couldn't understand what maggot had infested the Wallin men's minds, but it almost seemed as if they were trying to court her despite her warning from this morning. Were all the men in Seattle mad? Was it something in the Puget Sound waves? In the air? She knew brides were at a premium, but this was ridiculous.

She was highly tempted to dose them all with Peruvian bark and send them to bed before they infected anyone else!

* * *

Drew was shutting the horses in for the night when three of his brothers entered the barn. They stalked up to him, each trying to walk faster than the others. Simon thrust out a plate. "Here. Catherine thought you might be hungry."

James held out a cup from which half the cider had sloshed, if the shine on the side was any indication. "She sent us with your food."

"Actually," John said, handing him a fork, "Simon and James made fools of themselves trying to be gentlemen, and we all decided it was wiser to retreat to the barn for a while rather than confess our shortcomings to Catherine."

Simon stared at him, then shook his head, chuckle tumbling out. "He's right. Peace, James." He offered his hand.

James shook it with a grin. "Peace. For the moment. It never lasts long in this family."

Drew balanced the cup on the edge of the plate and eyed his brothers. "Let me get this straight. All three of you made a fool of yourselves over Catherine? Are you all trying to court her?"

James shrugged as he released Simon's hand. "Can you think of a better way to keep her in the family?"

"I believe there's good historical evidence that women generally frown on being kept captive," John pointed out. "You have only to look to the Romans to see that."

They were mad, the lot of them. Drew motioned them over to the bench his father had built along the stalls and sat with the plate in his lap. "It isn't easy adding a wife, you know," he told them as he forked up some of the mashed potatoes, gravy dripping. "She's your partner in all things. Remember how Ma and Pa used to act?"

Simon nodded as he sat beside him. "Every decision, every action taken together."

James raised his brows as he leaned against the wall. "That's a tall order. Based on some of the married folks I've seen in town, not every marriage is such a joyful union."

"But it should be," John protested, glancing among them. "'Therefore shall a man leave his father and his mother and shall cleave unto his wife, and they shall be one flesh.' That's what the Good Book says."

"That may be what the Bible says," Simon answered, leaning back on the bench and crossing his arms over his chest, "but Adam only had to worry about Eve. We might as well face facts. There aren't many women like Ma."

"Isn't that why Asa Mercer brought all those ladies?" John asked, frowning.

Simon eyed him as if he suspected his brother had been reading too many books. "The women Mercer brought out seem more interested in town life than helping make a home in the wilderness."

"And you think Catherine is different?" Drew challenged.

Simon dropped his arms and straightened. "Yes, I do. I haven't seen a thing about our lives to quail her yet."

"Neither have I," James agreed. "And we've thrown our best at her—cougars, wild men, John's cooking."

John picked up Drew's biscuit and threw it at his brother. James caught it and popped it into his mouth with a grin.

Drew set aside the cold remains of his dinner, no longer hungry. "Then you do intend to court her."

Simon eyed James, and James eyed Simon, then both looked to John. As if in concert, all three nodded. Drew felt as if the food he had just eaten might come back up.

Simon turned to him. "No, we aren't going to court her. She clearly favors you."

Drew blinked, feeling as if he'd missed a moment of the conversation. "What?"

"You heard me," Simon said, eyes narrowing. "You're the one to court Catherine Stanway, and we're going to help you do it."

Chapter Fifteen

The things he did for his family. Drew led his brothers back across the clearing for the main house, the stock safely enclosed for the night. He didn't agree with his brothers' logic that everyone in the family would perish without someone like Catherine to help them. He'd done pretty well keeping them all safe until now. He didn't agree with their assessment that she favored him. At times, he wasn't sure she even liked him. He certainly didn't agree that he needed their help to court a woman. As Beth had pointed out, once he set his sights on something, he was as apt as their mother to achieve it.

But if anyone in the Wallin household was going to court Catherine Stanway, he knew he'd go mad if it wasn't him.

The ladies had cleaned up after dinner and returned Levi to a chair next to the fire. Catherine sat nearby as if to keep an eye on him. Her gaze brushed Drew's as he entered, her smile lifting briefly before she looked away. Was this odd feeling in his stomach what other people called butterflies? Maybe he should have eaten more dinner.

Ma was seated in her rocking chair, a basket of mending beside her, needle and thread in hand. Flitting from one brother to another, Beth seemed to be trying to avoid their mother's gaze lest she be put to work, too. His youngest brother brightened as Drew and the others let themselves in.

"There you are, Simon," he proclaimed. "Go get your fiddle, and let's have a song."

"Because you're in such good condition to dance," James teased, coming to tweak the stockinged toe peeking out from Levi's splint. Levi scowled at the reminder.

"I have something else planned for tonight," Simon said. "Catherine, are you ready for that reading?"

She rose and went to retrieve the book from the mantel, where she must have set it before dinner. "Perhaps, but I do have a question about the selection you chose, Mr. Wallin."

Drew couldn't help but chuckle. His brother may have asked her to use his given name, but either she chose not to or the gesture meant so little to her she'd forgotten his request. She came to their sides and held out the open book. "Are you certain you want to read this part?"

Simon took the book from her and gazed down at it. "Hmm, perhaps not. I'll find something better. Give me a moment." He turned away, flipping the pages.

As if they knew what to expect, the others settled themselves around the room, James and John on the floor near Levi's chair and Beth, likewise, curled up at Ma's feet.

Drew knew he needed to say something to Catherine, who stood waiting patiently beside him. Simon would have been polished, James playful and John profound.

For the life of him, he couldn't think of an appropriate comment. He could hardly compliment her gown; she'd been forced to wear the same one for the past three days, and the blue skirts were beginning to sag from their adventures. She must own a mirror, so it made no sense to tell her that her hair was as soft as moonlight. And he refused to talk about her lips being as red as the wild woodland strawberries, for when he looked at her now he wondered what it would like to taste them.

Oh, but he was in trouble.

Annoyed with himself, he went to stand by the stairs.

James glanced over his shoulder as Drew passed. "You know Pa built those very well, brother. You don't need to hold them up."

Some help he was.

Catherine followed him. "Everything all right in the clearing? Any sign of the cougar?"

At least that was a safe subject that didn't remind him of what his brothers expected. "Everything seems quiet. My biggest concern was Levi, and he's doing surprisingly well."

She laughed, and the sound bathed him in light. "It would take a great deal more than a broken leg to unsettle your brother." She cast him a glance from the corners of her eyes. "But I do wish you'd tell your other brothers to cease fawning over me."

He nearly choked. "Oh, I expect the fawning has stopped for now."

She frowned as if she wasn't sure what he meant, but Simon called her just then, and she excused herself to move to his brother's side by the fire.

Drew couldn't deny that they made a fine-looking couple, with Simon all angles and Catherine all soft curves. But he'd never noticed how tiny his brother's eyes looked when he squinted at the words on the page. Did Catherine notice? Did she mind? Did she think Drew's eyes were squinty?

Please help me master my thoughts, Lord!

"I found just the thing," Simon was saying to Catherine, head bent as if to be closer to her. "I'll read the man's part, you the lady's." His large hand cupped hers as they held the book open together. Drew could imagine holding her hand that way, cradled in his. She'd smile that brilliant smile of hers, and the day would brighten.

As if Simon was as affected by her touch, he cleared his throat. Then he released her and stepped away.

"On second thought, I'm not sure I'm the best one to do this justice," he said with a rueful shake of his head. "Drew, come read."

Everyone turned to him, looks ranging from surprised to amused. The hint of a smile played about his brother's lips. He wasn't sure what Simon was doing, but he decided to go along with it.

Though Catherine's brows were up, she did not protest as Drew went to take his brother's place at her side.

Drew offered her a smile, then slipped his hand under hers. Her fingers were warm and supple, strong, he thought, from her work as a nurse. Yet he could feel the slightest tremor in them. He ran one hand farther up her wrist to steady her and heard her suck in a breath.

Now his hands were trembling as well, and he had a sudden urge to run for the door. Best to plow ahead. Glancing down, he looked to see where Simon had directed them to read. And then he very much feared he'd have to kill his brother, if the reading didn't kill Drew first.

"Right there, Mr. Wallin," Catherine said, her other hand coming to point to the stanza as if he might have mistaken his way.

Drew's smile was tight. So was his throat. "'He was a man of honor, of noble and generous nature,'" he began reading.

Levi snickered and was hushed.

"'Though he was rough, he was kindly,'" Drew continued. "'She knew how during the winter he had attended the sick, with a hand as gentle as a woman's.'"

"That's our Drew," James called out, and this time both John and Levi laughed.

"Let him be," their mother scolded. "Go on, Andrew."

He would never make it through this. Drew cleared his throat. "'Somewhat hasty and hot, he could not deny it, and headstrong. Stern as a soldier might be, but hearty and placable always. Not to be laughed at and scorned, because he was little of stature.'" He glared at his brothers to keep them from commenting. "'For he was great of heart, magnanimous, courtly, courageous. Any woman in Plymouth, nay any woman in England, might be as happy and proud to be called the wife of—'"

"Drew Wallin!" Levi yelled.

"'Miles Standish,'" Drew thundered.

Catherine did not so much as wince at his raised voice. Her tone was firm and polished as she took up her part.

"'But as he warmed and glowed, in his simple and eloquent language, quite forgetful of self, and full of the praise of his rival, archly the maiden smiled, and, with eyes over-running with laughter, said, in a tremulous voice, "Why don't you speak for yourself, Drew?"'"

Drew blinked. His father and mother had read them this poem countless times. The name should have been John, and he'd expected his younger brother to make much of it. Had Catherine really just said Drew's name instead?

He glanced out to find that everyone in the family was staring at Catherine. So he hadn't mistaken her.

She must have realized her gaff, for she was turning crimson. Her mouth opened and closed, as if she was trying to continue reading, but no words came out.

James hopped to his feet. "Here, let me take the next stanza. I'd be delighted to read, at length. In falsetto."

Levi cringed.

"Have pity on us, Catherine," Ma said with an encouraging smile. "Your voice is so much better than James's."

James threw up his hands. "And you claim to be my mother!"

"Hush," Beth scolded. She had scooted forward on the rug. "I want to hear more."

But Drew didn't think Catherine could take any more. He could hear the breath hissing out of her as if she was having trouble controlling it.

"John," he said, taking the book from her and closing it. "You've always been good for a puzzle. Come up with one of your twenty-question posers."

John grinned. "Delighted!" He rubbed his hands together. "Now, let me see…"

Levi and Beth leaned closer as if determined to guess what was on his mind. Ma cast Drew a glance before doing likewise. Simon and James, however, were frowning at him.

Drew turned his back on them, blocking their view of Catherine.

"It's all right," he said. "It was only a poem."

She nodded, fast and hard. "Yes, a poem. Just a silly poem. Thank you for pointing that out. If you'll excuse me, I should retire. It's been a long day." She started around him, and Drew turned with her.

"I'll walk you to the cabin."

"No!" She must have realized how firmly she'd spoken, because her color faded as all gazes returned to her again. "That is, there's no need for you to leave your family on my account. I'm perfectly capable of walking across the clearing."

"You forget," Drew said, taking her elbow and finding it tense. "There's a cougar prowling about. Until we're sure it's left the area, no one goes anywhere without a gun or escort."

She pulled back and glanced around the room until her gaze hit Simon. "Mr. Wallin, would you accompany me? Surely we have imposed on your brother enough today."

What did she think was an imposition? Carrying Levi back from the tree? He'd recuperated from that in less than a half hour. Had the slip of her tongue truly so overset her? Where was her commendable composure?

Simon straightened away from the wall. "Of course." He nodded to James. "We should turn in, as well. Come along, James."

Simon picked up the rifle, James a lantern. Then he went to open the door for Catherine. She paused beside Beth and Levi.

"If you need me tonight, come find me," she told them.

"I will," Beth promised.

Without another look in Drew's direction, Catherine exited.

John left Beth and Levi arguing over the answer to his riddle and joined Drew by the fire. "That didn't go as well as it should have."

"No, it did not," their mother put in, setting aside her mending. "Andrew Wallin, if you intend to court that girl, you'll need to work harder than that."

John met his gaze, and Drew thought his own must be just as panicked. The last thing they needed was for their headstrong mother to throw herself into the fray.

"No one said I was courting, Ma," he started, but Beth clapped her hands, hopping to her feet.

"Oh, you decided to court her after all!" She seized Drew's hand. "I have so many ideas."

Perhaps a young lady's opinion would help. His sister was entirely devoted to that society magazine after all. "Oh?" Drew said. "Such as?"

Beth's eyes glowed. "You could take her for a picnic by the lake."

"There's a cougar running about," John reminded her.

"All right," Beth said, undeterred. "A picnic in the barn, then."

"The barn?" Levi rolled his eyes. "What girl wants to be sweet-talked in a barn?"

"There will be no sweet talk," Drew said with all the solemnity he could manage. "Anywhere."

Beth shook her head. "Oh, Drew, there has to be some. That's what courting is all about."

"I thought you never wanted to court," John challenged.

"I don't want to marry," Beth corrected him. "That doesn't meant I don't want to be courted. Every girl wants to be courted."

Drew frowned. "Why?"

She stared at him as if appalled he had to ask. "Because it's wonderful! That's what that entire poem is about—the beauty of courting. Pretty words and longing looks and sweet sighs. Walking hand in hand, holding the prayer book together in church, sharing secrets." She peered closer at her brother. "Haven't you ever wanted to do those things?"

"No," Drew said. The panic he'd felt when he'd considered his mother's interference was nothing to the fear that bubbled up at Beth's outlandish ideas. "I appreciate everyone's help, but I'm capable of courting a woman on my own."

"If that was your best effort," Beth said, wrinkling her nose, "I don't believe you."

"That's enough, Elizabeth Ann," Ma said, gathering up her sewing. "I think it's time we all went to bed. Tomorrow will be another day, another opportunity." She smiled at Drew. "And I know you will make her a marvelous husband."

Drew only wished he had his mother's confidence. For he feared with all the demands on his life, he'd make a terrible husband for any woman, especially one as sought after as Catherine.

Catherine hurried across the clearing for the cabin, mist wrapped about her like a damp towel. Simon paced her on one side, rifle in the crook of one arm; James walked on the other side, lantern held high to light their way. Though the glow pushed back the darkness, she felt as if her escorts were walls closing in on her.

Why? Simply because she'd all but asked Drew to propose to her.

Where was her mind? Why had she slipped and used his name? The word *John* had been clearly written on the page. Her brother, Nathan, had once read the poem aloud to her and her friends over tea. She knew her part.

Why did her heart persist in offering Drew's name instead? Had she no control where he was concerned?

"I hope we didn't offend you, Miss Stanway," James said, twisting his head as if to see more of her face. "I didn't mean any harm."

"No offense taken, Mr. Wallin," she said, detouring around a rocky patch. "It was simply time for me to retire."

From inside the barn came the neigh of a horse and the fluttering cackle of chickens.

Simon's hand shot out to stop her. "Something's wrong."

Catherine felt as if the lantern had dimmed. "What should we do?"

He glanced back at the house, and then, as if deeming it better to keep her near, he nodded to his brother. "Stay close to James and follow me."

Together they set out for the barn. James pulled open the big door with a rattle of metal, setting the chickens to clucking again. The lantern's glow only reached the first few feet of the space, making Catherine feel as if they had entered a cave. As they ventured down the main aisle, she could see that the horses were backed up in their stalls, shifting and bumping against the wood.

Their eyes showed white. Nearby, the oxen lowed a warning, and a pig let out a squeal. James hung the lantern on a hook and went to quiet the beasts as Simon moved through the building.

Doubting she could be of any use in this instance, Catherine sat on a bench near the lantern, rubbing one hand up her arm. It did nothing to stop the chill that was overtaking her.

"James," Simon called, and his brother hurried to his side, bringing the lantern with him.

Before the darkness could swallow her, Catherine rose as well and went to join them by the rear door. On the ground outside, something lay in a heap that glistened in the light.

"What is that?" Simon demanded.

James climbed out onto the ground and bent over the mass, then raised his head and stared at his brother. "It's meat. A haunch of venison, I think. I don't remember John or Drew hunting today."

"They didn't," Simon said, head turning as if he was looking for someone or something in the darkened forest. "And neither did I."

Now James was looking around as well, and Catherine peered deeper into the shadows, fearing that she might see those amber eyes looking back at her.

"It's not like a cougar to leave its kill uncovered," James said, voice thick in the mist.

"I don't think it was the cougar." Simon cocked his rifle. "Someone left that there on purpose. Trying to draw in the cat, I'm guessing."

James jerked upright, lantern flashing with the movement. "You think someone meant to bring the cougar into Wallin Landing?"

"The same someone who poisoned the spring," Catherine murmured. And perhaps had beaten Levi?

Simon glanced her way. "Very likely. Come get the spade, James, and bury that thing."

James complied, scrambling back into the barn and handing the lantern to Catherine before going to find the shovel.

"I'll cover you," Simon promised, watching him. Before his brother could leave the barn again, Simon turned to her, face grim. "I'm sorry, Catherine, but I think you'd better sleep in the house with Ma and Beth tonight."

She wanted to argue. Return to the house? Face Drew and answer the questions she'd seen in his eyes? Meeting the cougar or their unseen enemy in the dark almost sounded easier.

Almost.

"Very well, Mr. Wallin," she said. "Your plan is sensible. But I hope you intend to explain all this to your brother." That might keep Drew busy enough that he'd have time to forget her mistake.

And give her enough time to convince herself she wouldn't repeat it.

Chapter Sixteen

Inside the house, Drew made sure Levi and their mother were situated for the night.

"You don't have to hover over me like a mother hen," Ma said as he tucked her in the big bed she'd once shared with his father. "I'm much better!"

She was, and he was so thankful for that fact. *If nothing else comes from this association with Catherine, Lord, thank You for sending her to help Ma.*

"Perhaps I just like to make sure," Drew told her, bending to kiss her forehead. "Humor me."

"I suppose I should be patient," she said, snuggling under the covers. "But it's not a trait I ever possessed. I was very proud of you for being so patient with your brothers and sister growing up. Don't lose that ability now."

Drew straightened so fast he nearly banged his head on the ceiling. "If I've been impatient with you, ma'am, I apologize."

His mother shook her head, nightcap brushing the pillow. "Not with me. But you and your brothers seem to think all you need to do is show Catherine a little courtesy, and she'll swoon at your feet." She narrowed her eyes at Drew. "A wife worth the having is a wife worth the wooing."

So she was still plucking at that string. "I'm not going to follow after her like a moon-sick calf."

"And who asked you to act so foolishly?" she challenged, flattening her fingers on the quilt. "Your pa liked to say we fell in love at first sight, but the truth is that it took time and proximity for love to grow." She reached out and took Drew's hand in hers, her gaze touching his. "Show her the man you are. If she can't appreciate that, then she's not the woman for you."

Drew nodded and pulled away, but the sound of the door closing downstairs made him pause. Footsteps crossed for the stairs, and he turned to see Simon leading Catherine up. His brother's face was tight, but Catherine's pallor struck Drew in the chest.

He was moving to their sides before they had reached the top. "What's happened? Are you hurt?"

Simon held up one hand. "She's fine. I think it best she spend the night up here. We need to talk." He nodded to Catherine before starting back down, as if assuming Drew would follow him.

Drew couldn't seem to move. He had no idea what had happened, but those same feelings he'd been fighting since he'd first met her wrapped around him, demanding action. He wanted to hold her close and promise to protect her no matter what.

As if she knew it, she managed a smile. "Go with your brother, Drew. I'll be fine."

"She can share my bed," Ma called, patting the covers and smiling in welcome.

Drew had to touch Catherine. He ran his hand up her

arm, then rested his fingers a moment on her shoulder. "I'll be in with Levi later if you need me."

She ducked under his hand and went to join his mother.

Downstairs, Simon explained what they'd found. "James is keeping an eye on the barn. I'll take the next watch, and John can take the watch after that. You stay with Ma."

Normally Drew might have bristled at his brother's high-handed tone, but now he could only agree that the best place for him was in the house.

"There's something else you should know," he told Simon. "Catherine suspects Levi didn't fall out of that tree."

His brother frowned. "How else would he have earned those injuries?"

Drew felt himself tensing just thinking about the possibility. "Someone beat him.

Simon's head snapped up. "Why? And why wouldn't he name the bully? That makes no sense."

Drew couldn't argue with him. "James might say he's annoying enough to have earned it, but I share your doubts. Let him sleep for now. We can ask him when he's had a chance to heal."

"Oh, we will," Simon promised. He turned to head back outside.

But when Drew returned upstairs and bunked down near a snoring Levi, he couldn't seem to get to sleep. Instead of the troubles that plagued them, his mother's words occupied his mind. She seemed to think it was easy to win a woman's heart, that all he had to do was be himself. He hadn't thought he'd been anything else, and Catherine didn't seem enamored.

He listened, trying to isolate her breathing among the other soft noises coming from the opposite side of the hearth. He could imagine her lying next to Ma, face relaxed in sleep, lashes fanning her cheeks. She was beautiful, she was talented, she was clever. Any man would be proud to marry her.

So how did a man show a woman he was interested in matrimony? Catherine didn't seem impressed by James's wit, and she didn't bloom under effusive praise. Not being married to her, he had only so many opportunities when it was appropriate for him to hug her, and it wasn't proper to give her expensive gifts even if he could find them readily in Seattle.

He thought back to how his parents had behaved. Pa always seemed to sit or stand close to Ma when they were done with work for the day, hand on her shoulder or arm about her waist. He'd thank her for what she'd done, even if it was her usual chores of cooking, laying in stores for the winter, washing, sewing or mending. At times, they'd work shoulder to shoulder, clearing a field, building a fence, raising a barn, raising a family. And Pa had always chosen the dirtiest work, the hardest labor, if that meant sparing her from it.

He could do that. He already valued Catherine's skills as a nurse. He could make sure she knew that. And while she was at the Landing, he could share every burden, even if that added to his own.

Maybe actions really could speak louder than words.

He rose the next morning prepared to tell his brothers that he didn't require their help in courting Catherine. But, as usual, his family had other plans.

The first person he saw when he came downstairs was James. His brother wore a black frock coat over his reclaimed vest, and carved leather boots peeped out from under his wool trousers. He adjusted his stiff collar, then pointed a finger at Drew.

"You, sir, are shabbily dressed to appear before your Lord."

Drew glanced down at the shirt and trousers he'd slept in. "I didn't plan on meeting my maker today."

James clasped his hands together. "None of us ever does, brother. Can I get an amen?"

"Amen," John obliged, coming in from the back room. He, too, wore a coat and trousers, but he'd wrapped one of Ma's aprons about his waist, and the smell of frying ham told Drew he was making breakfast. "Did you forget, Drew?" he asked. "Today's Sunday."

In truth, he had forgotten with everything that had been happening. Both his father and his mother had insisted that Sunday was the Lord's day, a time for worship and rest. Basic chores like cooking and feeding the stock had to be done, of course, but there'd be no logging or other major tasks started.

"I'll be back for breakfast and service," he promised his brothers before heading to his own cabin to clean up and change clothes.

When he returned a short time later, wearing his one good suit of brown wool, all his brothers had gathered around the table. Beth was digging a hole in the braided rug as she paced from the table to the stairs. His sister wasn't old enough, Ma insisted, for a fancy dress just yet, but she'd tied a ribbon at the waist of her blue gingham gown, and curls swung from either side of her face.

Maybe Catherine really did know her way around a curling iron as Beth had hoped.

Still, her agitation concerned him. "Is Ma all right?"

he asked, catching Beth's eyes as she swung past the table.

Her nod was a jerk of her head that set her hard-won curls to bobbing. "Fine, fine. And I want you to know, Drew, that it was my idea, and Ma loved it."

He thought she must be talking about the curls, but before he could tell her they looked nice on her, she stopped to glance up the stairs. Following her gaze, he caught himself staring.

Catherine was descending, hands carefully holding up the skirts of the dress his mother had given her to wear. He'd seen it any number of times over the years, but always packed away in a trunk. The elegant scooped neck with its lace collar topped a bodice that drew down in a V at the narrow waist, the blue-and-green-striped cotton brushed to a shine that rivaled the gleam of Catherine's hair.

It was the dress, his mother had told them, she'd worn to her wedding, and she'd never found a good enough reason to use it again, until now.

Drew felt his chest rising with the emotions inside him. Simon stood up from the table as if to escort Catherine, but Drew beat him to the foot of the stairs.

"Catherine," he said, offering her his arm.

"Andrew," she replied with a smile as she accepted. "Your mother said you all dressed in your Sunday best, but I hardly expected all this."

He heard the benches scrape the floor as the rest of his brothers climbed to their feet. Even Levi wavered on his splint.

"I am blessed with the company of a fine set of gentlemen," Ma said, following Catherine down the stairs in her favorite green wool gown. "And now two lovely ladies, as well."

Beth wasn't the only one to blush at her praise.

John's breakfast of ham, eggs and corn bread with honey was quickly consumed, and the dishes were put in the washtub to soak. Simon had already brought over his fiddle, John the family Bible. They all gathered in the front room for Sunday service. Drew made sure to position chairs near the hearth for Catherine and his mother, then took a spot not too far away.

"We've rarely had a minister come out this far," Ma was explaining to Catherine as they sat. "So we've had to improvise when it comes to worship."

"Today we're reading in Matthew, I believe," John said, moving another of the chairs closer and jerking his head to Drew as if he wanted his brother to take a seat.

Drew stayed where he was.

"Or should that be Levi?" Catherine asked with a smile to Drew before looking at her patient, who was sitting on a bench with his leg propped up again.

Levi stared at Drew. "You told her?"

James settled next to his youngest brother. "What can we say? You are an endless source of amusement."

"You're not," Levi retorted.

James pressed his hand to his heart as if gravely wounded.

Normally, Drew took the first reading, but he found himself strangely tongue-tied with Catherine watching him. Simon seemed to take pity on him, for he, too, directed Drew to the seat next to Catherine and read the passage himself. Still, Drew couldn't seem to focus, even when John followed with one of their father's favorite psalms.

"'My flesh and my heart faileth, but God is the strength of my heart, and my portion forever.'"

He ought to rest on the second part of that promise, but too many times he felt the first part. This family had a way of tugging at his heart, challenging his strength. Today, however, he had another concern about praying.

And how did a man pray for the strength to go courting?

Catherine felt as if the room warmed with each reading. God had been the strength of her heart. He'd seen her safely around the country, through months at sea, and now was helping her prosper in this new land. She was so full of thanks that when Drew's hand reached for hers, she did not pull away. The touch felt right, pure.

Hand in hand, they listened as Simon played a series of hymns, the last of which had the whole family singing. Something seemed to be rising in her heart like bread dough in the morning, and it took her a moment to realize it was joy.

Dangerous, a voice whispered inside her. Where one strong emotion bloomed, others would follow. But surely there was no harm in praise. It had been an eventful few days, and she was grateful God had brought them all through it safely.

But apparently others needed help as well, for Drew and his family had barely said "Amen" when there was a knock on the door, fast and furious. James, closest to the panel, jumped up to answer it as the other brothers rose to their feet, Drew once more putting himself between her and possible danger. But then, what else would she expect from a knight, even one in a brown wool suit that stretched across his shoulders?

James threw open the door, and to Catherine's surprise, Old Joe hobbled into the room with a nod to Drew and his brothers.

"Gents," he greeted. "Ladies. I'm right sorry to interrupt, but I got an itch I can't stop scratching."

Drew's voice was a warning rumble. "I'll not have Miss Stanway bothered. She's already refused your suit."

Beth wrinkled her nose. "*He* was one of those suitors?"

Around Drew, Catherine could see the prospector grimace. "Didn't come courting this time. Came for some doctoring." He yanked up on the sleeve of his shirt. "See?"

Beth and her mother recoiled from the puffy red flesh. Catherine rose and pointed to the door. "Outside, sir. I'll do all I can to help."

"Much obliged, ma'am." He hurried back to the door, fingers pressed against the rash. "It drives me so crazy at night I can't hardly sleep."

"Excuse me," Catherine said to the room at large. "I'll be back shortly."

Only Drew followed her out. She thought perhaps he still didn't trust Old Joe, but instead he looked to her as they paused on the porch. "How can I help?"

Catherine smiled in thanks. "Let me examine the fellow and then I can tell you what we'll need to ease his discomfort."

It took her a few questions to confirm what she'd suspected on first sight.

"Is poison ivy or oak prevalent in the area?" she asked Drew, who had remained at her side as Old Joe sat on the porch and Catherine stood over him.

"Not that I've noticed," Drew replied, rubbing his chin with one hand. "But there's a good-size patch of stinging nettles between here and the Rankin claim. Beth picks them sometimes and boils them for greens."

"You must have brushed against them without realizing it," Catherine told their visitor. "If you can get into Seattle, ask Doctor Maynard for some calamine lotion. If not, I've heard him say that the backs of bracken ferns can be rubbed against the rash for some relief. You might try that."

"You bet," Joe declared, slapping his hands on his dusty trousers. He rose and eyed Catherine. "Sure you won't reconsider, miss? You'd come in right handy during an influenza outbreak."

"She comes in handy all the time," Drew corrected him.

Though she had never trusted such praise, his sounded so heartfelt she blushed. "Good luck to you, Mr.… What is your last name?"

"Holzbrinkdannagermengin," he supplied with a grin. "And now you know why they'd rather call me Old Joe."

He started away from the porch, then glanced back at Catherine. "Might be a few other gents in need of doctoring in these parts. Mind if I send them your way?"

"Not at all," Catherine replied with a smile. "But warn them I only plan to stay another few days at most. After that, they'll have to come into town to help."

Old Joe shook his grizzled head. "Shame, that. Body could die between here and town. God bless you, miss."

Catherine waved as he walked toward the woods.

"He's right, you know," Drew said quietly beside

her. "A man could die trying to reach town for medical help."

Darkness seemed to be creeping up on her, as surely as the clouds building over their heads. "A man can die trying to do his duty, as well. That's what happened to my father and brother."

He touched her chin, drawing her gaze to his. "You would have saved them if you could have. I know it."

Tears burned her eyes. "I would have. Oh! I would, Drew. But I never had the chance."

"So now you help others. I will always be grateful for what you've done for my family."

His head dipped lower, and she thought he meant to kiss her cheek. Instead, his lips brushed hers, tender, sweet. Her eyes drifted shut, and for a moment, all she did was feel.

He raised his head and lowered his hand. "Will you walk with me?"

At the moment, she would have gone to the ends of the Earth had he asked. "Of course."

She wasn't sure where he meant to go with a cougar possibly nearby, but he returned to the house long enough to retrieve the rifle. Beth's face appeared at the window, grinning, before she ducked back.

Drew shook his head. "This way," he said, stepping down from the porch.

He led her on a wide track that descended past the house to the lakeshore. Today the waters were as gray as the clouds, but she spotted blue sky in the distance and something else.

"What is that?" she cried.

Drew grinned. "The mountain's out. That's Rainier."

Where she lived in Seattle she'd never gotten a good

look at the mountain, obscured as it often was by clouds or hidden behind tall trees. Now it rose in snow-capped majesty, as if it sat at the end of the lake itself. Gulls wheeled past with shrill cries like courtiers begging a boon.

"Pa loved this place," Drew said, gaze traveling across the water as if he could see his father even now. "He had big dreams—first a homestead, then a town site."

Catherine glanced around, then pointed to the upper curve of the lake, where a knoll thrust out into the water. "Along there, I imagine, with fine houses."

"And wide streets," Drew agreed. "Fit for riding or promenading." He chuckled. "Funny. Pa never struck me as the promenading sort. He was always busy working."

"Like you," Catherine said, watching him. "I get the feeling your mother's illness is the only thing that slowed you down, and then not by much."

"By too much," he said. "Fields need seeding, and we should bring in another load of timber for the mill to pay for a plow."

"You'll have time soon," Catherine promised him. "You can see how she's improving. And Levi should mend quickly. Things will return to normal."

"Normal." He snorted. "There is no normal out here. Every day can be a challenge."

Catherine smiled. "My friend Allegra calls it an adventure."

He turned his gaze on her, the blue-green as alive as the forest around them. "Do you like adventure?"

Once, no. She had been rather pleased with her life in

Sudbury. But then the war had come, and her father and Nathan had gone. And she'd sailed around a continent.

And into Drew's arms.

"My work is adventure enough, Mr. Wallin," she said. "Perhaps we should go back. I'd like to check on your brother."

He nodded and turned from the lake, but not before she saw his face sag. He'd wanted another answer.

So had she. She just wasn't sure she was ready to give it.

Chapter Seventeen

He had made progress. Drew told himself to be satisfied with that. But the feel of Catherine's lips against his had opened a window, flooding him with light. He didn't want to return to the dark.

They spent the rest of the day in family pursuits, playing chess, looking through Beth's sketches of gowns she wished to sew one day, making plans for the week to come. He knew Simon wanted to quiz Levi further on his injuries, but their younger brother looked so sore and worn out Drew advised Simon to wait another day. He couldn't see how digging for information now would help any of them.

And he didn't want to do anything that would spoil the day. His brothers, Ma and Beth were all teasing each other and laughing, with Catherine joining in as if she'd always been part of the family. Was he wrong to hope she might soon be?

Beth and Ma must have been enjoying her company as much as he was, for they begged her to sleep with them again that night. She cast Drew a smile as she retired upstairs.

"I hear the church bells ringing," James predicted, lacing his fingers behind his head and leaning back in his chair.

Drew only wished he heard them, too.

But tomorrow was another day, as his mother often said. So long as Catherine remained at the Landing, he stood a chance.

"That tree has to come down today," Simon said the next morning over a breakfast of dried venison, leftover biscuits and honey as the brothers minus Levi gathered at the table before dawn. "Captain Collings isn't going to wait much longer."

"Agreed," Drew said. "Can the three of you handle it?" He was having a hard enough time following the conversation. He'd made the mistake of peering into the ladies' half of the loft this morning, candle brightening the space. Catherine had been curled up on one side, hair loose about her face. The vision was going to make work challenging today.

"We need you," John answered him, joining them at the table, tin cup of coffee in one hand. "It will take two on the saw and another two with the oxen."

He knew his brothers depended on his skill with an ax and saw to bring down the big trees. But with a cougar around, he could hardly leave Catherine alone with Beth, his ailing mother and an injured Levi.

"It will have to wait, then," he said. "Someone who knows how to handle the rifle has to stay here."

James and John exchanged glances.

"That's easily settled," Simon said, licking honey off his fingers. "Teach Catherine to shoot."

"No," Drew said. He realized he'd just crumbled his

biscuit to powder, and dusted off his hands. "Out of the question."

"Why?" John asked with a frown. "She already understands the rudiments. She proved that when she fired to call us back."

"And being a good shot will only make her more attractive to her future husband if you fail to come up to scratch," James reasoned, popping the last biscuit in his mouth and talking around it. "She can bag the game, dress it and cook it. I'd marry a woman like that."

"That's the most ridiculous thing I've heard in a long time," Drew started, but Simon shoved to his feet and reached for the dirty dishes.

"It's settled, then. After Drew teaches Catherine to shoot, he can meet us at the tree." He glanced over his shoulder as he headed for the sideboard. "Unless you'd rather I spend the next hour or so with my arms around her, helping her hold the gun."

John's brows shot up as if he'd never considered teaching from that angle, but James grinned as if he approved of the technique.

Drew pushed back the chair. "I'll do it. But you'd better watch yourselves, because when Catherine learns to shoot, I wouldn't want to guess how she'll use that gun."

Catherine had spent the night next to Mrs. Wallin, sharing the big bed in the ladies' half of the upper floor. She could hear Levi's snoring and the snort as he stopped when Drew must have nudged him. After spending such a lovely day together, having Drew just on the other side of the hearth made it difficult to sleep. She kept remembering the faraway look on his face as he'd talked about the town his father had hoped to build. She'd been captivated by the image.

More, though, she was captivated by the man. Those large hands could swing an ax and bring down a massive tree, yet his touch to her chin had been soft, tender. He might argue with his brothers, but she could see the love between them. They all relied on him.

But she couldn't allow herself to rely on him. She didn't want to listen for his voice in the morning, the sound of his boots on the stairs. She didn't want to inhale the scent of him, feel the strength of his arms. She didn't want to look into his smile and feel herself trembling.

And she certainly couldn't spend time with this family without missing her own. When Levi grinned, she saw Nathan. When James teased, she heard her brother's voice. Even Mrs. Wallin's gentle correction reminded her of the way her father had taught his children.

She'd already had one family pulled away from her. She couldn't bear to lose another. And the thought of losing someone as close as a husband made her want to jump into the lake and swim for the far shore.

The sooner she left Wallin Landing, the better.

She woke to Mrs. Wallin's yawn. Sunlight brightened the room. Beth was humming to herself as she laid a cream-colored cotton gown dotted with blue forget-me-nots on the bed. Catherine thought it must be for her mother, but Mrs. Wallin nodded toward the dress and smiled at Catherine.

"That's for you," she said, green eyes crinkling in pleasure. "I thought you might like something else to wear today."

First the beautiful gown yesterday, and now this.

She felt a little guilty how happy the dresses made her. When she'd agreed to join the Mercer expedition, she'd known she would have to leave most of her clothing behind. Her single trunk and bandbox had carried only five gowns, one of which was a blue silk evening dress; several white aprons for her role as nurse; a warm wool cloak; a paisley shawl; and a supply of undergarments. But when Levi had abducted her five days ago, even those precious few belongings had remained behind in Seattle, and she'd been wearing her blue dress until yesterday.

Five days? Was that all it had been? She felt as if she'd known the Wallins her entire life.

"It's beautiful," she told Mrs. Wallin and Beth, holding up the simple dress against her frame. The bodice was gathered at the collar and waist, the lower part of the skirt cut on the bias to give it more flounce. The cotton was worn but clean, the blue flowers sprinkled over the cream material bright and cheerful. She'd have to belt the skirt with her apron to compensate for Mrs. Wallin's greater height, but otherwise it would fit. And she wouldn't need nearly as many petticoats to fill the narrower skirts. She felt positively buoyant as she came down the stairs.

Drew was waiting for her, leaning against the wall at the base of the stairs. His damp hair was combed in place around his heart-shaped face; his smile broadened when it met hers. The admiration in his eyes made her cheeks warm.

"Good morning, Catherine," he said, pushing off the wall. "I trust you slept well."

Manners. Being polite. Those things she could manage this morning. "Quite well, thank you. I looked in on Levi, but he was sleeping so soundly I didn't have the heart to wake him."

"Let him sleep," Drew advised. "He can take the day off. Tomorrow, I'll think of things he can do while sitting to keep himself busy. Simon and the others ate up the biscuits, but I can fry some eggs if you're hungry."

Him serving her? That she could not handle. "I'll just make some tea. I'm sure you have work to do."

He nodded, but he accompanied her as she headed for the stove. "When you've finished, I'll teach you to shoot."

Catherine stopped on the rug. "Shoot? I heal people, Drew. I don't maim them."

"No one says you ever have to aim at a person," he promised, pausing beside her. "But my brothers and I have to work today. Ma and Levi aren't as mobile as I'd like, and we need someone besides Beth who can handle a rifle in case the cougar returns."

She could hardly argue with that. Every time she thought about the woods she remembered that powerful body slinking through the shadows, eyes watching her hungrily.

"Very well," she said.

After a quick cup of tea, she and Drew ventured out into the clearing. The day was gray and overcast; she expected they'd see rain shortly. The mist rising from the lake drifted through the trees, leaving the clearing hushed and pebbling her skin with dew.

"The oxen are out at the tree we're cutting," he explained to Catherine, stopping not far from the spring. "The horses and goats are out to pasture. I moved the chickens to a pen by Simon's cabin, so it won't hurt anything if you aim at the barn." He nodded to where someone, probably him, had sketched a circle on the gray wood. "To start, we'll see if you can put a bullet inside that ring."

That shouldn't be so hard. Catherine took the gun from him and held it out as she'd seen Simon do. She remembered firing the other day, but the morning had been such a blur that she wasn't sure she could repeat her performance now. The wood of the stock felt worn under her hand, the barrel cool and slick. But the weight was no different than holding the porcelain-coated cast-iron tray of instruments while her father operated.

Of course, that porcelain pan hadn't propelled deadly bits of metal.

Drew pointed to the gun. "Pa brought this with him when he came West. There aren't too many like it. See the circular chamber? The gun will fire six times before you have to reload."

He sounded proud of the fact, so it must be a good thing. "How handy," Catherine said.

"It can mean the difference between life and death if you're shooting at something as big as a cougar or bear."

Something she hoped never to have to do. She thought he'd explain further, but he positioned himself behind her.

"Keep the barrel up," he murmured, putting one hand on her elbow. "Look down it to where you want the shot to go. See that little knot near the end? That's the sight."

Catherine squinted down the barrel, spotting the bump at the end. She pointed it at the circle. "Very well."

"Now," he continued, other arm coming around her as his breath caressed her ear, "put your finger on the trigger." He hooked her finger over the curved metal. "Hold your breath, and pull."

Hold her breath? She couldn't even find it! With his arms around her, she was held in his embrace. She could feel him behind her, the length of his body, the breadth of his chest, the strength of his arms.

"Catherine?" he murmured. "Is something wrong?"

Yes, but she refused to admit it. She swallowed and pulled.

The gun barked, bouncing upward and pushing her back against Drew. His arms tightened to steady her. But she wasn't steady. Her heart was hammering in her ears.

"Close," he said as the smoke cleared.

Blinking, she saw that a small nick had appeared on the edge of the circle.

"Now you know the gun pulls to the right," he said. "How would you compensate?"

How could he be so calm? Was she the only one affected by their proximity? She took a deep breath and raised the rifle again. "I imagine I aim farther left."

"Exactly." Was his breath hitching, as well? She didn't dare look at him. Once more, his arms came around her and positioned the gun. She pulled the trigger and felt her body press into his. Closing her eyes, she breathed in the scent of him.

"Better," he said.

Opening her eyes, she saw a hole closer to the center of the circle. Grinning, she glanced back at him. Sweat stood out on his brow as if he'd run a race, and his eyes were wilder than Puget Sound waves in a storm. They stood there, no more than a foot apart. She couldn't move. She wasn't sure he was even breathing.

Beth came out on the porch and started flapping out

her dust rag. "I saw you from the window. I'm so glad you're learning to shoot. How's she doing, Drew?"

He stepped away from Catherine, and the air felt cold, her limbs too heavy to possibly lift the gun. "Just fine. Try it alone this time, Catherine."

She knew women who would have pretended to misfire, just for the chance to be back in his arms. She wasn't that kind of woman. She lifted the rifle, sighted down its length, accounted for the pull and fired, rocking back with the recoil. Raising her head, she nodded in satisfaction at the hole in the center of the circle.

Beth applauded before darting back inside the house.

"Well done," Drew said, making no move to close the distance between them. "Beth can show you how to load it. You remember the way we call?"

"Once for danger, and twice for dinner," Catherine said.

That earned a smile from him. "Couldn't have put it better myself." He finally took a step closer, smile fading. "If you need anything, call. I'll come."

She nodded. She didn't dare do more than that. For if she opened her mouth she might just tell him how much she was beginning to need him.

And then he might never let her go.

Chapter Eighteen

The rest of the day, Drew waited for the sound of a shot that would send him careening through the forest to rescue Catherine. He imagined men circling the house, demanding her hand in marriage. He envisioned the cougar prowling up to the back door and scratching its way inside. He thought about whoever had poisoned the spring and left the haunch of venison returning to set fire to the house with her inside.

He was, in short, a mess.

"What are you planning to do, brother?" James teased him at one point after they'd felled the tree and set about removing the limbs. Drew had sat on a log to sharpen his ax and discovered the sun was suddenly much farther along its track.

"Any sharper," James warned when Drew looked up, "and you can give Simon a nice close shave."

Simon arched a brow and continued chopping at the branches.

He at least could focus. But how could Drew put himself into his work when all he could think about was Catherine? The brush of her hair against his chin when she was in his arms, the warmth of her body when the recoil had pushed her back against him, the deepening blue of her eyes as they'd stood gaze to gaze, the touch of her lips yesterday—how could any man forget?

Lord, You made us male and female, but did You have to make the female so deadly?

John slung a leg over the log and perched beside Drew. "Courting, as I understand it, is supposed to make a man giddy, not grumpy. But then again, we are talking about you."

Drew shook his head, lowering the ax. "I'm not grumpy, John, or if I am, it's no more so than usual. I know what you all want me to do, but I'm still not convinced I can do it."

John cocked his head, reddish hair falling against one cheek. "So you don't actually care for Catherine."

Drew's hand tightened on the handle. "I never said that."

"Ah, then you don't think she cares about you."

In truth, he'd doubted, but the way she'd reacted to being close to him said she wasn't entirely adverse to his company. "I'm not certain."

John cuffed him on the shoulder. "And that's why you court! It's an adventure. Enjoy it."

Catherine hadn't been keen on adventure yesterday. He couldn't blame her.

"Cougars, poisoned springs and abductions, and you think I need more adventure in my life?" Drew challenged, though he felt himself smiling.

John stood. "Every man needs the right sort of adventure, Drew. You're the one who has to decide whether that's Catherine. You know what Pa used to say."

"Pray about it before you talk about it," Drew replied. "Maybe I should."

"No maybes about it." John bent and picked up Drew's ax. "Why don't I help Simon, and you sit and think? You aren't much good to us right now anyway." With a good-natured smile, he strolled off, ax slung over one shoulder.

Drew leaned back on the log. Thinking, he had a feeling, was only going to get him into more trouble. But he'd never been the sort to hear the Lord's voice in answer to prayer. Then again, he'd never been one to pray overly much.

He had the notion he was supposed to close his eyes, but doing so in the middle of a busy logging group seemed foolhardy in the extreme. Instead, he raised his gaze heavenward, through the canopy of the forest, through the misty air.

Lord, I seem to remember a verse in the Bible about it being good if a man chose to stay unmarried. You know the work I have set before me. Won't a wife just get in the way of that?

"Hey!" Simon shouted. "James! Fetch me that saw."

Drew dropped his gaze to watch his younger brother trot across the cleared space with the tool Simon needed. They were a team.

A husband and wife could be a team.

It was an odd thought, yet he felt the truth of it. Certainly his mother and father were proof of the fact, and he'd seen how some of the wives in town were assets to their husbands.

But Catherine, Lord? She's not a hardy woman like Ma. She was born and raised in the city. She's used to finer things. She has a calling. Could she be happy clear out here?

That question didn't get answered until the evening. He and his brothers had finished the day's work without the sound of a single shot. They had been picking up their tools when the rifle called. Drew tensed, but the second shot was almost immediate.

"Dinner is served," James quipped, and they all headed back to the house.

Everything seemed to have gone well. Ma was helping Beth with dinner. Catherine had Levi's leg propped up on pillows on the near bench of the table and was sitting beside him. Ma must have given her some of the scrap clothing, because she was cutting it into lengths and Levi was rolling them up.

"Bandages," he said when Drew wandered closer. "She seems to think I might need them."

Catherine smiled. "It never hurts to be prepared, Levi."

"Except if you're digging your own grave," James said on his way to the door with the bucket for more water. "Someone might think you're ready to go and happily oblige."

That reminded Drew of a conversation he needed to have with Levi. He slung a leg over the bench and focused his gaze on his youngest brother.

"Do you expect to need more bandages any time soon, Levi?" he asked. "Are you planning to fall out of another tree?"

His brother busied himself winding up the strip of cloth. "No, siree. I've learned my lesson. I'll be more careful in the future."

"That's the thing," Drew said, leaning closer. "You've

always been good up in the trees. It's not like you to fall."

Catherine was watching him, lips compressed as if determined to let Drew lead the conversation. Levi shrugged and kept winding.

"You did fall, didn't you, Levi?" Drew pressed.

The bandage shook in his brother's grip. "Of course I fell. You don't think I'd break my own leg to get out of work, do you?"

"The thought had crossed my mind," James said, stopping beside them, water from the now-full bucket sloshing on the floor. "Either that, or you finally annoyed your friends sufficiently."

Catherine met Drew's gaze, but Levi shoved the bandage at her. "I have no friends."

"What about Scout?" Beth asked, bringing a pile of plates to the table. "You're always running off somewhere with him."

"He was the one who pointed us to where you fell," Drew told him.

Levi shifted on the bench as if he wanted to run off right then, but Drew knew his injury kept him from escaping their questions. "Scout Rankin is no friend of mine. He talks about being independent, being his own man, but he's the first one to do whatever that pa of his wants, even if it's..."

He swallowed and reached for the material Catherine still held in her hands. "Here, Miss Stanway. Let me tear that."

"Even if he what, Levi?" she asked, holding on to the old shirt.

"Doesn't matter," Levi said, head once more down. "I'm getting tired. Are we eating soon?"

Drew would have liked to question him further, but Ma and Beth put dinner on the table then. It wasn't until after the dishes had been cleared away and washed that Drew had a moment to talk, and then it was with Catherine.

Simon, James and John had headed to Simon's cabin to finish some chores there. Levi and Beth were playing the chess game their father had carved. Levi had never enjoyed the pastime, so Drew guessed he was trying to fend off more questions. Ma sat in her chair, the family Bible open in her lap. Catherine knelt next to Drew and started to add a log to the fire.

"Let me do that," Drew said, taking the rough wood from her hands.

He'd meant to do her a service, but she immediately bristled. "I'm perfectly capable of adding fuel to the fire, sir. I can even walk and talk at the same time. Some women are that talented."

Drew grimaced. He dropped the wood into the fire, and flames shot up the chimney. "I didn't mean any disrespect, Catherine. It was only a courtesy."

She sighed. "Is it a courtesy to do something someone could do for themselves?"

"Certainly." He sat on the floor beside her and crossed his arms over his knees. "Why do men open doors for women, help them up into wagons? It's a sign of respect."

"A sign of respect or a sign of dependence?"

Drew frowned. "Respect. Who'd want a dependent woman?"

She cocked her head, eying him. "You are a singular gentleman, Drew Wallin. Do you know that?"

He must have sat too close to the fire, for his cheeks

were getting hot. He shifted away. "I take it everything went well today."

"No sign of the cougar, no noise from the barn and Levi is healing nicely," she reported. "What did you think of his excuses before dinner?"

Drew glanced to where Beth was gloating as she took Levi's queen. "They sounded like just that—excuses. It seems he and Scout Rankin had a falling-out."

Catherine frowned. "To the point of a broken leg? Young Mr. Rankin hardly seems strong enough."

Drew shook his head. "It was probably an accident. Either way, Scout has to know I won't tolerate bullying."

"So does Levi," she said. "Perhaps he prefers to fight his own battles."

There was that. He'd be the last to stop his brother from taking responsibility for his actions. "I'll keep an eye on him."

She settled on the floor, skirts spread around her. "That shouldn't be hard for the next few days. Can you fell that tree without him?"

He wasn't about to admit his own lack of effort had kept them from finishing the job today. "We're nearly there. We should have it to the ship tomorrow."

"And when it's down? What next?"

He hadn't thought beyond the tree. "There will be more trees needed, for houses in Seattle, for businesses in San Francisco. There are always trees."

"Until there aren't," she countered. "One day you'll have this entire area cleared. What then, sir?"

He smiled. "Then we build Wallin Town, where men can turn timber into something more than log houses—ships and furniture and works of art."

She returned his smile. "And I'm sure you'll include

a fine hospital, with a staff willing to help women and children. It is a sad fact that some doctors neglect their needs or fail to take them seriously."

"Of course. And schools and churches and a civic hall for music and theatricals."

She tapped her chin with one finger. "And a library for John."

He chuckled. "For John and the rest of the community. Free for all."

"A noble calling, Mr. Wallin," she proclaimed. "I could see Wallin Town even eclipsing Seattle one day as the finest city in the Territory. You'll have your work cut out for you, but my father always said it was wise to plan for the future."

Perhaps that was his problem. He was so used to thinking about the present, counting heads, counting limbs, making sure everyone was fed and clothed and educated. His father's dream had been a distant thing, urging him on.

Perhaps it was time he started planning his own future, with Catherine.

Catherine was thinking about the future as she came down the stairs the next morning. To her, it seemed clear that her work at Wallin Landing was ending. Mrs. Wallin was up doing chores, cooking and cleaning for her family, and though she still tired easily, the danger was obviously past. Levi, as Catherine had told Drew, would heal quickly. A day or two more to make sure there were no complications, and then she could return to Seattle.

What she didn't expect was for Seattle to come to her.

Mrs. Wallin and Beth were tending the garden behind the house, Levi propped up on the porch with the rifle to keep watch. Catherine had insisted on helping them, bending and tugging out the vine-like weeds that seemed to flourish along with the carrots and peas. The day was still overcast, the sky a leaden gray above them. Birds called from the wood and swooped low over the lake.

"I've been meaning to ask you, Catherine," Beth said as she trained her peas up the lattice of sticks John had made for her. "Do the ladies really wear those big metal cages under their skirts like they show in *Godey's*?"

"Silliest things I ever saw," Mrs. Wallin said, pausing to adjust her sunbonnet. She'd given Beth and Catherine ones to wear as well, and Catherine was thankful for the long material at the back and sides that protected her neck from the little bugs she could see swarming down by the lake.

"I like them!" Beth protested, straightening. "I imagine they make you feel ever so graceful."

"They do indeed," Catherine replied, yanking out a weed from the rich, dark soil. "And they allow you to have the fullest skirts without the need for layers and layers of petticoats."

Beth nodded as if vindicated.

"Of course, they make it frightfully difficult to go through doorways," Catherine continued. "And sometimes, if you aren't very careful, they flip up and show your underthings to the world."

Beth look positively horrified. Mrs. Wallin laughed.

Levi climbed unsteadily to his feet. "Someone's coming." He aimed the rifle down the track leading south.

Rather inhospitable. Who did he think was heading this way? Then she remembered about the spring and the carcass behind the barn and took a step closer to Mrs. Wallin.

A wagon and team pulled into the clearing, tack jingling.

"There, are you seeing what I mean now, Mrs. Howard?" Maddie proclaimed from the back of the wagon. "Sure'n but she's working much too hard."

Catherine smiled as her friend Allegra raised a hand in greeting from the bench. In the lap of her fashionable full-skirted gray dress, her four-year-old daughter, Gillian, wiggled in her eagerness to be free, golden curls tumbled about her face.

Deputy McCormick jumped down and began unthreading the reins from the horses' harnesses. "Mrs. Wallin, Miss Wallin, Miss Stanway," he greeted with a tip of his black broad-brimmed hat. His eyes narrowed on the porch. "Levi."

Levi sat with a thud and lowered the gun.

As the deputy helped Allegra and Gillian down, Maddie climbed to the ground, shook out her cinnamon-colored skirts and hurried over to give Catherine a hug. "And how is my Catie-girl?"

Her Catie-girl couldn't help noticing how Beth was turning as pink as her gown, gaze on the wagon and finger twirling the tie of her sunbonnet. She couldn't be bashful of meeting new people, not after all her talk of socials and such.

Catherine glanced at Mrs. Wallin, who was smiling. "Any friends of Catherine are welcome," she told Maddie. "Why, I might not even be here if it wasn't for this dear girl."

Catherine thanked her, then introduced everyone

around as Allegra, Gillian and Deputy McCormick came to join them.

"I'm only sorry my husband couldn't come with us," Allegra told her. "He had pressing business in town. I was simply glad Deputy McCormick agreed to accompany us."

McCormick glanced at the porch again. "I had a reason to travel out this way."

Beth's color deepened. Levi's fled.

Mrs. Wallin invited them all into the house for cider. Only Levi demurred, claiming a need to keep an eye on the horses Deputy McCormick had let into an open patch of pasture. Though Mrs. Wallin looked disappointed in his response, Catherine thought Drew's mother took special delight in serving the rest of them from her pink-and-white dishes.

Catherine took more delight in the bandbox Maddie had brought with her.

"My clothes!" she cried, clutching it close.

"I feel the same way," Beth said with a grin.

Maddie had also brought a loaf of spice cake with her, the scent of cinnamon and cloves drifting up as Mrs. Wallin sliced off pieces.

"Oh, but my boys will be sorry they missed this," she said as she poured Deputy McCormick another cup of cider.

"And how many sons would you be having, then?" Maddie asked.

The question was polite, but Catherine could see the light in her friend's brown eyes.

"Five," Mrs. Wallin answered, pride evident in the height of her chin.

Gillian perked up from where she sat on the bench next to Allegra. "Can I play with them?"

Mrs. Wallin smiled at her. "I'm afraid they're a little too old. Drew is nearing thirty, Simon is twenty-eight, James is twenty-five, John is twenty and Levi is eighteen. But I'm sure Beth would be happy to play with you."

"Mother!" Beth dropped her gaze and gripped her teacup so hard Catherine thought the handle might snap. "I'm not a child!"

Mrs. Wallin frowned. "Who said you were?"

Deputy McCormick rose from his place at the end of the table and held out a hand to Gillian. "Come along, urchin. There's a goat or two around here somewhere that needs petting, if I remember correctly."

Beth hopped to her feet so fast her cup rattled in its saucer. "I'll be happy to show you."

McCormick nodded. "Much obliged, ma'am."

As the three set out, Mrs. Wallin stood, as well. "Now, you ladies just visit. I want to bring Levi some of this cake. He's taking this guard duty so seriously." Plate in hand, she moved toward the rear door.

Maddie slid along the bench until she bumped into Catherine. "And what about you, Catie, me love? Are you taking your duty seriously?"

Catherine sipped from her cider before answering. "Mrs. Wallin is feeling much better, and I am convinced the youngest Mr. Wallin will heal nicely from his injury." She was just as convinced he'd stayed outside to avoid having to talk with Deputy McCormick.

Maddie tsked. "And was your nursing the duty I was meaning?" She lowered her voice. "How are you and the eldest Mr. Wallin getting along?"

Catherine broke off a bit of the moist cake with her fork. "He has been very helpful in the nursing process."

Maddie glanced at Allegra with a frown, then returned her gaze to Catherine's. "Has he sung you no songs? Tried to steal a kiss under the moonlight?"

Catherine felt her face coloring as she remembered the kiss they'd shared. It hadn't been under the moonlight, but she'd still felt moonstruck. "Certainly not," she told Maddie.

Allegra blew out a breath that stirred her dark hair. "Well, what's wrong with the fellow?"

"Nothing," Catherine protested, and Maddie crowed.

"You see? Wasn't I telling you that, Mrs. Howard? There's not a thing wrong with the fellow, at least nothing marrying a good wife wouldn't fix."

"That's quite enough," Catherine said, picking up her teacup with two fingers. "Mr. Wallin and I are both quite indisposed to courting."

Maddie picked up her own cup and pointed her little finger at Catherine, nose in the air. "La-di-da, but aren't we above such things, now?"

Allegra shook her head with a smile. A slender beauty with coal-black hair and stunning blue eyes, she had been one of the leaders among the women Asa Mercer had brought to Seattle. She'd organized a school aboard ship so that they'd all know everything they could about their new home, and she ran the town's lending library from her home near the territorial university.

"No one says you must marry, Catherine," she replied now. "But it seems you couldn't choose a finer fellow. I asked around town, and everyone I talked with holds Mr. Wallin in the highest regard. He always fills his contracts on schedule, and he and his family have been very generous in donating wood for civic and church projects."

That did not surprise her. Drew was so conscientious about his responsibilities to family. It seemed he extended that responsibility to his neighbors, as well.

"Sure'n but he's a pillar of the community," Maddie agreed. "Especially as he's as sturdy as a pillar. Why, I can't imagine a thing that would ever threaten the man."

Catherine blinked, then set down her cup. "But something has." She went on to tell her friends what had happened at the Landing, including her suspicions about Levi's injuries and his response that even Scout Rankin was not his friend.

Maddie made a face. "Rankin. I've heard his name in town. There was a scrawny lad wandering about trying to interest gentlemen in stopping by his father's property for a good chicken dinner. I thought he might be needing a cook or cleaning woman, so I asked Mrs. Elliott, who has the running of our boardinghouse. She advised me to stay away from the man. Said he could drink Puget Sound dry."

"That could be nothing but gossip," Allegra reminded her. She slid off her end of the bench and stood. "I'm sorry to cut our time together so short, Catherine, but we'll need to go soon if we want to reach Seattle by dark. I'll fetch Gillian. Why don't you tell Deputy McCormick your concerns?"

Should she? She didn't want to give the lawman more to consider when it came to Levi. Drew had enough on his hands. But if Deputy McCormick knew something that could help Drew protect his family, wouldn't Drew want to hear it?

Chapter Nineteen

Drew dunked his head in the spring pool and shook the water from his face. It had been a long day. They'd sheared off the last of the branches and dragged the fir down to the stream. Bracing the log by ropes and poles, they'd worked the oxen to maneuver it down into Salmon Bay, where sailors from the *Merry Maid* were waiting to take it to the ship. A carpenter was already aboard to help them varnish the mast, step it into place and rig it properly. One more job done, and no one hurt.

John came out of the barn where he'd penned the oxen. He took one look at Drew and shook his head. "That is no way to approach a lady." He pulled a comb from his hip pocket and handed it to Drew. "We want you neat and tidy to court Catherine."

Drew accepted the carved wooden comb, another example of his father's handiwork, but his annoyance must have shown on his face, for John stepped back with a grin. Either that, or Drew looked even worse than he thought.

"And smelling nice," James agreed, joining them by the pool. He took a sniff near Drew and reared back, waving a hand before his nose. "Where's that cologne Simon bought from the tinker?"

"Gone," John informed him. "I used it to start that pile of wet wood burning last week."

Drew pushed away from the spring. "I'm fine. If Catherine can't appreciate a man who works, she's not the bride for me."

"Drew?"

The looks on his brother's faces would have told him who had called him even if he hadn't recognized the voice. James stepped aside, and Drew saw Catherine standing just behind him. The pink of her cheeks suggested she'd heard at least part of their conversation.

Drew nailed a smile on his face. "Good evening, Catherine. We were just about to join you for dinner."

James and John murmured their agreement and hurried for the house, James with an arch look to Drew.

"I hoped to catch you," she said, taking a step closer, "before you went inside."

He didn't think it could be about anything good, but he made himself lean a hip against the stone wall of the pool and say, "Oh? About what?"

She blew out a breath as if she wasn't sure how to tell him, and he tensed for the worst.

"Deputy McCormick was here today," she said, one finger rubbing another in front of her gown, which was the color of the lilacs that grew in the wood. She hadn't had it with her before, and the wide skirts and fancy white piping along the bust and waist told him the dress didn't belong to his mother, either. Had McCormick brought her clothes? Was he courting her, too, now?

"Why?" he asked. "More trouble?"

"He said it was a social call. He brought my friends Miss O'Rourke and Mrs. Howard to visit."

Drew relaxed a little. So that was where the dress had come from. A shame his brothers hadn't been here to meet the feisty redhead.

"I don't think he was telling all the truth," she continued. "He seemed inordinately interested in Levi. And he didn't seem surprised to see him in a splint."

Drew frowned. McCormick was as hard as the cedar Drew felled, but he couldn't see the lawman beating his brother. "Did he have words with Levi?"

"Not that I noticed. He seemed more interested in observing. But I thought he should know about the troubles you've been having, so I told him." She closed the distance between them, gaze turned up to his. "I hope you don't mind."

"Why should I mind?" Drew replied. "You were looking out for my family. What did the deputy make of it?"

"He said our problems were similar to what's been happening at the other farms between here and town. Only no one's been hurt there."

"So whoever is behind this singled out Levi," Drew said, hearing his voice deepen.

As if she heard it, too, Catherine laid a hand on his arm. "There's more. My friends mentioned a Mr. Rankin. I take it he's the father of Levi's friend Scout."

Drew nodded. "But you saw Scout. I'm having a hard time imagining him beating Levi."

Catherine cocked her head. "Or perhaps looking the other way while his father did it?"

Drew didn't know what to believe. "Why shield someone, even an old friend, who treated you so badly? No, something else is at the bottom of this. Did McCormick have any suggestions as to what we can do, how we can protect ourselves?"

"Just to be vigilant," she said with a shrug that spoke of her own frustration at the vague advice. "He said he'd do the same. I'm sorry, Drew. I wish I had something more for you."

Drew shook his head. "You tried, and for that I'm grateful."

He'd followed such a statement with a kiss before. It seemed only natural to do so again. But this time when his lips met Catherine's, emotions exploded around him like Mr. Yesler's fireworks on the Fourth of July. He couldn't think, could only feel. He wrapped his arms about her and cradled her against him. She clung to him, arms coming around his waist, hands pressed to his back, as if she wanted him closer. The world fell away, until all that was left was Catherine.

Nearby, a rifle roared.

Drew's head jerked up, and he put Catherine behind him, sheltering her, fists up and at the ready.

Levi stood on the porch, gun in one hand. "Do I need to fire again, or do you get the message?" he asked, face tight.

Drew wiped his lips, still tingling from the kiss. "We'll be right in."

Levi nodded, hung up the rifle and hobbled inside.

Drew turned to Catherine. She looked as though she wasn't sure whether to laugh or cry.

"Drew, I..." she started even as he said, "Catherine, I..."

He smiled at her. "Go ahead."

She seemed to take him literally. "Thank you. Excuse me." She hurried for the house.

Drew followed more slowly, trying to master his emotions. He'd thought her so calm, her feathers never ruffled. But there was a fire inside her. He could feel it calling to him. Was this how his father had felt about his mother?

Not for the first time, he wished his father was there to ask. Drew had managed to figure out everything else the past ten years, from how to weld his quarrelsome brothers into an effective logging team to where to plant vegetables during a chilly spring.

But when it came to falling in love, he hadn't a clue.

Catherine found it hard to eat dinner that night. Levi had surprised a fat hare in the garden, and the stew was savory with the tender meat. But every time her spoon touched her mouth, she remembered the pressure of Drew's lips, his fierce embrace and the way she'd reacted. All she'd wanted to do was hold him closer and sway with the emotions he raised in her.

She could not be in love. She'd shut the door on feeling. She had to remember her calling, her purpose. Anything else was not to be borne.

So she refused to be alone with Drew the rest of the evening. That was surprisingly difficult, given that they were sharing the main room of the cabin with six other people. She started by offering to help Mrs. Wallin with her mending. Drew's mother agreed with a smile, and Catherine took a chair next to hers and accepted the red flannel shirt from her former patient.

"Such a time they have working," Mrs. Wallin said with a shake of her head that made her red-gold hair catch the light from the fire. "They're forever ripping or tearing something. That one's Drew's—a hole in the sleeve."

Catherine felt as if the fabric warmed in her hands.

She set it aside and rose. "Would you care for some water? I could do with a cup."

Across the room, Drew had been leaning against the wall while his brothers sat at the table, Simon whittling, James rubbing linseed oil into an ax handle and John reading. Now James elbowed his younger brother.

"Did you hear that, John?" he said, overly loud. "Catherine wants water."

John eyed Drew. "Someone should fetch it for her."

Drew straightened away from the wall.

Panic pushed Catherine to the other side of the room. "No need. I'm fine." She collapsed on a chair next to Beth. "What does *Godey's* have to say about the new hemlines, Beth?"

The girl grinned at her. "That the more narrow silhouettes are very becoming. I was thinking about making a new dress, a nice one for church and socials and such."

"And taking tea with the governor's wife," James teased.

Beth ignored him, rising from her chair. "I'll go get my sketches and show you." She glanced around the room. "Drew, why don't you keep Catherine company until I return?"

Again, he straightened off the wall, and Catherine racked her brain for a way to avoid him.

This time she had an unexpected ally. "My leg's paining me," Levi announced. "Maybe you could have a look at it, Miss Stanway, if you're not too busy with other matters."

Catherine hurried to his side. "Of course I'll take a look, Levi. That's what I'm here for." Not to fall in love and risk her heart.

Levi had been sitting on the bench of the table, leg straightened out in front of him. James vacated his chair for Catherine, and she sat and examined the splint. Everything seemed in place, and she could detect no sign of swelling.

"Where does it hurt?" she asked Levi.

To her surprise, he glared at his hovering brothers. "Can't a man have a little privacy?"

"In this family?" James asked with a grin. "No." But he allowed John to lead him over to the fire. Simon went to sit beside his mother. Drew relaxed back against the wall, though Catherine could feel him watching her and his youngest brother.

"What's troubling you, Levi?" she asked.

He lowered his voice. "I saw you talking with Deputy McCormick. What did he say about me? What did you tell Drew?"

So that was the problem. Catherine kept her voice lowered as well, fingers skimming the wood of the splint. "We talked about the other accidents that have happened recently. I believe Deputy McCormick sees a pattern."

"Then he's smarter than he looks," Levi muttered.

Catherine eyed him. His face was paling, and he'd crossed his arms over his chest.

"What do you know about this, Levi?" she asked.

He narrowed his eyes. "Why do I have to know anything? Why is it always my fault?"

"No one said it was your fault," Catherine argued. "But if someone hurt you or threatened your family, you must tell us."

"I don't have to tell you anything. We did just fine on our own until you came along."

Catherine recoiled from the anger in his voice. "If you ask me, Mr. Wallin, it's not your leg that pains you. It's your conscience."

"And if you ask me, you ought to go back to Seattle where you belong!"

His voice had risen, and everyone in the room glanced their way. Beth, returning with her sketches, paused on the stairs. Drew moved to his brother's side.

"That's enough, Levi. Your injury may explain your temper, but you should apologize to Catherine."

Levi was breathing hard, as if the air had grown too thin. "Sorry," he muttered. "I want to go to bed now. John, will you help me?"

"Surely," John replied, coming to join them. He put an arm under Levi's and helped him to his feet. Together, they moved toward the stairs.

"I'm sorry, Catherine," Drew said, and for a moment she wasn't sure what had made him apologize, his actions earlier or his brother's now.

James returned to their sides. "Am I getting old, or was brother Levi testier than usual tonight?"

Simon ventured over, as well. "What did you expect? He's a young man with nothing to occupy his thoughts or utilize his energy. Something was bound to snap."

Was that it? Sometimes she thought Nathan had gone off to war because he couldn't bear being left behind by his friends and father. Was Levi acting out because Drew hadn't given him enough responsibilities?

"Perhaps he should come with us tomorrow," James said. "We'll keep him busy."

Catherine shook her head. "I fear a logging camp is no place for healing."

Drew eyed her. "Have you ever seen men log?"

"No," she admitted. "But I'm certain it's hard work."

"No argument there," James said. "Sometimes I positively grow faint." He collapsed back against Simon, who pushed him up with a grimace.

"It might surprise you what we have to do, Catherine," Simon said. He glanced at Drew. "I say we bring her out with us tomorrow morning. Watching us work should give her a fair idea of whether it's a suitable place for Levi."

It was a logical suggestion. She really couldn't determine what was safe for her patient otherwise. Yet some part of her was more curious to see Drew in his element.

He glanced around at his brothers, his eyes narrowed, as if he suspected treachery of some kind. Finally, he sighed and nodded. "Very well. If you're willing, Catherine, we'll need you to be ready by dawn."

She was willing and ready at the appointed time. She'd dressed in the flowered cotton gown Mrs. Wallin had loaned her, deeming it far more practical than her fuller skirts. A sunbonnet shielded her hair from the cool morning mist.

James set out first toward the west, ax poised over his shoulder. Simon and Drew carried saws and a burlap sack each that clanked as they walked. John bore the rifle, gaze shifting around the brush as they traveled along a well-worn path through ferns and thick green bushes where white flowers burst in clusters. Someone in town had told her they were called rhododendrons.

"Have you seen any more of the cougar?" she asked Drew, who was walking beside her. His checkered shirt was tucked into dusty trousers, which in turn were tucked into heavy boots. By the way they sucked at the mud, she thought the bottoms might carry spikes.

"Only some tracks down by the lake yesterday morning," he said. "We're hoping it headed for better hunting."

So did she. She glanced around the forest. The mist obscured the trees, touching her skin with soft fingers, but she could see a brighter patch to the east where the sun was trying to burn through.

At length they reached an area where the trees had been cut away, stumps like teeth jutting up through the wild grape and blackberry vines. A single tree remained in the center. Catherine gasped at the sight of it.

James grinned. "Why, Catherine, don't you like our little sapling?"

"Sapling?" she sputtered. "It's huge!"

John went over and patted the rough bark. "And several hundred years old, a mammoth of the forest." He sighed. "A shame it's come to this."

Catherine felt a similar sorrow. The tree soared into the air, so high she had to hold the bonnet to her head from craning her neck. Birds darted among the upper branches, and lichen clustered around the base.

"Must you cut it down?" she asked Drew.

"That's our job," Simon said as he passed, long-toothed saw bouncing over one shoulder.

Drew pointed up the bark. "See the holes? They were made by woodpeckers seeking bugs. The tree's sick, Catherine. If we don't fell it, it could infest all the trees around it."

"Not to mention knock half of them to the ground when it falls in the next windstorm," James said cheerfully, going to help Simon.

John held out the rifle to Catherine. “If you wouldn’t mind? With Levi at home, we’re a man down.”

She took the gun gingerly from him. Though she felt confident she could shoot it now, she still didn’t like the idea.

“That’s something for Levi,” Drew said. “He could keep watch for danger. Most animals shy away from the noise of the axes, but a few get curious enough to come too close for comfort. Holler if you see any that concern you.”

She nodded, and he went to join his brothers at the tree.

Now that she looked closer, she could see where they’d notched it earlier, the cuts of the ax pale against the weathered bark. John and James hacked away on the opposite side, then Simon and Drew drove in wedges with a sledgehammer to hold the back cut open.

James brought over the big saw and positioned it along front cuts. Simon joined him on one side, while Drew and John took up the other. Slowly, then gathering speed, they rocked the metal through the wood, the blade humming.

Catherine could see their muscles strain under the cotton. Soon sweat darkened their necks, and the shirts clung to their backs. They were a testament to strength and power, their bodies moving as one with the song of the blade.

And Drew was their leader, the commander of this little army, directing his brothers, encouraging them. His was the voice that rose above the noise, the head that never bowed with the effort. The sun broke through the mist and turned his hair to gold. She could not look away.

Beside her, something rustled in the brush. She tore

her gaze from Drew and aimed the rifle at the spot, but whatever it was must have had its curiosity satisfied, for she saw no movement and heard nothing more.

"Scatter!" John's voice echoed through the clearing. "Widow-maker!"

All four brothers dropped the saw and dashed away from the tree.

"What is it?" Catherine cried, clutching the gun.

Drew was frowning up the tree as if trying to spy the danger himself.

"There," John said, pointing. "I thought I saw it shift."

Now Catherine saw it, as well. Halfway up the tree, a massive branch had broken off. Right now, it lay wedged between two other branches, its tip pointing down, but the vibration of the saw could easily have sent it plummeting.

Right onto Drew and John. She shivered at the thought.

"I'll go," Drew said. "Brace the cut and rig the rope." His brothers moved to comply.

"What are you doing?" Catherine asked with a frown.

He offered her a grim smile as he walked away from the tree to give his brothers room to work. "Removing a danger before it removes one of us."

John and James put more wedges around the big saw to keep the tree from shifting while Simon began swinging a weighted rope. Up it went, over one of the larger branches not far from the broken one. He tugged down on the weight and went to wrap the rope around a stump. Once he was certain it was secured, he brought the other end to Drew.

Catherine stared at Drew as he looped the rope around his waist. "You aren't going up there."

"One of us has to," Simon said, coming to tug on the rope as if to make sure it would hold his brother. "He volunteered."

James and John came to join him, spitting on their hands before taking hold of the rope. They were going to haul Drew into the tree!

"Are you sure this is safe?" she asked, feeling a tug of panic as strong as their hold on the rope.

"Safer than leaving that up there," Drew answered.

"Never fear, Catherine, dear," James said. "We hardly ever drop anyone."

Catherine choked. "Hardly ever?"

"He's teasing," Drew assured her. "We've done this many times, and we've never been hurt."

"Ever since Pa was killed by a falling branch," John explained, "we tend to take such matters seriously."

Catherine took the matter just as seriously. She wanted to order them all back to the house and lock them inside. As if Drew understood, he took a step closer.

"Trust me, Catherine," he said. "We know what we're doing."

She felt as if the mist had returned to clog her senses. "Promise me you'll be careful."

He smiled. "I promise. I'll be back by your side before you know it." He touched her cheek. The warmth only pushed her panic higher.

She shoved the fear down. He needed to focus, not worry about her. "Good luck," she made herself say.

With a nod, he turned to the tree.

Drew positioned his spiked boots against the trunk

and nodded to his brothers, who began pulling back on the rope. One hand braced on the rope, the other on his ax, Drew leaned back and took a step higher. In a moment, he was nearly perpendicular to the tree, moving slowly upward, one step at a time.

Simon, James and John kept hauling, their own feet braced on the damp ground, hands tight on the rope. Catherine tilted back her head and watched as Drew reached the branch and swung his ax. Each time the blade fell, his body jerked against the tree, and she was certain she felt the tree tremble. She trembled along with it. Then one more cut, and the branch broke free. Drew pulled back one boot and kicked the branch away. It twisted in the air to fall.

Right on the rope.

Simon, James and John stumbled forward with the weight as Drew was jerked higher.

"Get it off!" Simon shouted, and John released the rope to scramble forward, yanking at the massive limb.

"It's no good! We need at least two of us to cut it." He stared at Simon, and Catherine felt his fear.

Simon looped the rope around his waist, then pulled a knife from his belt and drove it hard into the ground as if to help anchor himself. "Go," he told James, who released the rope.

James had taken two steps toward their axes when there was a snap as loud as a gunshot, and the rope whipped upward.

Catherine cried out, then threw up a hand even though she knew she couldn't reach him, as Drew tumbled down the tree.

Chapter Twenty

The world reeling around him, Drew clutched the rope and tried to dig his heels into the bark. The spikes on the bottoms of his boots refused to find purchase. He felt every bump on the way down. He was going to die.

Lord, protect Catherine and my family!

He was a few feet from hitting the ground when he jerked to a stop, the rope burning against his chest. Blinking, he looked up to see the line tangled among the branches.

John reached him first, knife out and sawing at the cord. "Are you all right?" he begged.

He was alive and in one piece, something he hadn't believed possible a few moments ago. *Thank You, Lord!* The rope snapped, and he dropped lightly onto the ground to suck in a breath.

"I'm all right," he started to say, but Catherine had beaten his other brothers to his side and was thrusting the rifle at John. She put her hands on Drew's shoulders and peered up into his eyes, her own smoky with fear.

"Where does it hurt?" she demanded. "Can you breathe? Speak, man!"

Drew tried to smile at her. "Only a nurse would ask a man to breathe and speak at the same time."

Simon and James, who had also come running, pulled up beside her. He could see them frowning at her, but he could feel her body shaking.

"You hit eleven branches on your way down," she informed him, as if she'd counted each one. "And you struck your back at least twice. You could be bleeding internally, have fractured a dozen bones..."

He caught her close and held her in his arms, thankful he still could. "I'm all right," he repeated against her hair. "You have no reason to fear."

She clung to him a moment before pushing away. "I'm not afraid!" she cried. "I am furious! What sort of antic was that? How could you risk your life? Don't you know your family depends on you? Do you want to leave them orphaned?"

Her words hit harder than the tree, and his breath rasped out of him.

"He isn't our father," Simon said quietly. "We can take care of ourselves."

"Can you?" Catherine whirled on him. "I didn't see you volunteering to climb that tree. And you," she turned to James as Simon reddened. "You take nothing seriously. How can your brother rely on you? And you," she turned to John, who dropped the gun and held up his hands as if surrendering. She threw up her own hands. "I have no opinion about you."

James grimaced, but John looked stricken at being an afterthought.

"You asked me out here to determine whether it's safe for Levi to return to work," she continued, undaunted, gaze stabbing each in turn like the flash of a knife. "Of course it isn't safe. It isn't safe for any of you. If you want my advice, you will find another line of work, immediately!" She turned and stalked out of the clearing.

"Go with her," Drew told John. "She finds you the least offensive."

"Small comfort," John muttered, retrieving the gun. "Apparently I have so little personality I failed to make any impression." He jogged after Catherine.

Simon blew out a breath. "Forgive me for demanding that you court her, Drew. She is obviously not the bride for a lumberjack."

"Oh, I don't know," James said, scratching his chin. "She could probably fell a tree by pointing out its shortcomings. It would certainly make this job easier."

"Enough," Drew said. He threw off the last of the rope, wincing as his sore muscles protested. Catherine had been right about one thing—he had bruises on bruises. "She's trained to heal. You can't blame her for objecting to someone getting hurt. To her, it must look as if we take chances intentionally."

"Wild men that we are," James agreed, bending to loop up what was left of the rope. "Still, Simon is right. This is how we make a living. People need this wood for houses, for ships, for furniture. We can't just stop working because it looks dangerous."

"It doesn't just *look* dangerous," Simon said. "It *is* dangerous. Any woman who can't live with that fact has no place in the wilderness."

"Clear off the branch," Drew said. "I'm going after Catherine."

Neither of his brothers protested as he limped away.

Catherine must have kept going at a goodly clip,

because Drew didn't catch up to her and John. And it took him a little longer than usual to reach the Landing, given his injuries.

On the way, he kept thinking about what he would say to her. She was right on all counts—Simon didn't like to take chances, James treated the world as if it were designed for his entertainment and John would crawl inside a book and stay there if Drew allowed it. But they were all good men and would make fine husbands one day—for the right woman.

And she was right about their work, as well. When the saw had whipped past him years ago, he'd been fortunate to walk away with a lacerated hand. His father hadn't been so fortunate. Every year loggers were crushed by falling logs or trampled by oxen. What they did was dangerous.

The past few days had been particularly challenging with the cougar and Levi's injury, but even on the best of days accidents could happen, people could get sick. He did everything he could to keep his family safe and healthy. What more did she want from him?

He had nothing left to give.

At last he reached the Landing and hobbled out onto the grass. He didn't see Catherine right away, but John met him at the edge of the clearing.

"She's in your cabin," his brother reported, face pinched as if he'd been the one to fall down a tree, "and she asked Beth to help her change into one of her gowns. She wanted to know whether I'd drive her back to town or whether she had to walk."

"Go help James and Simon," Drew said. "I'll talk to her."

He started across the clearing, but his mother came out of the main house to wave at him from the porch.

"Everyone all right?" she called.

"Fine, Ma," he said, gritting his teeth to saunter up to the cabin as if he hadn't a care in the world. No need to worry his mother when Catherine was worried enough for all of them.

"But why must you go?" Beth protested as she watched Catherine finish buttoning up her dusty blue gown. Mrs. Wallin's pretty dress lay draped over a chair, along with the sunbonnet. Nothing looked out of place in the cabin. It was as if she'd never been there.

She drew in a shaky breath. It was for the best. Her work here was done. Mrs. Wallin was well; Levi was healing. Drew said he was fine, although she'd seen the pallor on his face and watched the skin darken on his hands where he'd hit them against the tree. She feared the number of ways he could be hurt, but felt equally certain he'd never allow her to treat him. If he and his brothers were determined to risk their lives, she didn't have to stay and watch them die.

But she couldn't say that to Beth. The girl had to live out here with her brothers; it was probably a kindness that she didn't realize how close to death they walked.

"Doctor Maynard needs me in Seattle," she told Beth, knowing the statement for the truth, as well.

"We need you here, too," Beth argued, hands worrying in front of the apron on her pink gown. "What if Ma gets sick again or Simon pushes James out of a tree?"

Catherine's stomach flip-flopped. What if one of them got hurt? Who'd tend their wounds? Who'd nurse them to health?

Lord, You can't ask me to stay. You know the need is greater elsewhere.

"You all survived before I arrived, Beth," Catherine said, moving toward the door. "And if Simon pushes James out of a tree, maybe it will knock some sense into him."

"You don't mean that!" Beth followed her to the door. "Please, Catherine, don't go! It was so nice having another girl to talk to. I never got to show you how to make flapjacks or milk the goats. We could have had fun!"

Living here was hardly fun. Being around the Wallins hurt deeply. And the thought of losing Drew made her physically ill.

"You can come visit me in town anytime you like," Catherine offered, pausing at the door. "You'll most likely find me at the hospital." Where she could deal with patients on a purely clinical level.

She opened the door to find Drew on the porch. His hair had fallen into his face, and a bruise darkened one cheek. She had to fist her hands to keep from reaching out to him.

"You don't have to go," he said. "I'm fine."

But he wasn't. She didn't have to lay her hand on his forehead to see that he was sweating. She could hear his breath coming fast, as if it hurt to draw anything deeper. He should be lying down, putting a cold cloth on his bruises, being examined for broken ribs.

But not by her. She knew if she put her hands on him now, she'd be holding him close and never letting go.

"All the more reason for me to leave," she said, picking up her bandbox and stepping around him. "There is nothing more for me here."

As if the very earth disagreed, Wallin Landing

seemed to leap toward her, surrounding her. Everywhere she looked, she saw memories: sending Levi into the pool, firing the gun to bring Drew and his brothers a-running, sitting by the fire and listening to his dreams, being so sweetly held and kissed.

She straightened her spine and cast him a glance. "No John, I see. Very well. I'll start walking."

Drew's arms came around her. For a moment, she closed her eyes and gave in to the feeling of warmth, of safety. But it was all an illusion. He could be taken from her at any time.

"You don't have to walk," he murmured. "I'll drive you. Are you certain this is what you want?"

He leaned back and gazed down at her. She could feel herself slipping into the blue-green of his eyes. *Stay*, some part of her urged. *Take whatever life gives you and enjoy it while it lasts.*

But she couldn't. Her heart wasn't strong enough. Already she felt as if she were shattering into a thousand pieces.

"This is for the best," she made herself say. "I'll wait while you harness the horses."

He let her go and headed for the barn.

Beth touched her arm, blue eyes swimming. "Please, Catherine, I know Drew cares about you. I thought you cared about him."

Catherine watched him cross the clearing. His shirt was torn where a branch must have caught it. Though he tried to hide it, she could tell he was limping. He was a battered, tattered fellow, yet he had never looked more honorable or more dear.

"I do care about your brother," she murmured. "That's why I have to leave."

* * *

Maddie at least was glad to see Catherine when she walked into the boardinghouse late that afternoon. She took one look at Catherine's face and hugged her close.

"Is there a fellow I should be scolding?" she murmured, "for putting such a look on your face?"

"No," Catherine said, drawing back. "I'm the one who should be scolded, for putting myself in such a position."

She could not forget the silence between her and Drew as he'd driven the wagon back to Seattle. She'd heard every creak of the wheels, each thud of the horses' hooves. He'd kept his gaze ahead, as if she weren't sitting beside him, wishing him to speak, praying he'd stay silent.

"Ma and Beth will miss you," he'd said at one point, and she nearly asked whether he'd miss her, too. But she didn't want to know. Oh! She didn't want to know.

Now Maddie followed her upstairs to the room they shared. All she wanted to do was change out of this dress into something fresh, something that might not remind her of how she'd spent the past few days. But the room with its twin beds covered in bright wool blankets and its window overlooking Puget Sound felt tighter than she remembered. It was as if even the air in town wasn't as clear, as deep.

"What happened?" Maddie asked as Catherine pulled out her trunk from under the bed and drew out her favorite brown dress. "I left you with a handsome man. Could you not be bringing him back with you?"

At least Maddie hadn't changed. "I sent you a handsome man," Catherine countered, rising to begin unbuttoning her gown. "Did a Mr. Ward call on you?"

Pink crept into Maddie's cheeks. "Mr. Ward, the thespian? Oh, he's as charming as the day is long, so he is. But I'm not sure I'm the lass for him."

"Oh?" Catherine glanced up with a frown. "Why?"

Maddie twisted her fingers around each other, avoiding Catherine's gaze. "Well, two Irish people? You know what everyone will say—there they go a-breeding! And a man with ideas about acting and such. No, no. If I marry, sure'n it will be to a man with gold in his pockets and the respect of the community behind him, someone I can be proud to stand beside."

Money and position. Catherine knew many women back East who had married for those reasons. "I always thought a marriage required more than that," she told Maddie as she pulled off the blue gown. "Love, for one thing."

"Oh, now don't you be getting on your high ropes the moment you get back, Catie, me love," Maddie warned her, flopping down on her bed. "Isn't position why you refused that lumberjack out in the wild?"

Catherine tossed the gown on her bed. "Mr. Wallin never asked me to marry him. And it's not his position that troubled me."

Maddie cocked her head. "Was he such a gadabout, then, courting any woman who took his fancy?"

She couldn't leave her friend with that impression. "Not at all," she said as she drew the dress over her head. The fine brown wool was fitted, the skirts narrow and it said the wearer would brook no nonsense.

"A more faithful fellow you'll never find, I'm convinced," she told Maddie. "But what he does for a living, where he lives, there are so many dangers, Maddie. I don't think I can bear it."

"Ah," Maddie said, straightening. "You want a husband who will treat you like a fine porcelain doll, keep you safely wrapped in pretty blankets."

"Certainly not!" Catherine shuddered at the image. "I wouldn't stand for such treatment. I've worked too hard at my profession to want to give it up. I help people, Madeleine. Sometimes I give them back their lives."

Maddie stiffened. "Begging your pardon, me darling girl, but only the Lord gives life. I've seen you be His hands. Yet doesn't the Good Book say that any act done without love means nothing?"

Catherine marched to the little table near the window, picked up her brush and began attacking her hair. "So simply because I don't engage my heart with every patient who walks in the door, you would have it I've done nothing worthwhile. I don't believe that."

In the mirror over the table, she could see Maddie watching her. "I'm not casting aspersions on your work, Catherine. I'm questioning your motivations." She gentled her tone. "Sure'n you can't bring back your father and brother."

"No," Catherine said, hand stilling on the brush. "But I do my best to see that no one else suffers such loss."

"And you can keep yourself from suffering, I'm thinking," Maddie said, rising from the bed and crossing to her side, "by making sure you never let anyone close enough that you start to care."

The words slammed into her, piercing her chest. She shut her eyes, but she couldn't shut out the truth.

"Very well. I don't want to hurt like that again. I don't think I'm strong enough. Is that what you want to hear?"

Maddie's arms came around Catherine, and she

opened her eyes to meet Maddie's gaze. "No, me darling. I want to hear that you realize love is worth the risk that you might be hurt again."

Tears were coming. She could see them sparkling in her eyes in the mirror, along with Maddie's mournful smile.

"I'm sorry, Maddie," she murmured. "I'm not sure I believe that."

Maddie gave her a squeeze before releasing her. "Well, that's progress, isn't it, now? Once you would have told me you didn't believe it at all."

Catherine smiled at her friend through the tears. "Only you would see my doubts as progress."

Maddie nodded as if the matter were settled and picked up the brush to run it through Catherine's hair, the strokes gentle and calming. "Doubt can be good if it brings you to the truth. And if it's that Mr. Wallin who's made you wonder, I'll be saying a prayer for you both. Now let's get you prettied up so you'll be ready when he comes back for you."

Something inside her leaped at the thought, but she couldn't let her friend hope in vain. "He isn't coming back, Maddie."

"Oh, he is," Maddie insisted, twisting up a hank of Catherine's hair and pinning it in place. "I saw his face as you came to the door. He's hurting as much as you are, so he is. A man like that isn't going to give up. I'd say he'll be back within the week, so you better decide what you'll say when he proposes. And if it's anything less than yes, you and I will have words, me darling."

Chapter Twenty-One

Drew returned to Seattle three days later. He hadn't intended to. They didn't need supplies. The days were warming as May went by, and the leafy tops of Beth's carrots were already waving in the garden. They didn't need medical help. Ma was back to her regular routine, Levi was hobbling around on a crutch that John had made for him, and Drew's bruises were fading.

At least, the bruises on the outside of his body.

No, the reason he had to return to Seattle was because he'd never know peace otherwise.

"You let her get away?" James had protested from his place on the rug when they'd all gathered in the front room the night Catherine had left. "And you call yourself a man?"

His mother, seated in her rocking chair, had tsked as she'd worked on knitting a new pair of socks. Beth at her feet had looked from one brother to another.

"I thought things were going so well," she'd protested. "Levi said you kissed her."

James had hooted as if he quite approved, but Ma had silenced him with a look.

"If she let you kiss her, I don't see how you could have lost her," John had said from his place beside James. "You've never failed to bring in a deer or bring down a tree you set your mind to."

They'd had no idea what they were talking about. Wait until they fell in love. Leaning against the stairs, Drew had shaken his head. "Catherine is hardly a tree."

From the opposite wall by the window, Simon had crossed his arms over his chest. "But the same principles apply. You determine your objective, plan your approach, gather your supplies and act. You knew the objective was to keep a nurse in the family. We gave you a plan and offered our help. You had all the supplies you needed." He'd pointed a finger at Drew. "You didn't act."

"For shame, Simon Wallin," Ma had said, frowning at him over her knitting. "I never taught you to think of a lady that way. Why, you make falling in love sound like a battle!"

Simon had colored as he'd lowered his hand. "Apologies, ma'am, but I tend to think of courting that way."

"Another reason I'm still waiting for a daughter-in-law." She'd set aside her knitting and risen to come to Drew's side. Her green eyes had been solemn. "What happened, Andrew? I was under the impression you cared for Catherine."

Drew had pushed off the wall. "I care. She doesn't want to be part of this family. That's all that matters."

His mother's face had softened. "How she feels about us is less important than how she feels about you. A lady can put up with a great deal for the right man."

"Then apparently, ma'am, I'm not the right man."

He had felt the protest building around him, shining

in his sister's eyes, shouting from his brother's tensed shoulders. He'd had enough.

"This topic of conversation is closed," he'd told them all. "I wish you a good night."

He'd felt their surprised gazes follow him as he'd crossed the room and left the house.

Returning to his own cabin had seemed like the best way to remove himself from the criticism, but even there he'd found no rest. Catherine had seemed to linger in the air. One chair had been out from under the table, and he'd fancied he could still feel the warmth of her against its back. His quilt had held the scent of lemon and lavender he'd come to think was hers alone. And one pale blond hair had gleamed in the moonlight on the wood floor. He'd bent to retrieve it, stroking one finger down the length.

Oh, but he was lost.

What do You expect of me, Lord? She hesitates to fire a gun, she hates our work, she's as bossy as the day is long.

And despite what he'd said to his mother, he'd known then and now that Catherine sincerely cared about his family, maybe as much as he did.

In the end, her love for his family wasn't what had driven him back to Seattle. No, he had come for Catherine. For all her propriety and high ideals, there was something vulnerable about her. Spending time with her, watching her ply her trade, holding her in his arms, he'd caught a glimpse of her heart, and he wanted more.

He found her at the hospital, as he'd expected. Several people sat or stood along the white walls of the dispensary, waiting for Doc Maynard to see them. One man cradled his arm; another rocked back and forth, moaning. Catherine moved among them, speaking softly, laying a hand of encouragement on shoulders, offering advice on how to deal with the illness or injury. She was wearing a dress of a warm brown. The color contrasted with her pale hair, and the tailoring outlined her figure. With her apron wrapped about her, she looked competent, confident.

So beautiful he couldn't look away.

He took off his wool cap and held it in his hands as he paused in the doorway. Now that he was here, he couldn't think what to say to her. How did one family compare to the needs of the many here in town? How could his feelings vie with her calling?

Before he'd even taken a step, she looked up and met his gaze. Her eyes widened as she straightened, then she hurried toward him.

"Drew, what's wrong? Did Levi's leg fester? Did your mother have a relapse?" She clutched his arm. "Please tell me Beth's all right. Simon? James? John?"

"Fine," he assured her before she could ask after the stock, as well. "We're all fine, or at least they are. I came for me."

She pressed her fingers to her lips as if offering up a prayer. "Oh, no! Your fall must have been worse than I thought." She gripped his hand and towed him to the nearest chair, pushing on his shoulders to make him sit. "You should have had one of the others drive you in," she scolded. She ran a hand up his arm as if checking for injuries, and his heart started hammering.

"Where does it hurt?" she asked. "Your arms? Your legs? Your back?"

Drew caught her hand and pressed it to his chest. "My heart."

Catherine gasped, and he thought she must have understood him, but she jerked her hand away. "Doctor Maynard!" she cried, dashing for the door. "We need you!"

As the other waiting patients stared at him, Drew stood. "No, Catherine, you misunderstand. I'm fine."

Doc Maynard strode into the dispensary. His white apron was speckled with a dusty red. "One more life in this world. What's wrong?"

Catherine drew in a deep breath. "Apparently nothing. Please forgive me. And give my congratulations to Mrs. Stevenson."

He nodded, then smiled at Drew. "Come to steal my nurse again, Drew?"

He was about to deny it when inspiration struck. "Actually, yes," he said. "I'd like her to come out and take a look at Ma and Levi. I'll return her tomorrow."

Maynard waved a beefy hand. "Certainly. We can make do a day or two without her this time. But not much more." He turned to the man waiting nearest him and began asking questions about his condition.

Catherine moved back to Drew's side. "I thought you said everyone was fine at the Landing."

"They are," Drew replied, "and I'd like to keep them that way."

Catherine's eyes narrowed. "As you can see, we have a great need here."

Though he felt like a selfish oaf for asking her to abandon these people for him, he couldn't very well talk about their future in such surroundings. He needed her somewhere they could discuss matters, reach some agreement.

Where he could hold her in his arms and tell her how much she meant to him.

"Come with me, Catherine," he urged. "I know everyone will be glad to see you, and you can make sure Levi's leg is healing straight."

Still she eyed him. He thought she might be holding her breath. He was holding his. Finally, she nodded. "Very well. But this time we stop by the boardinghouse before we go so I can alert Maddie and bring a few things."

Relief coursed through him, and air rushed into his lungs. She was going to give him a chance. Perhaps on the drive or at the Landing, he could convince her to think differently about him.

"Anything you want," he told her. "And thank you."

She should have refused him. By his own admission, everyone was fine at the Landing. What good could she do there? Her heart would only break when she left him again.

She'd had a hard enough time the past few days. Each time the door opened at the hospital, she'd expected Drew to walk through it, coming to tell her something horrible had happened. Or Simon to tell her Drew lay dying from the injuries she'd chosen to ignore. How could she claim to be a nurse and leave the man she loved in pain? Why had she let fear rule her better judgment?

Yet how could she go back and beg his forgiveness when she still wasn't sure how to deal with those fears?

Now she glanced over at Drew as he drove the team along the track out of town. He had been quite the gentleman, escorting her to the boardinghouse and waiting on the porch while she'd told Maddie the circumstances and packed her bandbox. She'd let him carry it to the wagon for her while Maddie had supervised from the porch.

"What's this?" he'd asked as Catherine had handed him a book.

"Culpeper's Complete Herbal," she had told him. "I promised John a copy. I simply wasn't sure when I'd see him again to give it to him."

His smile had been warm as he'd placed the book behind the seat. Very likely he'd thought she'd been hoping he'd come for her.

He wasn't entirely wrong.

"You be taking all the time you need, now, Mr. Wallin," Maddie had called in encouragement as he'd lifted Catherine onto the bench. "Sure'n Catherine could do with a change of scenery, and I'm thinking you have some fine scenery up where you live."

Catherine had frowned at her, but Maddie had merely laughed and waved a hand as they'd set off.

If Drew noticed Catherine's scrutiny at the moment, he didn't show it. More than anything, she wanted to know why he'd made the trek into town to fetch her. He'd said something was wrong with his heart. Was he truly hurting as much as she was, as Maddie had claimed? Why didn't he say something, explain his reasoning, share his feelings?

Tell her he loved her too much to let her go.

"Have you had many patients lately?" he asked.

Polite conversation again? Once she would have welcomed it or sought her own safe topic. Now her disappointment was like bitter medicine in her mouth.

"Enough to keep us busy," she replied, shoulders of

her dress brushing a red-throated rhododendron as they passed. "There's a rumor another doctor may be coming on the next ship from San Francisco."

"That's good news."

In the silence that followed, she could hear the horses' hooves sucking at the mud of the track. She couldn't go on this way. *Lord, help me. Give me the words to tell him what's in my heart, what I fear.*

"Drew, I…" she started, even as he said, "Catherine, I…"

He smiled. "Forgive me. What did you want to say?"

Catherine couldn't look at him. How did a woman tell a man she cared for him so much it frightened her? She fixed her gaze ahead, into the trees, then frowned. "Is that smoke?"

Drew had been looking at her. Now his head whipped around. Rising above the towering firs was a plume of gray, growing larger every minute.

"Something's on fire," he said, and he slapped the reins to urge the horses faster.

Not the Landing! But even if it wasn't Drew's home, the fire looked too close for comfort. How fast did a fire travel among the trees? Could it outrun a person? A horse? How many would be harmed if it wasn't contained?

As if her fears had infected him, Drew called to the team, pushing them forward. Catherine clutched the sideboard as the wagon careened down the track. The forest was no more than a green blur on either side. Something leaped across their path, and she realized it was a deer, fleeing the flames.

Lord, please protect Beth and Drew's brothers. Protect dear Mrs. Wallin. Please keep them all safe!

They rattled into the clearing, and Drew hauled back on the reins to bring the horses to a stop. Flames licked up the side of the barn, darkening the white circle Drew had drawn for Catherine to practice shooting.

The Wallins had formed a line from Mrs. Wallin and Beth working the pump outside Drew's house to Simon closer to the barn, and were passing buckets of water toward the fire. Drew looped the reins around the brake and put his hand on the sideboard to jump down. The team reared in their traces, whinnying in fear, knocking him back beside Catherine. She put out her hands to steady him.

"I'll calm them," he promised as he straightened. "Take Ma and Beth to the lake. You'll be safe there."

"I'm not leaving you!" Catherine insisted, but he was already climbing down, speaking to his horses. A moment later, he was running toward his cabin.

She wasn't sure how she could help fight a fire, but she knew she could ease his mind about his mother and sister. Gingerly, she picked up the reins, then had to pull as the excited horses tried to plunge forward.

Beth ran to the wagon and climbed up beside Catherine. "Drew and the others are going to keep fighting the fire," she reported, face flushed. "He wants us to protect the stock."

James and John had dropped their buckets and raced into the barn. Now they reappeared through the smoke, each leading two goats, some chickens nearly smothered in their arms.

Beth gathered the frightened hens into the back of the wagon while her brothers loaded in the bleating goats. Catherine couldn't catch sight of Drew. Where was he? What was he doing? Would he be safe?

Mrs. Wallin had gone to the house and returned to dump an armful of her quilts at Catherine's feet. Handing her husband's daguerreotype to Beth, she climbed up beside Catherine and cried, "Go!"

Still, she couldn't see Drew in the smoke that billowed about the clearing. She had to trust him to make it through, to come back to her. Just as he trusted her to keep his mother and Beth safe.

It was the hardest thing Catherine had ever done, but she slapped down on the reins and left him.

Chapter Twenty-Two

With Mrs. Wallin on one side and Beth on the other, Catherine guided the team through the trees, following the track she and Drew had walked on Sunday. Nathan had taught her how to drive years ago. He'd thought himself so clever to be better than her at something, the teacher rather than the pupil at last. She'd humored him, though she'd known the skill wasn't critical. Where she'd lived she'd either walked or traveled with friends or family. Besides, her father rarely surrendered the reins to his son, let alone Catherine. Now she blessed Nathan for teaching her, for the knowledge allowed her to bring the horses down the hill and onto the shore by the lake.

If she looked out over the blue water, cresting in places in a rising breeze, she could almost pretend everything was normal. Birds darted back and forth across the lake: gulls with their black-tipped wings, swallows with their mouths open. Mount Rainier rose in the distance, like a mother watching over her children at play. Only the hint of smoke in the air told of the fight going on among the trees behind them.

Beside her, Mrs. Wallin had her hands clasped in her lap, and her lips moved presumably in prayer. Catherine sent up a prayer as well, but it felt so small against five lives, three homes and the work of two generations.

She hated not knowing, not doing more. A part of her had always wondered whether there might have been something she could have done if she'd been there with her brother and father on the battlefield. Was God giving her a chance to help now?

She rose from the bench. "Wait here. I'm going back."

"No, don't!" Beth clutched Catherine's skirts. "Oh, please, Catherine, don't leave us. What if the cougar is still around?"

"Then I won't be much use to you," Catherine replied. "We don't even have a gun."

Mrs. Wallin touched her daughter's hands. "It's all right, Beth. Let her go. She knows her mind." She nodded to Catherine as Catherine climbed down to the ground. "Help them. We'll keep the stock safe. You save my boys."

Save her boys. What faith she had in Catherine.

As she lifted her skirts and started up the hill for the Landing, Catherine knew she didn't have that kind of faith. She wasn't sure why the Lord didn't keep some people, like her father and brother, safe, why some had to die so young or when so needed. Despite her best efforts, things just seemed too chaotic, too out of control.

These things I have spoken unto you, that in me ye might have peace. In the world ye shall have tribulation, but be of good cheer. I have overcome the world.

She drew in a breath, feeling as if the truth of the remembered verse had touched her physically. The Lord had made no promises that life would be safe and secure. He'd only promised to be with her through it all.

And that was a promise she could keep for Drew.

She hurried through the trees and out into the clearing at the edge of the Landing. Though Drew's brothers continued to throw water at the fire, their faces grimy from the smoke, the blaze was beginning to gain the upper hand. Tongues of flame licked greedily through the slats on the barn. The oxen had been let free and were running from one side of the clearing to the other in their fear, the rumble of their hooves accompanying the crackle of the burning wood.

Above the noise rose the bang of metal on stone.

Catherine spun to face the pool. Drew stood, one leg in the water, the other straddling the wall. He lifted a massive sledgehammer over his head, muscles straining, and brought it down. Stone and mortar flew from the blow. He was trying to break open the pool, and she saw in an instant his purpose. If he flooded the barn, he'd cut off the fire at its base and hinder its progress. He raised the hammer again, shirt taut across his chest, gaze fixed on the wall as if it were his enemy. Once more he was a knight, going to battle for king and country.

For all he held dear.

She wanted to cheer him on; she wanted to speed his work. She glanced around, looking for some way to help, and her spirits plummeted.

The woodpile was smoking.

The towering mass of logs, raised on a platform and braced by a pair of struts at either end, all but covered the side of the barn closest to the pool. When Drew battered down the wall, the wave might put that fire out in the pile, but the water would never reach the underlying flames in the barn. And neither Drew nor his brothers was in any position to move the wood.

But she was. She might not be able to hack through a wall or carry off dozens of chunks of wood, some as big around as her waist, but she knew how to break through a strut.

Glancing around, she spotted any number of axes on the grass, dropped, most likely, when their owner had run to join the bucket brigade. A good many she wasn't sure she could even lift, much less swing. But there, stuck in the wood of the porch, she spied a hatchet!

She ran and yanked free the tool, then dashed across the clearing for the woodpile. The movement must have caught Drew's attention, for she heard him call her name, his voice strained. No time to respond, no way to quickly explain, and she needed all her strength. She drove the hatchet into the wood at an angle, as she'd seen Drew's brothers do at the tree, pulled it free and drove it in at the opposite angle. Again and again she struck, watching, praying, as the little V widened.

"Catherine!" Drew's voice was like distant thunder.

"It's all right," she called, pulling back the hatchet. "I'm almost there." She swung it into the strut.

The wood snapped, peppering her with splinters. She stepped back as the pile began to shift. With a rumble, the logs started tumbling out onto the ground.

Something wet sloshed into her shoe, and she slipped. Turning her head, she saw a wave of water churning toward her. The pool was breached, water pouring across the land. She was caught between it and the falling wood.

She struggled to gain purchase in the mud, skirts heavy with water. A log bounced off her foot. She gasped, and strong arms wrapped around her, lifted her, carried her out of the way.

Cradled her close and kept her safe.

Drew set her on the porch, and she had to force her fingers to release her hold on his shirt.

"Stay here," he said, backing away, face drawn and eyes wild. "If anything happened to you, I'd never be whole again."

Catherine reached out a hand to him. "I know. I feel the same way. Let me help!"

A cry went up from the barn. Drew turned, and Catherine saw James dash out into the light. He splashed and kicked up his heels in the remaining puddles as the wave of water spread out across the Landing.

"Yee-haw! You did it, Drew! It's out!"

Catherine sagged against the porch support, clutching the rough wood. *Thank You, Father!*

Levi, who had been manning the pump, hobbled closer to the barn as if to make sure. Now Catherine could hear Simon and John calling to each other as they beat back the last of the flames.

Before her, Drew's shoulders sagged, the past few moments apparently having taken a toll. Catherine climbed down from the porch and put a hand to his shoulder. "You did it, Drew. Everyone is safe."

He took her in his arms, held her close and buried his head in her neck. His damp hair caressed her cheek.

"We did it," he murmured. "I saw the fire starting in the pile, but I couldn't leave the spring to stop it. But if those logs had fallen on you, Catherine, if the water had knocked you under it..."

She felt him shudder. She rubbed his back. "It didn't. I'm safe. Your family is fine."

He raised his head and gazed down at her, eyes haunted. "This time. What about the next time or the time after that? I can't be everywhere, with everyone."

Catherine gave him a squeeze. "That's God's job. And I'm learning we should do our best and leave the rest to Him."

"And His helpers." James grinned as he approached them. "Very nice work on the woodpile, Catherine. Remind me never to leave my hatchet out when you're angry."

"Hatchet, sir?" Catherine answered with a smile. "I have my sights on an ax, two handed, perhaps."

"Better watch out for this one, Drew," James said. "She thinks big."

"One of the many things I love about her," Drew replied.

Catherine could not make herself move from his embrace. Love? Oh, yes, she felt it, too, bright and pure and strong. But though she was beginning to wrestle with her fears from the past, she could see he was still consumed by concerns for the ones he loved. Would he be willing to add her to the list?

Love. He hadn't sought it, had not earned it, but he could see it shining in Catherine's eyes and feel it in the touch of her hands. There was so much he longed to say to her, things they needed to work out, but once again, his brothers had other ideas.

Simon and John strode out of the barn, tossed aside their shovels and crossed to Drew's side. Grime striped their faces, and Simon's green eyes looked pale in their red rims.

"It's out," he announced. "But what I want to know is how it started."

Drew released Catherine, but kept one arm about her waist. He couldn't seem to let her go completely.

"None of us would be so careless," John said. "If Beth hadn't called us when she smelled the smoke, the fire could easily have spread to the forest and threatened dozens of farms before it was through."

Catherine nodded toward the barn. "I think Levi may have an answer for you."

Drew looked to where his youngest brother was walking toward them, leaning heavily on his crutch. His face was white under the smear of mud. He stopped a few feet from his brothers, as if afraid of coming too close.

"It's my fault," he said, voice cracking. "Someone started the fire on purpose, and I know why."

"Surely even you couldn't make someone this mad," James teased. He clapped his brother on the shoulder, nearly oversetting him on his crutch. "Although you must admit that you have the unique ability to annoy a body without trying."

Drew was interested in how Levi would respond. His brother shifted on the crutch as if he'd like nothing better than to run away again. "Oh, I annoyed someone, all right. I didn't intend to. But I may owe someone money."

"May?" John frowned as Drew felt his shoulders tighten. "Either you owe it or you don't."

Drew couldn't remain silent. "Why would you owe anyone anything?" he demanded. "You have all the food, clothing and shelter you need."

"And maybe I wanted more!" Levi's head came up,

and he glared at Drew. "Maybe I wanted something of my own, something I earned all by myself."

Drew reared back from his brother's vehemence, but Simon leaned closer.

"What have you done?" he demanded.

Levi turned his glare on his second-eldest brother. "It was just a friendly game of cards. Scout goes into town and rounds up folks to join his father. I thought, why not me? I'm grown now. I can enjoy a hand of cards or a good cigar if I want."

"I imagine a bottle of gin was involved, as well," John said with a shake of his head. "I've heard there's plenty of that rotgut stuff at the Rankins."

"I didn't drink," Levi said, as if that would be any worse than what he'd already confessed. "I kept my head. And I was winning a lot. I was good at it." Suddenly, he sagged. "Only then I wasn't. Mr. Rankin said I could pay him back when I won, but I couldn't stop losing."

Drew couldn't seem to grasp the idea. "You chose to gamble away what little you earned from logging? When did this happen? You've had plenty to do here."

Levi shrugged. "I did, until Ma got sick. Then you sent me back to the Landing. I was bored, and Scout needed help rounding up clients. Besides, Mr. Rankin hosts his games at night. It wasn't hard to slip away… until she came." He nodded at Catherine.

Anger licked up Drew. Did Levi dare blame Catherine for his shortcomings? She evidently had as little liking for the comment, for her eyes narrowed.

"Then it's a shame I didn't come sooner, Mr. Wallin," she said.

She was getting all prim and proper again, but Drew

couldn't blame her. He felt the same way. He'd thought he'd raised his brother better than this. He wanted to strangle Levi and lock him in the house for safekeeping at the same time.

One of the oxen thudded through the mud, head low and call plaintive. The last of the smoke drifted from the barn. As much as Drew would have liked to question his brother further, they had bigger concerns at the moment.

"We'll settle this later," he said. "For now, there's work to be done. Simon and James, fetch back Ma and Beth and the stock. John and I will make sure all the sparks are out and get the oxen penned again. Levi, start supper. I don't know whether anyone is in the mood to eat, but I want something on the table just in case."

As his brothers scattered, Catherine touched his hand where it rested on her hip. "How can I help?"

"Keep an eye on Levi," he said. "It seems someone has to."

He watched as his brother stumped up the porch, head bowed.

"We'll help him," Catherine said, watching Levi, as well. "He's lost his way, but he's not lost."

Drew could only hope she was right and that he could reach his brother.

And Catherine.

Chapter Twenty-Three

It was a solemn dinner that night. Though Levi had managed to put together a stew with dried venison, carrots and potatoes, as well as a pan of biscuits, no one seemed interested in eating. Simon had returned with Mrs. Wallin and Beth, and the men had built a makeshift pen for the stock until they could repair the fire damage to the barn.

Simon must have told their mother about Levi's confession, for the first thing she did when she returned was to cup her youngest son's face in her hands.

"What's done is done," she'd said, green eyes meeting blue. "Now you must make things right."

Levi had nodded, blinking back tears.

Although Catherine knew Mrs. Wallin was wise to counsel action, she wondered how the boy would go about settling the matter. It was clear to her he was in over his head and up against people with no regard for life or property.

Of course, she knew something about feeling out of control. Despite her best efforts, she had come to love this family. Especially the man who held them all together.

Drew sat at the head of the table, gaze traveling from one sibling to another as if he were counting heads, making certain everyone was safe and fed. He didn't eat until their plates were filled, didn't rest until they were dreaming. And if their sleep was peaceful, it was because they knew he was standing guard. A prayer for him came easily.

Father, they called You the Good Shepherd. I had forgotten that until I met Drew. He thinks he's doing what his earthly father asked, but I think he's doing what You expect and more. Show me how to help him.

Mrs. Wallin and James had cleared away the dishes and were in the back washing up when Drew spoke to Levi again. "How much do you owe?"

His brother seemed to shrink in on himself. "Two hundred."

"Dollars?" Beth asked with a gasp as Simon hissed in a breath.

Catherine felt her stomach drop. It had cost her three hundred dollars to sail from Boston to Seattle, money she'd saved from the sale of her father's house. Two hundred would surely be a huge burden to this family.

"Where did you lay your hands on so much money?" John asked with a frown as if he could not make the sum add up in his head.

"I told you," Levi snapped. "They let me play on credit."

"Knowing your family would make good on your debt," Simon said with a shake of his head.

"I never asked you to pay my debt," Levi protested,

clutching his crutch as if he wanted to swing it at someone. "I told Scout I'd pay his father back. They just didn't like waiting."

Catherine felt ill. "If they torched your family's barn and beat you because they disliked waiting, I shudder to think what they'll do once they know you can't pay."

"We'll pay," Drew said, voice low and hard. "This harassment must end before anyone else is hurt."

"But we can't let them get away with it," John argued. "What they did is wrong."

"Not to mention potentially deadly," James said, coming back into the room with a towel slung over his shoulder. He lay a hand over his heart. "Not that I hold it against them, seeing how Levi so abused their trust."

"'Vengeance is mine, saith the Lord,'" Mrs. Wallin quoted, following James back to the table. "I don't like what Mr. Rankin's done, but I won't see more of my boys hurt because of it."

They were missing the point. Why was this their fight to begin with?

"Surely this is a matter for the sheriff," Catherine said, glancing around at them all. "Deputy McCormick said there had been other harassment out this way. Levi can't be the only one to fall into the Rankins' trap. If we tell Deputy McCormick our suspicions about Mr. Rankin and his son, he'll have enough information to at least warn the man off, perhaps even jail him."

"But suspicion is all we have," Simon reminded her. "McCormick isn't going to arrest anyone unless he has proof."

Catherine lay her hand on Levi's shoulder. "And Levi's word and injuries aren't enough?"

Levi cast her a quick glance. She thought he looked surprised that she considered his word important.

"He claims to have fallen out of a tree," John pointed out.

"And he hasn't actually been the most trusted and respected of citizens," James added.

Levi slumped under her hand. "I really mucked it up this time."

"Yes, you did," James agreed. "But never fear. We still need an annoying little brother to make the family complete, so you might as well keep playing the role. Unless we could get that Gulliver Ward fellow to stand in last minute." He glanced around at his family, as if seeking approval.

Beth shook her head at his silliness, but Catherine felt Drew's sigh.

"Levi made a mistake," he said, and she thought he took it personally. "Rankin made a bigger one by destroying property and threatening lives. But the fact of the matter is that Levi owes him money. Like it or not, deserved or not, the debt must be paid."

The conviction in his voice seemed to build her strength, as well.

Simon did not seem to share it. He leaned forward. "And just how do you intend to pay it? You don't have two hundred dollars."

Drew's jaw tightened. "I'll go to Yesler, offer him a contract on timber for his sawmill and ask for an advance."

John snorted. "Yesler doesn't pay on time even after we deliver the wood. I doubt he'll give us money ahead of receipt."

Now Drew's shoulders were tensing, as well. He was trying to protect his family, as he always did.

"I'll find a way," he insisted. "I refuse to see this family endangered."

"And you think the rest of us will sit by contentedly?" Simon asked. He rose from his seat, gaze on Drew's. "I heard Pa that day. He made you head of this family. I know the sacrifices you've made to raise us all. Your clothes wore out, but you made sure ours didn't. You were the first one out in the fields in the morning, the last in at night."

So he saw it, too. What Catherine couldn't understand was why he sounded so angry about it.

Simon bent and braced both hands on the table so that he and Drew were eye to eye. "You did your job, Drew. We're grown men. It's time you started letting us have a say in how things go around here."

Catherine leaned back from him. She still disliked his tone, but she realized that he was right. If Drew's brothers took more of a hand in keeping Beth and Levi safe and supporting their mother, it would surely ease Drew's mind. Maybe enough to start the family his mother hoped for him.

Perhaps with her.

Drew was watching his brother. "I never told you to hold your peace," he said. "Not about family matters."

"No, but you act as if we're all your responsibility." Simon straightened. "When something threatens one of us, it threatens us all. I have sixty dollars saved from my cut of the timber. That can go against Levi's debt."

"I have forty," John put in. "I can do without a few books for a time."

"I brought you *Culpeper's*," Catherine offered, and he beamed.

James fingered his shirt. "I have thirty, but I owe twenty at the mercantile." He shrugged. "Mr. Howard has commented more than once on my taste in clothing. I could probably get him to pay twenty for my waistcoat."

Sacrifice, indeed. Not to be outdone, Beth took a deep breath.

"I have three dollars from gifts," she said, twisting a strand of hair around one finger. "I was saving it for my social dress, but James is right. When will I attend a social?"

Catherine touched her hand. "Sooner than you think."

Levi glanced around at them. "I can't take your money. I don't deserve it."

"You certainly don't," James said. He patted his brother's shoulder. "I believe that's why it's called a gift."

"That's one hundred and thirty-three," Simon said. "If we put in the hundred from Captain Collings, we've more than enough."

"But that money was to go for a plow," John protested. "And we'll need lumber to repair the barn."

Catherine clasped her hands together on the table. "I am paid two and a half dollars a week at the hospital. I've saved five dollars, and I have it with me. You are welcome to it."

They all stared at her.

James spoke first, tugging down on his smoke-stained shirtsleeves. "If you had told us you were such an heiress, Catherine, I might have tried harder to wedge my way into your affections."

Drew's hand came down on hers, warm and firm. "Thank you, Catherine." He looked to his brothers. "It seems we're all in this together, then."

Together. A family. Oh, but that was what she hoped they soon might be.

They set out the next morning. Drew wasn't sure what to expect at the Rankins', but he'd agreed that Catherine should come with them. She'd fought for her place at his side when they'd laid out their plans around the table last night.

"Having a lady with you may make him think twice about his behavior," she'd insisted, eyes bright with fervor.

Levi had snorted. "You've never met Mr. Rankin."

"You're right," she'd admitted. "I haven't had the pleasure."

"Believe me, it's not a pleasure," James had assured her.

"He's proved he cares about nothing but money," Drew had agreed. "He could have killed us all or damaged acres of timber by torching the barn. It's not safe for you to come with us, Catherine."

"Then it's not safe for you to go, either," she'd insisted. "You cannot expect me to sit idly by while you are in danger."

His brothers should have done more to help him counter her logic, but instead they had all grinned at her.

"I've always admired a woman willing to fight for those she loves," James had said. "That and one with a good head of hair."

She had ignored him. "And Scout. I promised myself I'd look in on the boy. I'm convinced his father is beating him."

That might be, but the thought that Catherine might fall under those fists as well had made his back stiffen, his fingers tighten. He'd wanted to argue further, but she'd laid a hand on his arm. "If anyone is hurt, Drew, I want to be there to help."

As always, that logic he could not defeat. So Catherine was walking in front of him when they left at first light that morning.

"Be careful," she murmured as they started into the trees. "You don't know how Mr. Rankin will react. If he gambles all night as Levi said, he may not take kindly to visitors so early in the morning."

Drew was counting on it.

Only an old game trail, heavily overgrown, led between the two claims. They went single file, Simon at the head, Drew at the back. James held the bushes so John could help Levi and Catherine could come through with her wide brown skirts. The boy had tried to remain behind, worried that his injured leg would slow them down.

"You started this," Simon had told him. "It's only right you be there to finish it."

Now they moved quietly, his brothers with axes in their hands and knives at their waists. James carried his rifle, but Drew had warned everyone use their weapon only for protection. Catherine carried her bandbox, which she'd packed with the bandages Levi had rolled and some medical supplies she had brought from town this time. Drew only hoped she'd have no call to use any of them.

The Rankin cabin was set near the shore of the lake, drowned trees lying like giant needles in the mud all around it. Scout had once bragged that his father let the water do his clearing for him.

But it didn't look as if Rankin had worked on his land in any other way. Blackberries had overtaken the vegetable patch, and a few chickens pecked among the weeds of the yard. The log cabin looked nearly as deserted, standing silent as they approached.

The Rankins had never bothered to install glass in their windows. Shutters closed up the house like the shell of a turtle. Only smoke trickling from the chimney, rising to meet the gray clouds, said someone might be home. But a new hitching post had been built in front of the house, resin still dripping from the timber, and the dirt around it had been packed solid, as if any number of horses had waited for owners busy inside. Somewhere near to hand, Drew caught the acrid scent of fermenting grain.

As his brothers fanned out across the yard, Catherine behind Simon for her protection, Drew nodded to Levi, who limped up to the door and banged on it. "Mr. Rankin? It's Levi Wallin. I have your money."

Inside came thuds and a raised voice before Benjamin Rankin yanked open the weathered door. A large man with ample folds around his thick neck and a protruding belly, his eyes squinted against the light. The sneer on his flabby face quickly vanished as he spied Drew and the others in the yard.

James raised the rifle, but Drew thought Catherine's glare was far more effective in making the man take a step back.

"We don't want any trouble," Drew assured Rankin. "Pay the man what you owe, Levi."

Levi shoved the sack of silver and gold coins at the man. "Two hundred, just like we agreed."

Rankin spat a stream of something yellow into the yard, as if the sight of the money left a bad taste in his mouth. "You forgot the interest."

Drew stiffened. So did Catherine and Levi.

"Interest?" his youngest brother cried. "You never said anything about interest."

Rankin shrugged with a roll of muscle and fat. "Didn't think I had to. Goes without saying that there's interest on a loan. You get to use my money. I get a consideration." He opened the sack and dug a thick finger into the coins, making them clink against each other. "I see no consideration here."

"How very inconsiderate of us," James quipped. "What do you say, Drew? Shall we pay Mr. Rankin back the same way he paid Levi?"

Simon smacked his ax handle into the palm of one hand.

To Drew's surprise, Catherine strode forward, eyes flashing. "Levi already paid your interest, Mr. Rankin, with his blood. And so, I believe, has your son, Scout. I demand that you show us the boy."

"You demand?" Rankin laughed, the sound like the creaking of a badly oiled door. "You have no rights on my property. A man can treat his boy any way he likes."

Catherine looked him up and down, standing tall and trim in her tailored brown wool. "And he can treat himself as he wishes, as well. You certainly have. Veined nose and bloodshot eyes—the effects of too much alcohol. Ample girth, too much food of the wrong sort.

Shortness of breath and wheezing laugh, indications of an asthmatic condition brought about by excessive exposure to tobacco smoke. If you do not mend your ways, Mr. Rankin, I predict you will shortly die of heart failure."

Drew took a step closer, fully expecting Rankin to light into her verbally, if not physically. Instead, the man squinted his eyes at her. "Who are you?"

"Catherine Stanway," she replied. "Trained nurse and assistant to Doctor Maynard. And I strongly suggest you take my advice and see to your diet and surroundings immediately."

Rankin glanced between her and Drew. "Is she crazy?"

Drew smiled. "Not in the slightest. Ma nearly died of a fever. She nursed her back to health in a couple of days."

"Took care of Old Joe's rash, too," James called. "For which we are all grateful." He shuddered, as if even the recollection of the puffy skin was painful.

Scout crept up beside his father, one hand tugging at the man's sleeve. "She knew about my nose, Pa, before I ever said a word."

Rankin frowned, rubbing one finger against his own nose. "So what it is you want, ma'am?"

Catherine lifted her chin, gaze still militant. "You will cease striking your son. I suspect you'll need his goodwill should something horrid happen to you."

Rankin glanced at Scout as if he'd never considered that possibility before.

"You will drink at least eight glasses of water a day," Catherine continued, "and take a turn around the yard three times, rain or shine. You will watch your diet, choosing vegetables over meat for a time. And you will stop drinking alcohol."

Rankin grimaced. "I ain't no teetotaler."

"If you wish to live," Catherine said, "you will be."

Drew took another step forward, towering over them all. Pride for Catherine vied with anger over what Rankin had done to his family. "And your business with us is over, Rankin. You leave the Wallins alone."

"And the Wallins will return the favor," Simon added.

Rankin looked from one of them to another. He must not have liked his chances, for he squared his shoulders. "I don't like your attitude, Wallin. Sheriff might have something to say about this bullying."

Bullying? And this from a man who had perfected the art? But another voice spoke from behind them.

"As a matter of fact, the sheriff has quite an opinion on the matter."

Rankin turned white as Deputy McCormick stepped out from behind a tree, rifle resting in the crook of his arm. He nodded to Drew.

"Wallin. We saw the smoke from out this way yesterday, but I couldn't come investigate until this morning. Thought I'd better check on all the farms in this neck of the woods. Any trouble here?"

Drew glanced at Rankin, who had all but disappeared into the shadows of his cabin, leaving Scout on the step, blinking at the light.

"Our barn caught fire yesterday," Drew told the deputy. "You might ask Mr. Rankin if he knows anything about that."

Rankin's piggy eyes were bright in the darkness.

"Shame when hay just catches fire by its own self. Been known to happen."

Scout dropped his gaze.

"True," McCormick mused. "Funny how so many fires have sprung up out this way, though. Maybe you and your boy ought to move into town, where we can keep an eye on you."

"A fine suggestion," Catherine agreed. "It might improve your health, Mr. Rankin."

Rankin's smile turned oily. "Thank you both for your concern, but we're doing just fine out here. I think Mr. Wallin is right. His family and I are finished with our business for now." He gazed up at Drew. "Any interest on that loan is forgiven, seeing as how young Levi is such good friends with my boy, and your lady friend here is so helpful about my health. And you're all welcome at my table anytime."

"Don't hold your breath," Levi said, turning away.

"Actually, do hold your breath," James suggested. "For say ten or twenty minutes. I guarantee it will improve the neighborhood immensely."

Rankin slammed the door on them, leaving Scout standing on the step. Catherine immediately drew him aside, and Drew heard her start to question the boy about his own health.

McCormick waited as Drew and his brothers gathered around him, then spoke with a low voice as if mindful of Scout and Catherine not too far away. "I take it you have reason to believe Rankin burned your barn."

"Among other things," Drew murmured. "But we have no proof to offer you. It's our word against his."

McCormick's smile was grim. "No question in my mind which a judge would believe. I'll keep watch here for a while until you get home. And the sheriff and I will be keeping an eye on Rankin." He glanced at the house and shook his head before returning his gaze to Drew's. "That's some lady you have there. Never thought I'd see any miss who could stand up to Rankin."

"I never thought I'd see a lady who could stand his smell," James added. Simon cuffed him on the shoulder.

"I expect she'll need to return to town soon," McCormick continued, ignoring them. "Do you want me to fetch Miss Stanway back with me?"

His brothers were all watching Drew, waiting for his answer.

"Not just yet," Drew said. "First, I need to propose."

He wasn't sure which of them had the biggest grin.

Chapter Twenty-Four

The air smelled cool and sharp as Catherine walked back through the wood with Drew and his brothers. Rain would be here soon, but she didn't mind. She felt as if they'd achieved a victory, both in removing Mr. Rankin's threats from over Levi's head and in letting him know they would brook no further nonsense.

She glanced back over her shoulder where Scout Rankin walked just behind her. Seeing her look, he straightened from his slouch and managed a smile. She'd thought it best to keep the boy at Wallin Landing for the day to give his father time to calm down and think about what she and the others had said. And perhaps he and Levi could mend their differences. The boy had already confessed that he'd tried to stop his father, to no avail.

Beyond him, Drew smiled at her as well before she turned front again, cheeks heating. He looked as if he wanted to say something to her, but this walking single file through the woods certainly wasn't conducive to conversation. She could hardly wait to return home.

Home.

Her smile deepened as the woods opened up to reveal the cabin and barn, the horses trotting about the pasture, the chickens pecking in their yard. Mrs. Wallin had set the large cast-iron kettle on a fire in the clearing, and the pile of shirts and trousers next to it said she was about to start the laundry.

Beth had made her own path from the tub to the ruined wall Drew had opened in the pool, where the spring bubbled below the level of the break. The way her face brightened at the sight of her brothers told Catherine how little she'd liked waiting. Catherine knew the feeling. She'd waited for her father and brother to come home, and they never would. This time, she'd been the one to help.

Lord, I thought I was the healer, but I've been blind. Everything I've done was to try to take control because I doubted You. You didn't send my brother and father to their deaths—they chose to fight. You didn't force me out of Sudbury—I ran. I can see You've given me a chance with Drew. Please help me find a way to tell him how much he's come to mean to me.

She glanced back again and caught her breath as Drew moved into the sunlight. His head was high like the trees he felled, his smile brighter than the spring sun. Something fluttered in her stomach, and she let Scout pass her so she could wait for Drew to reach her side.

He came to a stop beside her and lowered his ax. She couldn't look away as he bent his head to hers. "Thank you," he murmured before he kissed her. His arms came around her, fierce, protective, as if he'd never let her go. She nestled against him, returned his kiss and trembled with the joy that tumbled through her.

"Ahem."

Catherine blinked and realized James was standing next to them, hands clasped behind his back. Seeing he had her attention, he wiggled his blond brows.

"It appears, Miss Stanway, that you have compromised my brother's reputation, and I want to know what you intend to do about it."

Catherine glanced at Drew even as her cheeks heated.

Drew frowned at his brother, but she saw merriment in his eyes. "You better hope she doesn't need a gun to get me to the altar, because we both know her aim is questionable."

"Oh!" Catherine cried in indignation. "I can hit the broad side of a barn."

James snorted, then hurriedly turned the sound into a cough.

"I'm not worried," he told Drew when he'd recovered. "I figure Simon will be the one standing up beside you. I'll be safely in the throng of well-wishers."

"No throng would be safe with you in it," Drew countered. "Now, go on. Catherine and I weren't finished talking."

"Oh, talking he calls it," James said, but he bowed and sauntered back to where his other brothers were telling Beth and Mrs. Wallin about their reception at the Rankins.

Drew had kept his arms around her, and she did not mind. His warmth seeped into her heart like water on parched earth.

"Deputy McCormick wondered if you wanted an escort back to Seattle," he murmured. "I told him I had something I needed to ask you first."

Her heart started beating faster. "And what would that be?"

He pulled back to meet her gaze. "Catherine, nothing would make me happier than for you to agree to be my wife. But I've long known that whoever marries me marries into this family. Ma has her way of doing things. Beth could talk the paint off a wall. Simon must have the last word, James the last laugh. John thinks he knows everything, and Levi hasn't realized how little he knows. We're not the easiest bunch to get along with."

"You're not the most difficult, either," she countered. "You love each other, support each other."

"Argue with each other, fuss at each other."

"Work together toward a common goal. I envy you that. But as much as I love your family, Drew, I cannot marry you for them. That wouldn't be fair to you."

He released her. "Is there nothing I can say, nothing I can do, then, to win your heart?"

Catherine cocked her head. "Do you want to win it, Drew? I know the burden you've put on yourself to keep this family safe. Even with your brothers taking a bigger role, are you willing to add more to the family—a wife, perhaps someday children? Are you willing to speak for yourself, Drew?"

That was, of course, the key question. He wasn't sure why he was surprised she'd asked it. Certainly his family thought nothing of him taking a wife. Look how they'd campaigned on Catherine's behalf.

He knew every argument against her, every reason a marriage wouldn't work. Yet when he tried to imagine life without her, the future looked dark, empty.

"I want to speak, Catherine," he told her. "But I feel

like that Miles Standish fellow. I'm not the most eloquent man. I can't play a love song like Simon or quote from some book like John. But if it's pretty words you want, I'll try."

She took his hands, fingers spreading to wrap around the edges of his. "Then perhaps I should go first, before I lose my courage."

Anything that scared her ought to terrify him. "All right," he managed to say.

She took a deep breath and met his gaze. "You know I love this family, Drew, but everything that's happened over the last week has proved something to me. When we were all in danger, it scared me to think of losing my family. But what truly made me fearful was the thought of losing you."

She squeezed his hands. "What I'm trying to say is that I love you, Drew Wallin. You are a fine, noble, honorable man. Any woman would be proud to stand beside you."

She seemed to think he should just smile and nod in agreement. But his brain had seized on one statement and wouldn't let go.

She loved him.

Against all odds, this clever, talented, amazing woman loved him. He finally understood what James meant about it being a gift, for he knew he could never earn her love, but would always be grateful for her.

He was pretty sure a smile and nod was not the appropriate way to respond to such feelings. He pulled her into his arms and kissed her.

Catherine closed her eyes, glorying in the feel of Drew's arms around her, his lips caressing hers. The sound of the Landing, the clamor of her heart, the lingering smell of smoke faded away, until he filled all her senses. He had not said the words, but she could feel his love in the way he cradled her against him, hear it in murmur of her name. She had traveled thousands of miles to find a new life, and the journey had led her home, to him.

Slowly, he raised his head, and she smiled at him. She thought it must be a besotted sort of smile, a bit crooked and trembling about the edges. His matched it.

"I promised myself I would do things properly this time," he said, "but I seem to have a hard time being proper where you're concerned."

Catherine laughed. He released her to go down on one knee on the ground, gaze lifted to hers.

"Catherine Stanway," he said, deep voice echoing around the clearing. "I love you. Will you do me the honor of becoming my wife?"

"Say yes!" Beth cried, and was quickly hushed.

Drew's cheeks darkened. Catherine cupped his face with her hands, feeling the hint of stubble peppering her palms. "Yes, Drew. Yes. A thousand times yes. Nothing would make me happier."

He rose and gathered her close once more. "I'll fix up the cabin, whatever you want. And I'll build you a dispensary so you can nurse from the Landing. Someday, when we have a hospital, you can lead it. You have a gift, Catherine, and I want to see you use it."

He might not be a poet, but he'd just found every word she needed to hear. "Thank you," she murmured. "For understanding, for making me part of your family. I'll be a good wife for you, Drew. I promise."

He smiled. "How could you be anything else?"

"Simon!" James called. "Fetch your fiddle. Methinks I detect cause for celebration."

Catherine glanced over her shoulder at her new family and found them all grinning at her. Mrs. Wallin wiped a tear from the corner of her eye.

Beth rushed up to them. "Oh, a wedding! You must let me help. We'll need flowers and a cake and a special dress. I saw the latest prints in *Godey's*, yards of lace and long veils of the sheerest net."

"Beth," Drew started.

"And a quilt! Ma has to make you a quilt. I'll help. It might take a few months."

"Beth," Catherine warned.

She was patting the tips of her fingers together, eyes bright. "Oh, there are so many people to invite—all the Mercer belles and Mr. Yesler and Doc and his wife. We'll need to talk to Mr. Bagley, of course. I wonder if the brown church will be big enough. Maybe we'll have to see if they'll let us use the white church."

"Elizabeth Ann Wallin," Mrs. Wallin said. "Leave them be."

With a blush, Beth hurried off, humming to herself.

Catherine shook her head. "It seems we'll have no trouble planning a wedding."

Drew chuckled. "I had no idea it was such an undertaking. Months, she said. I hope you'll have pity on me, Catherine, and not make me wait that long."

Catherine smiled. "You speak to the Reverend Bagley and see how soon he can fit us in. So long as our family is around us, I'd be happy to be married at any time."

And so, two weeks later they gathered at the brown church. After being at the Landing, Seattle looked crowded to Catherine, the muddy streets teeming with people, but perhaps that was because she had so many attendants at her wedding. She still found it hard to believe—her, marrying a brawny lumberjack. It was nothing she could have imagined and everything she'd ever wanted.

She stood at the back of the church, pews of carved dark wood stretching on either side, beams open above like the boughs of a forest. She wore Mrs. Wallin's blue-and-green dress, which she now knew had served as the lady's own wedding gown more than thirty years ago. The skirts might be narrower than she was used to, but the fine material and love behind it made it the most beautiful dress she'd ever worn.

Maddie, wearing a jade-green dress she'd sewed for the occasion, was standing between her and the altar. Behind Maddie stood Allegra in a similar gown, Doctor Maynard's wife, Susanna, in darker green, then Beth in her first social dress, paid for courtesy of Maddie's laundry earnings. Waiting at the front, Drew stood with his brothers beside him, hair slicked down, all in dark suits and high collars. Only James looked comfortable in them.

It was most likely the largest wedding party Seattle had ever seen, but she would have had it no other way.

Next to her, Doc Maynard squeezed her arm. "I'm honored you chose me to give you away, Catherine." His eyes twinkled. "But then, I seem to be always giving you away to these Wallins."

Catherine smiled. Doc had already packed up a number of supplies and instruments for her to take with her to the Landing for her dispensary.

"A lady should have family beside her when she weds," she said now. "And I am blessed with the most wonderful family, even if we don't share the same mother and father."

"Ah, but the good reverend would remind us we do share the same Father," he replied with a wink. "And I think we've kept Mr. Bagley and your charming groom waiting long enough."

Catherine nodded. They started down the aisle, the congregation standing as they passed. She spotted Sheriff Boren and Deputy McCormick, boardinghouse owner Mrs. Elliott and all the women who had come with her on the Mercer expedition, some married and some, like Maddie, determined to remain single.

Unless You send them someone like Drew, Father. Someone who can find the way to their hearts. Thank You for being patient with me, for helping me understand. My family chose to leave me. I can choose to stay.

Reverend Bagley beamed at her as she reached the front of the church. "Who gives this woman to be married?" he asked, adjusting his spectacles on his thin nose.

"I do," Doc Maynard said. "And if you don't recognize me by this time, Daniel, I'd say you need to polish those glasses."

The minister frowned at him as the congregation laughed.

As the room quieted again, Drew moved to Catherine's side. Looking up into his eyes, she felt as if his arms, and his love, were holding her even now. Her heart was so full she barely heard the words of the ceremony.

Thank You, Lord, for this gift. I will never take it lightly.

"I now pronounce you man and wife," Mr. Bagley said. "You may kiss the bride."

Drew took her in his arms and pressed his lips against hers, sealing their promise. Her husband, his wife, forever, no matter what happened.

A cheer went up behind him. As he broke the kiss with a smile, Catherine could see James and John clapping each other on the back, Simon actually grinning from ear to ear and Levi doing some sort of dance with his crutch along the front pew.

The reverend coughed as if trying to remind them of proper behavior in church, then gave it up and grinned as he raised his hands in benediction.

"Ladies and gentlemen, friends and family, I give you Mr. and Mrs. Wallin."

Their guests clapped and cheered as Drew and Catherine made their way down the aisle.

"You are my hero," Catherine told him. "I didn't think I would ever be this happy again."

They stepped out onto the porch. Seattle rain fell softly like a blessing. Drew's brothers spread out on the steps, demanding the right to kiss the bride on the cheek.

"Go ahead," Drew said, moving aside. "Just remember one thing. I know the trouble you went to to make sure your brother courted his bride. I think the best Catherine and I can do is return the favor."

James, who had just pecked Catherine on the cheek, straightened. "You mean you're going to marry us off?"

Catherine bit her lip to keep from laughing at the shock on his face.

"Yes, I do," Drew said. "Turnabout is fair play. I think we should start with Simon."

Simon raised a brow. "You can try, brother, but I haven't seen a woman yet who can meet my criteria for a bride."

"Sure'n that's because you've been looking in the wrong places, me lad," Maddie said, nose in the air as she passed. She twitched her jade skirts to one side. Then she seized Catherine's hand. "Come along, me darling girl. Toss your bouquet, and let's see who's next to wed."

The other women hurried past to gather at the foot of the stairs, faces alight as they gazed up at Catherine. She caught James and John eyeing them appreciatively.

She turned her back and tossed the flowers over her shoulder. Then she whirled to see who had caught the bouquet.

Most of the women looked downright disappointed to see the flowers nestled in Beth's hands. Beth was staring at Maddie.

"You threw it at me!" she accused.

Maddie's brown eyes were wide, though her cheeks were turning pink. "Sure'n it bounced off my fingertips."

While the others congratulated a confused Beth, Drew put his arm about Catherine's waist. "Perhaps we should add your friend to the list of those needing help finding a match."

"Perhaps," Catherine agreed. "But you surprise me, Drew. I never took you for a matchmaker."

"With the right teacher, a man can learn anything," he said, holding her closer. "And starting right now, I aim to learn all the ways I can show my wife how much I love her."

Catherine smiled up at him. "An admirable goal. And

I intend to show my husband my devotion, as well. I predict the process will take a lifetime."

And it did.

* * * * *

Dear Reader,

Thank you for choosing *Would-Be Wilderness Wife*, the second book in my Frontier Bachelors miniseries. If you enjoyed the story, I hope you'll consider leaving a review on a reader or retailer site online.

As I was writing the book, I couldn't help thinking about one of my favorite musicals, *Seven Brides for Seven Brothers*. I picture Drew and his brothers having that kind of loving, teasing relationship. Let's just hope Catherine and Drew can find a few more brides for the rest of the Wallin clan, and a groom for Maddie, too!

I love to hear from readers, so be sure to come find me online, whether at my website at reginascott.com, my blog at nineteenteen.com, or on Facebook at facebook.com/authorreginascott.

Blessings!

Regina Scott

COMING NEXT MONTH FROM

Love Inspired® Historical

Available April 7, 2015

WAGON TRAIN REUNION

Journey West

by Linda Ford

Abigail Bingham is reunited with former flame Benjamin Hewitt when she joins a wagon train headed west. Will the Oregon trial offer a second chance for the socialite's daughter and a charming cowboy?

AN UNLIKELY LOVE

by Dorothy Clark

Marissa Bradley is drawn to Grant Winston, but his livelihood is to blame for her family's destruction. Can Grant find a way to maintain the family business and to have Marissa as his wife?

FROM BOSS TO BRIDEGROOM

Smoky Mountain Matches

by Karen Kirst

What starts as a strictly professional relationship grows into something more between boss Quinn Darling and his lovely employee, Nicole O'Malley. Until Quinn discovers Nicole's been keeping a secret that could derail their future together.

THE DOCTOR'S UNDOING

by Allie Pleiter

Doctor Daniel Parker doesn't want a fiery nurse telling him how to run his orphanage. But Ida Lee Landway's kindness—and beauty—slowly chip away at his stubborn exterior.

LOOK FOR THESE AND OTHER LOVE INSPIRED BOOKS WHEREVER BOOKS ARE SOLD, INCLUDING MOST BOOKSTORES, SUPERMARKETS, DISCOUNT STORES AND DRUGSTORES.

LIHCNM0315

SPECIAL EXCERPT FROM

Love Inspired® HISTORICAL

On the wagon train out West, will Ben Hewitt find love again with Abigail Bingham Black—the woman who broke his heart six years ago?

Read on for a sneak preview of Linda Ford's WAGON TRAIN REUNION, the exciting beginning of the new series ***JOURNEY WEST****.*

Benjamin Hewitt stared. It wasn't possible.

The man struggling with his oxen couldn't be Mr. Bingham. He would never subject himself and his wife to the trials of this journey. Why, Mrs. Bingham would look mighty strange fluttering a lace hankie and expecting someone to serve her tea.

The man must have given the wrong command because the oxen jerked hard to the right. The rear wheel broke free. A flurry of smaller items fell out the back. A woman followed, shrieking.

"Mother, are you injured?" A young woman ran toward her mother. She sounded just like Abigail. At least as near as he could recall. He'd succeeded in putting that young woman from his mind many years ago.

She glanced about. "Father, are you safe?"

The sun glowed in her blond hair and he knew without seeing her face that it was Abigail. What was she doing here? She'd not find a fine, big house nor fancy dishes

LIHEXP0315

and certainly no servants on this trip.

The bitterness he'd once felt at being rejected because he couldn't provide those things had dissipated, leaving only regret and caution.

She helped her mother to her feet and dusted her skirts off. All the while, the woman—Mrs. Bingham, to be sure—complained, her voice grating with displeasure that made Ben's nerves twitch. He knew all too well that sound. Could recall in sharp detail when the woman had told him he was not a suitable suitor for her daughter. Abigail had agreed, had told him, in a harsh dismissive tone, she would no longer see him.

It all seemed so long ago. Six years to be exact. He'd been a different person back then. Thanks to Abigail, he'd learned not to trust everything a woman said. Nor believe how they acted.

But Binghams or not, a wheel needed to be put on. Ben joined the men hurrying to assist the family.

"Hello." He greeted Mr. Bingham and the man shook his hand. "Ladies." He tipped his hat to them.

"Hello, Ben." Abigail Bingham stood at her mother's side. No, not Bingham. She was Abigail Black now.